Dedication & Ac

This book is dedicated to my [illegible]
who got me home.

Editing and proofing: Mary-Anne McNulty
(If Mary-Anne had paid every time she read this book, then all my readers could have had free copies!) Her perseverance, skill and good humour have been a catalyst to the release of my book.

Cover concept sketch: Michael Lynch, a truly hidden talent.

Front and back cover: Martina Doherty, a class act.

A huge thank you to 'Sarge' and Paul whose generosity greatly assisted the publishing of this book.

Special thanks to local author, Jane Buckley, who showed me the pathway to self-publishing and gave so selflessly of her time and shared valuable personal experiences during the publishing of her book Stones Corner, Turmoil.

Special thanks also to Mary-Anne (again), Martin, Gerry, George and Daniel for their support, advice, guidance and critical comment during the writing process.
You were loved and hated in equal measure!

"How vain it is to sit down to write when you have not stood up to live"

(HENRY DAVID THOREAU)

Foreword

As a debut author let me introduce myself and my book. In many ways those two topics are intertwined. I'm Eamonn Lynch, a proud Derryman, a son of my late parents, a father to Emma, a grandfather to Davin and Penny, a brother to seven and hopefully a good friend to those whose paths I've crossed over the years. *(That was beginning to sound a bit like Maximus in Gladiator when he faced Commodus in the Colosseum, but I assure you that, unlike Maximus, I am not seeking vengeance in this life or the next!)* To describe myself as a writer or an author still seems somewhat of a stretch. However, stretching at my age is strongly advised by all good doctors!

For several years I have written poems and short stories, just as a hobby. *Get That Boy Home* seemed like a natural progression. The fact that it finally got published is more down to the encouragement of family, friends and indeed a few strangers who read and enjoyed the manuscript, than to any personal vanity or ambition on my part. If you enjoy reading my book half as much as I enjoyed writing it, then we will be twice gratified. Readers of this book will have deducted that my prowess at mathematics is not up to Dan Feeney's high standards!

The book follows the life and times of fictional character, Dan Feeney, and takes him through his childhood in Derry during the 1950's and 60's and into the developing Troubles and beyond. My book falls into the genre of historical fiction, but like many of those books, personal recollection and experience is strongly woven into this tale. His story could be echoed by many from my city during that period. Indeed, the reach of the Dan Feeney story could well be transposed to other cities and countries throughout the world where uprisings occurred. Revolutionaries are born out of circumstance, not ambition.

I have tried to provide authentic commentary of those difficult days through the prism of Dan Feeney, introducing humour, innocence, danger, tragedy and sadness into his chaotic life. This is not a book solely about the Northern Ireland Troubles; it's a book about a young boy who became a man against the backdrop of the political and social struggle that many consider was the genesis of the Troubles. It's also a book about how all of that impacted on him. Historians can grapple with the historical facts of those times. Dan Feeney will take you in there with him, and give you the perspective and experience of the ordinary boy and man during those extraordinary times. You can laugh at him and with him, you can be on his side or against him, but I suspect that you won't forget him.

Robert Frost once said, *No tears in the writer, no tears in the reader. No surprise in the writer, no surprise in the reader.* Well, I can certainly attest to the writer's tears and surprises during my time writing this book, but I will leave it to you, the readers, to hopefully deliver fully on Frost's aspirations.

Contents

1

Never Judge the Book…

As far as Dan Feeney was concerned, there was a lot more to jogging than sweaty, middle-aged men adorned with branded sportswear and plugged into their iPods struggling along that lonely road back home, dreaming of the hot shower to come and the natural endorphins promised by the local GP. Anyway, you'd think medical science would have moved on enough that such highs could be prescribed in tablet form instead of having to undergo all that pain!

Believe it or not, joggers actually think a lot when they're out pounding the highways, byways and riversides in an attempt to repel the relentless gallop of time and ensure they hurt and sweat enough to know that it must be doing them good. Granted, that's an incongruous deduction, but they would argue the validity of this theory to the death. And some do, often before there's enough mileage on their Nike 'Stratocasters' to justify the cost of purchase. Perhaps jogging should be upgraded to a blood sport. Dan's rock metaphor for trainers emanated from his belief that jogging brought music to his feet!

Deep down they knew they were not 'real deal' athletes,

but they believed they might have been if they'd chosen sport before chocolate and fish suppers in their mid-twenties. This was amply compensated for in the knowledge that, when real athletes whizzed by them, they were missing out on a perspective and perception of life that could only be attained at jogging pace.

This story amplifies and personifies the vista of the jogging classes.

It was a cold but dry November Sunday morning. For Dan, 2007 had been another fairly uneventful year, bar a sojourn to Cape Verde back in June which put another nail in a coffin full of failed relationships since his marriage break-up a decade earlier. At 54, he had become disillusioned and cynical about his prospects of finding another companion with whom he might share his past emotional carnage and failing sex drive!

These days he loved and hated women in unequal proportion, with a current ratio of 90:10 in favour of dislike. But that ratio was as flexible as Dan was fickle, and could often change with a simple smile from a member of the fairer sex; all part of the burden of incurable romanticism that he carried somewhat neurotically. His days as anything resembling a stoic man were long gone due to the painful anvil of experience associated with his life. In his favour was that he usually got up from all the knockdowns. He hadn't yet worked out if this was a quality or a defect.

Derry was still recovering from the usual Saturday night melee of drink, music and late-night kebabs, as well as a mosaic of vomit-smeared pavements resulting from the aforementioned kebabs. Dan was awakened by the shrill sound of his Nokia mobile phone alarm. It was 8.30am and the trumpet had sounded for his 9am jog. Tentatively, he extended his right leg outside of the quilt and was immediately met with the obnoxious onslaught of cold air that goose-bumped his leg enough to convince him to retract said leg and spend ten more minutes in the safe haven of death by duvet.

By 8.55 he was suited and booted with a cocktail of Nike, Adidas, and Reebok sports attire. Then, the ritual stretching of tendons and muscles in the back, neck, shoulders and legs. Dan didn't know what good this all did, but he saw other veteran joggers perform these exercises so he assumed it must be a good idea. Last but not least he plugged himself into his beloved iPod, which promised him an oasis of his favourite songs to counteract the incremental pain of running that was about to descend in the next hour.

At exactly 9am he unleashed himself onto the riverfront, which hugged his apartment block, and immediately set off at a sedate pace that would change regularly depending on whether Credence Clearwater was belting out 'Proud Mary' or Dolly Parton was wooing him with 'I Will Always Love You'. Aesthetically this may have been ungainly but it usually got him from A to B.

Within a minute he was lost in the triple functions of breathing, listening and looking ahead. Who said only women could multitask? Speaking of women, Dan's first encounter of the morning was with that phenomenon known as 'power walkers', members of an Amazonian cult who could be instantly identified from behind by the dropping bulges that protruded generously from under their 'yellow pack' fleeces. A learned friend of Dan's reckoned this was steatopygia, but he just thought they had fat arses!

Power walking, in Dan's sardonic state of mind, was the domain of comfort-eating women who had a clinical aversion to smiling and seemed to confound science by walking that fast, that often and yet got fatter by the week. They usually hunted in packs of two, three or four. They would have liked to march in greater numbers, but such a profusion of cellulite could only be accommodated in market towns like Aughnacloy and Cookstown. Secretly, Dan knew there was another reason why four was the limit. Not more than four women could be together for more than five minutes without falling out with a least one of the pack. Thoughts like that asserted his belief that maths was one of his stronger subjects!

Power walkers seemed to have an inherent dislike of joggers, who they saw as a threat on their beat. And aside from that, they just didn't like the thought of men being allowed out unsupervised. They never gave way to them as this might have been seen as bowing to male supremacy. Any thoughts of submissiveness to the male species could only be countenanced during the weekly shag, when there was total darkness and no witnesses.

As Dan approached them on the outside at the council offices, three thoughts polluted the textured tones of Rod

Stewart as he reminded mankind that the first cut is the deepest. *Do men actually live with these creatures? Where do power walkers go when their legs give out on them?* And his third brought an impish smile: *Wouldn't it be great to run between them and break their cycle of gossip?* He chuckled inwardly as he gave them the wide berth they deserved and said 'hello' just to annoy them and interrupt their train of slander.

On the plus side, Dan was pleased for their husbands who at least wouldn't have to pretend to give a fuck for the next two hours! Rod Stewart gave way to Spencer Davis, who wisely counselled him to keep on running. Within a few seconds, the power walkers were confined to the dustbin of the overtaken. Dan would have preferred just to put them in the dustbin, but he knew that would create problems of scale and aesthetics for Derry City Council, not to mention the issues of waste disposal and global warming.

The astute reader may have deduced by now that Dan didn't like power walkers! Yet for an instant, he thought an oncoming one gave him a look and a smile. However, with the current war that was going on in his head about women, he just dismissed it, although a backward glance that almost tweaked his sciatica seemed to suggest the girls were giggling among themselves. A few early gasps for air reverted his thoughts to a more pressing matter, that of completing the run without dying through lack of oxygen!

Dan had just taken the turn at the wharf and was heading towards Mandarin Palace (nearly On The Waterfront) when he saw four tourists at the side of the city pleasure cruiser the Toucan One; or was it the Onecan Too? Again Dan was amazed at his mathematical prowess and longed for a spreadsheet to solve this riddle.

Derry's cruise ship was a cross between the African Queen and the Bounty after the mutiny, in that it was a bit of a rust bucket with hardly anyone on it. Such cynicism was somewhat unfounded, though, as this little ship had been to the fore in getting locals and tourists to sample some of the beauty and life around the River Foyle and the warmth and mirth of Derry craic in the renaissance years following the end of the troubles in 1998.

Dan would have gladly signed up to that idea had the sewage of the city not featured in both glorious technicolour and toxic smell within three feet from the cruiser (and if someone had remembered to tell the Continuity and Real IRAs that the war was over). These were minor details, however, to the city fathers who put such a vigorous spin on local tourism. Selling the city was not one of their greatest achievements. They featured the river (with all the shite suitably airbrushed out) on all the billboards and brochures, but in this frenzy of promotion they adorned the skyline along the river with the backsides of supermarkets, shopping centres and DIY outlets and then threw in a car park on the river side of the road for good measure.

Why they hadn't adorned the riverfront with cafés, restaurants and bars, as would be the case in other European cities, would eternally mystify Dan. At this moment his mind diverted to a competition he had in mind that might help tourists to discover the city better. It was called, 'Where the fuck is the Millennium Forum?'

But conscious of his duty as a citizen, Dan greeted the tourists with a hearty hello. He hoped they weren't queuing for a trip on the Onecan Too, as it didn't sail for another four hours. Not to worry, while they waited they could count the number of cars in the car park and factor in the number of turds in the vicinity of the ship and this would give them a rough idea of how much of a shite decision it was to put a car park there. Once again a penchant for maths had saved the day!

The music had changed again and now Bruce Springsteen was gravelling out 'The River'. *Bet there was no car park beside his fucking river.* Dan looked across at the City Hotel on his right. It had been built about 100 yards from the former City Hotel, which the IRA demolished in a bomb attack in 1972. It could have been put back in the same place but decisions beyond his comprehension by wiser and better men, behind closed doors, had decided its fate.

A couple had just descended the hotel steps and were crossing over, hand in hand, to go for an early morning stroll along the riverside. Dan instinctively knew that this was not a normal liaison. He quickly surmised that they couldn't be married and that they weren't from Derry. This was based on the fact Derrymen didn't hold their partners' hands in daylight and they usually exited furtively from local hotels in darkness after they'd touched with a 'strange bit' on a Saturday night. He reckoned these two lovebirds were from out of town and were having an affair.

An air of judgment fleetingly infiltrated his thoughts but was quickly quelled when he remembered his messy divorce 10 years earlier, in which a number of inappropriate liaisons in Irish hotels were cited by his wife in her grounds for divorce. Dan took his self-admonishment on the chin but then reminded himself of the sterling work he'd done for Irish tourism during those heady days, and that indeed his contribution was perhaps the catalyst for the Celtic Tiger.

The run from the City Hotel to the Craigavon Bridge was largely uneventful, with the exception of Steve Earle and Sharon Shannon livening up his pace with their sparkling rendition of 'Galway Girl'. He thought he might put this on repeat on his iPod as it lifted his spirits and legs simultaneously, but two thoughts stopped the momentum. *If I reach into the inside pocket of my running shorts and try to adjust the iPod someone might see me and think I'm a pervert.* His second consideration clinched the decision to let the music play as selected: *If I stop to adjust this iPod someone might think I can't stick the pace.* With that, he injected a little more energy into his step and wiped sweat from his brow in the hope that any onlookers would have him pegged as a serious athlete.

As he approached the bridge, he had been running for 10 minutes and was at that, 'If I turn back now, no one will see me' stage. But they say that God works in mysterious ways and the traffic lights at the bridge were green, which happily meant that cars had the right of way. Dan stopped gratefully. There were no cars within 200 yards but he waited till the lights changed anyway before he skipped off again towards the old GNR railway line, known to locals as 'the line', with the fleet footedness and energy of a decomposed Yeti. Granted, a skipping Yeti was probably not a pretty sight and possibly an oxymoron. But Dan could also slot in comfortably under this dichotomy, so he 'skipped' forth!

As if by magic, Kris Kristofferson was jaggedly reciting, 'He's a walking contradiction, partly truth and partly fiction, taking every wrong direction on that lonely way back home.' Instinctively Dan looked over his shoulder just in case Kris was following him. *Fucking uncanny.*

His next encounter was the usual Sunday morning banter with the street drinkers who congregated at the Foyle Valley Railway Museum. They were always there when he passed. They had been moved on many times from more central parts of the city to ensure they did not detract from the ambience of Derry, the modern European city with shite flowing freely along its riverbank and plenty of places to park along the river, but fuck all to do when you get out of your car.

To emphasise consistency to this theme, it was rumoured that the city council paid £60,000 a year of ratepayers' money to keep the museum closed and had actively resisted attempts from a local entrepreneur to reinvigorate the site by providing a range of services for the community and create employment for local citizens. At this moment Crosby, Stills, Nash and Young filtered 'Deja Vous' through his iPod. This all seemed familiar to him!

Dan's thoughts were interrupted by an intoxicated, 'lift those legs, ya boy ye' from one of the street drinkers. In spite of his cynical approach to life, Dan had a soft spot for people who were down on their luck. He'd had close up and personal experience of the disease of alcoholism and knew that the fact he was running past them and not drinking with them was an act of divine providence.

His cynicism reached new heights when he wondered if the strategic plan for the city involved pushing the street drinkers a few miles further out the line so that they eventually crossed into Donegal and became Bertie Ahern's problem. Dan pressed on with feelings of deep gratitude and total powerlessness engulfing him.

A few minutes later he was on familiar territory as he approached the area skirting Foyle Road and Bishop Street. Dan was born and bred there and was still steeped in the nostalgia of his boyhood Huckleberry Finn days. There wasn't a day he jogged here that he didn't relive some childhood adventure.

Prior to being an undiscovered philosopher, poet and lyricist, unappreciated political analyst and unquestionable expert on how to fuck your life up in one easy lesson, Dan had enjoyed an idyllic childhood in which the river played a huge part. In those days, however, he did not realise that all the shite had such a negative impact on tourism.

In an instant, Van Morrison's 'Brown Eyed Girl' infiltrated his mind and once again he was lost in nostalgia, this time a doomed affair with a brown-eyed, big-busted babe from down the country who took him to heights of passion he had never known, and when she got him there threw him off the peak without a parachute. This reminded Dan of a lyric from a song he wrote, 'She gave me wings and I could fly, but when she left she took the sky'. In his mind, this was sure-fire hit material, as the pop charts were always saturated with such self-indulgent shite. The fact he hadn't pursued offering his song to the music industry perhaps reflected a dilution of his initial thoughts of having written a hit song; he just wasn't ready for the world to know he had been dumped!

For a number of years after, Dan had convinced himself she would repent like the good Presbyterian she was, beg his forgiveness and once again offer her ample bosom for inspection and foreplay. But for some strange reason, she had decided to stay with her multi-millionaire husband who lavished her with unimportant tangibles, among them a Ferrari sports car and a holiday villa in the Seychelles. *Some day she'll get her priorities right and realise what really matters,* Dan stubbornly asserted.

Dan headed out towards the Daisy Field. Many hours of his childhood were spent in this field. Football, the circus and the amusements all flooded into the happy memories that momentarily invaded the music. The Daisy Field was a field with no daisies, converted some years previously into a utility site for travellers. Strangely, the travellers had abandoned the site – maybe they were more perceptive than the street drinkers and could see they were being herded towards the Donegal border to become 'a hernia' for Bertie.

Then another thought stopped him in his tracks - metaphorically of course, as he was still running. Derry was a predominantly nationalist/republican city with aspirations for the unification of Ireland. Maybe the edging of the street drinkers and the travellers towards the Donegal border was part of a subtle master plan of creeping osmosis towards a united Ireland, he mused.

Prior to some mature study that amassed him two O-levels, he thought that creeping osmosis was something that could be eradicated with weed killer, but now he knew it had something to do with a united Ireland! Within a few years, everyone could be moved to the outskirts and into the 'free state' and the unionists wouldn't even notice. The next time he was in Donegal he thought he would speak to his friend in Donegal fisheries and let him know to expect a lot of shite in the rivers in the next few years.

Nostalgia flooded in again as he motored on out the Line. He was old enough to remember when trains bound for Dublin steamed by as he frantically backed towards the hedges for fear of being sucked in as the train passed. At the age of thirteen, he'd had teenage fumbles with local girls out there. He had fumbled in other areas too, but it all started out there. A sense of accomplishment and emotional closure overcame him as he now identified the source of his life-long awkwardness with women.

Just then he spotted two blondes in the distance. He knew they were blondes by the colour of their hair. He might have been a bit of a fumbler but he wasn't blind! Always keen to impress the ladies, even in spite of his current cynical phase, he upped his pace as they approached. *I wonder will they be impressed by my athleticism and physique? Well, they would be if their native language was Braille*, he retorted to himself as he looked down at his portly stomach. To counteract, he sucked in vigorously and searched for an appropriate chat-up line. However, that wasn't necessary. As he looked up he saw the approaching blondes were well beyond pension age. One was actually more blue rinse than blonde. The other indeed had blonde hair, but with black roots hatcheted deeply into her crooked parting. *I'm now a fucking blind fumbler.*

At this point, the iPod moved on to introduce Johnny Nash's 'I Can See Clearly Now'. *Good for Johnny*, Dan conceded. *I wish that song had come on two minutes earlier.* His marketing tendencies immediately kicked in as he visualised this little scene in an advertisement for Specsavers, and he undertook to mention it the next time he went for an eye test.

Dan was now approaching Brown's Field, which was his turning point that day. Next week he would try and make it to Anthony's Rock. He had no idea who Brown and Anthony were but presumed they were two former tourists who got lost and died in the wilderness from hypothermia while out looking for the Millennium Forum.

As he turned, his first thought was, *How the fuck am I going to make it back?* Obviously, Peale's *Power of Positive Thinking* had resonated all those years earlier. Dan realised he was nearer to Donegal than home, and for a moment he considered running on to the border so that he would be in the united

Ireland before the street drinkers and the travellers. But he wasn't sure if he would get the hot shower and the natural endorphins when he got there, so he headed back home to avail of his favourite part of jogging.

Dan's mind turned to his failed marriage as Simon and Garfunkel mellowed out 'The Sound of Silence'. In over twenty years of marriage, this was a constant theme, and he reckoned he and ex-wife Bridget had sufficiently underused their vocal cords during those years of many long silences, some of which lasted several weeks, so as to ensure full volume till death and beyond.

The river to his right looked so still and glass-like and made the raw sewage resemble shite stuck to a large window. A few deep breaths later and he was striding towards the Daisy Field again.

Then it happened; the dreaded dog in the distance syndrome. About 100 yards away a man and a dog approached. Dan had a deep fear of big dogs. How was he going to get past the oncoming mutt without getting eaten or crapping himself? A cold sweat started to form over the warm sweat that was already there. Dan didn't know the scientific impact of this concoction but it certainly impacted his nerves. He dared not look in case it might draw the attention of the hound. There was no way out other than the river on his right, and even in his state of abject fear he preferred a tetanus jab for a dog bite to swallowing some power walker's shite from the river. The dog barked sharply. Oh fuck I'm dead, he thought, but as God had it, the white poodle passed by without mauling him!

As Dan was heading back in the line he saw the Craigavon Bridge a few hundred yards away in the distance. The bridge indicated to him that he had 75 percent of the run completed. The bad news was that he had 25 percent to go and his shins were hurting. He would have delved deeper into whether the glass was half full or half empty only he had stopped drinking years ago, so this metaphor didn't apply. However, the mathematician in him had calculated that he would be home in 15 minutes.

As he passed the street drinkers again at the railway museum, he was glad they had not yet been moved to the border because he wanted to check house prices in Killea before the unification of Ireland.

A feature of the running surface from his apartment all the way out the line was that the council had provided a cycle path. As he crossed the road at the bridge and was taking a corner, a cyclist nearly took him off his feet. Cyclists in Derry were very territorial and didn't like the fact that joggers often strayed onto their designated path. This guy was no different and grunted a few expletives from his fallen position.

Dan looked down and immediately identified him as a taxi driver from a local firm. 'When you fuckers stop blaring your horns at 3am and stop parking in the middle of the road, then I'll stop running on the cycle path,' he said. At that the cyclist got up, pointing to his cut knee. 'You should have got a taxi because you can't ride that fucking bike,' Dan taunted. The taxi driver got rather agitated but Dan soon disappeared towards the Foyle Embankment, comforting himself in the thought that taxi drivers might be next in the osmosis to Donegal but hoping they didn't settle in Killea.

Tiredness was kicking in and Dan's breathing was sending out distress signals. The couple having the affair were 50 yards in front of him. When they saw him coming they flagged him down. *Hope they're not trying to enlist me for a threesome as I'm too knackered,* he thought. *If they'd just asked me on the way out.*

Dan stopped to give them the bad news. The man produced a camera and in his broad Derry accent explained that they were married yesterday and were going on honeymoon later that day. He asked Dan to take a photo of them with the River Foyle as the backdrop. Dan was still in shock that a Derryman had used a local hotel for honourable and legitimate purposes.

He took the camera and waited until the happy couple readied themselves. As he looked through the lens he wondered would the Foyle's raw sewage feature in this photo or would the council airbrush clean this photo too. The sewage deficiencies in the Foyle seemed to preoccupy Dan a lot and, in an unsolicited Darwinian moment, he reckoned that if he ever wrote a book he would call it *The Origin of the Faeces.*

Secretly Dan was glad of the breather that this little encounter had facilitated. The newlyweds thanked him for stopping and he did a token muscle stretch to impress them before setting off again with that extra spring in the step that only a wee rest and the thought of the imminent Sunday fry could bring. As he passed the City Hotel he checked to see if it had been restored to its former site but alas, not yet.

On approaching the Onecan Too, he noticed that the tourists were still there but were contentedly seated on a bench and seemed to be reading a book of some kind. Dan slowed up to see if he could make out what they were reading. To his amazement, it was the Millennium Forum programme of events for autumn/winter 2007/08. *Where the fuck did they get that?* He initially consoled himself with the knowledge that all the events would be over before the tourists could locate the theatre, although there was a lingering thought creeping in that they might have got the programme at the Forum box office.

As he passed the council offices close to his home, another wave of power walkers approached. The iPod appropriately moved on to the Travelling Wilburys' 'End of the Line'. The less intellectual reader may think he was referring to the fact that he was near home, but Dan thought it poetic as the gruesome girls looked well past their best years. This time they were head-on. Dan looked at their sullen faces and wondered were power walkers immune to natural endorphins and why were they so glad that they were sad. It had been rumoured that two of them were caught smiling and were barred from walking on the riverfront in case they might encourage more tourists and joggers.

Locals, who had obviously observed from behind, had renamed the riverfront Fat Ass Alley, but following an objection from the more affluent walkers, it was renamed Big Bum Boulevard. Dan pondered on this and thought it interesting and probably a physical impossibility that so much affluence and effluence passed each other every day!

Outside the Italian restaurant, some early morning breakfasters were having their coffee and croissants. *How very cosmopolitan,* he thought. *It was far from coffee and croissants that we were reared. The nearest we got to cosmopolitan was to get a German bun and a drink of American cream soda once a week, and now they're having European breakfast by the fucking river.* But in spite of his cynicism, he was pleased with the city's recent progress in the aftermath of the Troubles.

Dan was nearly home and the feel-good factor was already beginning to kick in. The hot shower and the natural endorphins would have to wait until after the fry was downed. He stopped outside his apartment building. He was glad that Derry was a modern city today, otherwise he would have had to stop outside his flat.

As the lift ascended to the first floor he reflected on the last hour. On entering the apartment he thought that perhaps he wasn't the good judge of character that he prided himself to be. After all, the tourists found the Millennium Forum, the couple at the City hotel were actually married, the two blondes were a bit of a letdown and the dog hadn't attacked him.

This was a lot for Dan to accept and certainly not on an empty stomach. So as he readied the frying pans and watched the sausages, bacon, eggs, tomato, potato bread, beans, and white and black pudding sizzling he sunk his teeth into a Mars bar and instantly knew what heaven really was. *This is the whole essence of jogging,* he reckoned. *This is what athletes miss out on.* Once again he was feeling good and the earlier errors of judgment had momentarily faded away in the midst of this gastronomic cacophony and kaleidoscope of calorie-laden delights. It took almost as long for him to think of that description as it did to eat the fry.

Twenty minutes later he was feeling sick and bloated. *I shouldn't have eaten that sixth sausage,* he rationalised. Dan wondered how he would make it to the shower. But not being a quitter he got there and within seconds was lavishing his body with shampoo and shower gel. As the hot water cascaded from above and washed the soap from his body he was again in a state of oneness with the universe. Except for one thing. In all the years he had been jogging and having this special hot, invigorating post-jog soak, he was disappointed that no one had invented a way to keep a Mars bar dry and free from soap in the shower. Maybe *Dragon's Den* would someday provide the solution.

Undeterred, he washed the soap off the chocolate and ate it greedily. Soon the endorphins would provide that final pleasure to the ritual of the Sunday morning jog: peace of mind. But today it didn't seem to happen. His mind was still tortured by all the wrong assessments he'd made earlier and he couldn't let go. Then, as if by magic, a thought entered his consciousness that reassured him all was well: *At least I was right about the fucking power walkers...*

2

Best Days of Your Life…

Dan Feeney's somewhat cynical and jaundiced views on life and living were not a gift from Santa or the tooth fairy. They were fertilised to a large extent within the Catholic schools system and blossomed tragically over the next 40 years.

Dan's school days were largely unremarkable from the point of view of academia. Apart from emerging with majors in cynicism, apathy and low esteem and a belly full of contradictory indoctrination, Dan's academic achievements are best described as sparse in terms of certificates, degrees and diplomas.

He knew that he knew things; it was just he struggled to incorporate some of that knowledge into his daily living. You see, not as many people as you'd expect seemed to be interested those days in the corporal works of mercy, plenary indulgences and the rosary (with or without the litany to the saints).

Dan entered the 'Wee Nuns' primary school in the late 1950s. This was the beginning of an education that was to be inflicted on him by nuns, Christian Brothers and priests, all of whom incrementally guided him towards the eternal rewards of heaven while at the same time making his life hell on earth. What was on offer was the certainty of damnation to the everlasting fires of hell for those who didn't measure up to the requirements of being a good Catholic.

Strangely, even at the tender age of five, Dan didn't quite get the selling point of what the nuns were peddling. They called it religious instruction and in later years he came to appreciate why, as the children were certainly not allowed to question or debate the instruction that was provided.

Sisters Angelis and Immaculata were the head honchos at the Wee Nuns. They didn't teach Spanish there, but Dan was an ardent fan of the Lone Ranger and Zorro and so became bilingual at a young age. At five he didn't know much about paradoxes or contradictions, but hindsight had taught him that these ladies were neither angelical nor immaculate.

Beneath the veneer of education, these two 'angels' seemed to excel in the instillation of fear, guilt and incontinence into the minds and bladders of innocents. In later years Dan was to come to believe that their early role models were high up the food chain in the Spanish Inquisition. At times, though, the nuns did make them feel special. After all, Catholics were the only ones who could get to heaven and who had a total monopoly on God. Even at a young age, Dan often struggled with the teachings of the clergy. He could never quite visualise what the three persons in one God actually looked like and also struggled with heaven being up in the sky and wondered how did Catholics suffering from vertigo cope.

Add to that a talking snake offering apples to the early settlers and one could understand how Dan had some conflict with the information being given by the 'good' sisters. However, these were the days before civil rights protests, so he said nothing about his youthful scepticism just in case he might annoy the sisters enough to be chastened by their canes. You see, the sisters also believed that beating up on wanes was good for the soul. Dan often wondered why they didn't beat the crap out of each other as well so they could benefit spiritually as much as he did.

Somewhere in the midst of being guided in the ways of the Lord, the nuns also seemed to manage to teach English and arithmetic to lost souls such as Dan. He was a keen student, as he liked things that made sense, and more importantly had an avid fear of nuns brandishing canes.

'One and one are two, two and two are four, four and four are eight' et al was the mantra around the class every morning, but at least this was better than wondering how long he would have to spend in purgatory before he got into heaven, or what venial and mortal sins looked like when they hit your soul.

His last year at the school was largely devoted to preparing for his First Confession and First Holy Communion. At the age of seven, young Catholic children were introduced to these two sacraments.

The First Confession was by far the worst. It involved going into a darkened box and telling a priest through a grill all the sins committed since the last time he'd grilled you.

The benchmark was the Ten Commandments and it was extremely difficult for children to understand them, never mind break them. In 1960, adultery, murder and coveting thy neighbour's wife were not high on Dan's agenda. In later life, he was to try some of them out, but that was a story for another day.

After a few attempts, Dan got the hang of confession and used to rattle off the same sins each week. The fact that he always threw in at the end that he told lies seemed to cover the fact that he was still telling them to the priest in the confessional box. After he told his sins, the priest would mumble at him in Latin and then give him his penance of a few prayers to say to cleanse his soul.

Priests were like that; they used to say things in Latin, like the mass and benediction. It kept them aloof from the proletariat. In hindsight, Dan reckoned that it may have been their chat-up lines to young boys given the number of revelations of child sex abuse instances many years later.

As Dan hadn't read the Book of Revelations, he wasn't sure if it contributed to the scandals. Or perhaps they just needed to keep it all a secret from the punters to keep them attending these rituals and the money flowing in, as to say it all in English might have emptied the chapels. Interestingly, in recent years he had attended a few empty chapels, so his theories still had oxygen.

Dan vividly remembered his First Holy Communion. This was a big day for young Catholics. From the Church's perspective, the initiates would receive the body and blood of Jesus compressed into a little white wafer. Just like the three persons in the one God, this confused Dan. He often wondered how so many people could eat the same man who died 2000 years earlier, and yet there always seemed to be plenty left and he didn't decompose. Dan reckoned that Jesus would have been a candidate for Weight Watchers if he were around today!

The good news was that, after his first act of juvenile cannibalism, the nuns threw a party in the school and they all had cakes and lemonade to wash down any cadaver remnants that were stuck to the roof of the mouth or lurking between the teeth.

The best part of the day was yet to come. That was the ritual visit to friends and relatives to show off the First Communion suit and be rewarded with a few bob at each visitation. Dan collected seven pounds seven and sixpence which, with inflation applied, would be worth about £400 these days. So, he was a wealthy boy that day and he still had the acne into adulthood to prove that he'd spent it all on sweets over the next week.

Having been fully integrated into the Catholic schools system, he was then despatched to the local Christian Brothers' school for lesson two in how to live in eternal fear without wetting yourself too often. The Christian Brothers were a contradiction from the start, in that they were neither Christian nor brotherly. Their promise to Catholic parents was, 'Bring me the boy and I'll give you the man.' Unfortunately, they didn't explain the torture methods they would use in their marketing brochure.

The need to make men out of boys seemed a priority to Brother Desmond, who began class with English, maths and religious instruction. The instruction from the brothers was basically a more manly way to ram down the throats of Dan and his fellow victims the fact that bad boys were bound for the fires of hell.

The school day often ended with Brother Desmond getting the boys to rearrange their desks to form a boxing ring, then he randomly selected two young gladiators to don boxing gloves and fight each other until one could fight no more. Those who would not fight were given six slaps with the strap and then made to get in the ring and fight anyway, so the boys soon learned to accept the gloves if they were thrown in their direction. Dan was selected many times, probably because even on a losing day he never gave up, a trait that was to cause pride and pain in equal measure in later life.

Dan's next four years under the tutelage of the Brothers confirmed the undoubted link that educators of that era saw between learning and corporal punishment; a lovely soft term for beating up on wanes, he thought. It was a relatively simple formula; if you didn't learn and remember what the Brothers wanted you to learn, then you got beat up.

There were three types of punishment. The conventional leather strap was holstered in the right or left-hand pocket of the brothers' soutanes, and these religious gunslingers drew them out to administer six of the best to any terrified schoolboy who had got their dander up, resulting in either sore hands or a sore arse depending on whether they were feeling kind or not.

The soutane was a long black skirt-like garment similar to that worn by priests. Dan thought it strange that those who set out to make a man of him should dress like a woman. Perhaps it was to lull the boys into a false sense of security - or maybe cross-dressing was just their thing!

For more spontaneous results they used the flying duster that they hurled through the air, aimed at the offending boy's head. Finally, there was the 'knock the bejaysus out of you' approach, which was used more at sporting events.

One unspoken but important element of a Christian Brother's duty was to bring Irishness and culture to the boys of Derry. Part of this involved twice-weekly trips to the playing field to learn how to play Gaelic football and hurling. Choice wasn't an option in those days, so everyone was herded there to play a man's game.

Soccer was banned and anyone caught playing it was punished. Dan was one of the lucky ones, as he loved sport and excelled at Gaelic football. But there were some boys who were different and their lives were made pure hell at those pitches.

Dan recalls one particular incident when he was running up the park with the ball toe to hand. Tony Stewart, a hefty yet effeminate lad who liked dolls more than balls, was marking him. Dan cruised past him to shoot and score a point. Simultaneously the brother thought it was time he made his point as well, and Tony was manhandled towards the sideline and beaten almost senseless by the *brave* brother. For years, Dan's consciousness was branded with that image of his classmate's head being banged several times against the rusty corrugated tin fence, with Tony screeching, sobbing and roaring in pain and terror.

And that was the way it was. Nobody complained or stood up for each other when the brothers pounced. At a deep level, Dan hated himself for not standing up to this abuse, but at ten years old, fear was the winner every day, so the brothers enjoyed a free hand. They knew the power they had and they abused it on almost every occasion. His only comfort was to know that the next time he was running up the wing and saw Tony approaching, he cut inside to allow someone else to tackle him, much to the distaste of the ranting brother. It wasn't much but it kept the brother away from Tony, for a while at least.

The Brothers' primary mission was to get the boys through the 11-plus and into grammar school. Other less spoken of targets included teaching them about Irish heritage, history, culture, music and sport and ensuring that the 11-year-olds who left the Christian Brothers school left as men. To a large extent, they succeeded with Dan; he passed the exam and had learned enough about Ireland's history and culture to know it was his duty to free the North from the English invaders who had raped, plundered and pillaged his country for 800 years. Inside that prepubescent boy with the sweet soprano voice, there was a semblance of a man trying to get out.

On top of that, he was a regular on the school football team and won the all-Derry 80-yard sprint at the schools sports day in the Brandywell. None of your metric crap in those days. A yard was a yard; unless of course it was a backyard, a shipyard or the gasyard, in which case it was miles bigger than a yard!

In later years Dan was to learn that only Derry's Catholic schools were represented at the sports day, so he would never be sure whether he was the fastest 11-year-old in town or not. But he was fast; there was no denying that. It was a talent that would save his life some years later.

His memories of that day still remained. It was a sunny, Sunday afternoon and all the top sprinters who had come through their school heats lined up nervously on the sideline of the hallowed turf at the Brandywell Stadium, awaiting the signal to start. Suddenly a gun went off (many more guns went off years later in this area, but more about that anon) and the boys exploded off their marks (again, the Brandywell area was to know all about explosions some years later too).

Dan was never headed as he blazed the trail to the winning line. He had won something at last and was the best sprinter in his year. He was jubilant and enjoyed his moment of glory before being herded off the running track to make way for the next race. No Olympian lap of honour was allowed in those days.

Dan waited for the next two hours, wondering what his prize would be. And then the announcement came over the tannoy, 'Would the prize winners of the under 11 80-yard sprint come to the sideline to receive their prizes?'

With nervous and excited anticipation Dan ambled towards the prize giving area. He was congratulated by a teacher from a rival school and handed the first prize. No, it wasn't a gold medal, it wasn't a bike or even a watch or a transistor radio. It was the 1964 *Rawhide* annual. And to make matters worse, it had no pictures apart from the cowboy from the title on the front cover.

In an instant, Dan learned the life skill of how to look pleased when you're bitterly disappointed. The boy who finished second to him got a plastic fishing rod, which he immediately coveted, as anything was better than a book with no pictures. Readers will note that the Ten Commandments from the Wee Nuns had not fallen on deaf ears, as Dan had now learned how to covet thy neighbour's goods. Dan tried unsuccessfully to swap his first prize for the other boy's second prize. So as well as being a champion sprinter, he had also managed to stain his soul with a sin before he left the stadium. The nuns would have been so proud to see his guilty face.

In today's world of counselling, therapists and analysing the shite out of everything, Dan's act would probably be viewed as the outworking of low self-esteem and rejection coupled with a hint of manic depression. He would probably have been given another book with no pictures telling him how he should feel and who to blame, together with a cocktail of anti-depressants to numb his sense of aloneness. The reality was that the fishing rod looked better than the *Rawhide* annual and he just fancied a swap.

Dan returned home and announced he had just become the all-Derry champion sprinter. This was met with initial disbelief followed by, 'Ah that's grand, son,' from his mother. And so ended the most successful moment of his life. Recognition in a family of ten was not easy to achieve, but in later years Dan certainly got their attention on a grand and sustained scale.

After the 11-plus exam was over, the Christian Brothers appeared to be possessed by aliens. They became friendly, funny, likeable and easy-going in class. It was as if their mission was over. The strap was permanently holstered, the duster was only used to clean the blackboard and the fists remained unclenched until the end of term. Apart from English, maths and the mandatory dollop of religion, the brothers taught them some Irish and French to prepare them for college. Sport was played more often and without the threat of a hammering if you made a mistake.

Those few weeks were, without doubt, the best days of Dan's school life; up to then at least. History would ensure they remained in that exalted position, as his days at St Columb's College did not contain any memories that could be remotely characterised as happy.

He did have many memories of his college years, but they were ones that would catapult him into adulthood with a certain amount of knowledge and lots of simmering anger, cynicism and sarcasm, but little in terms of life skills, confidence and self-worth.

In hindsight, Dan reckoned that institutions such as St Columb's gave birth to the influx to Derry of the 'rent a therapy' mentality, which was imported from America during the late 1970s. Many students of his generation left college so fucked up that the imminent joys of sex and rock 'n' roll required the stimulant of copious amounts of drink and drugs to achieve those pleasures. In fact, following some personal experiences in later life, Dan came to believe that if you went to a counsellor without an emotional or mental disorder, they would give you one to take away at no extra cost.

Dan had four older brothers, all of whom had preceded him at 'the College', as it was known, and all of whom he looked up to. His younger brother by ten years, 'a wee late wan', as Derry mothers liked to say, was to succeed him at the school, thus completing the full house of Feeney brothers.

Dan had an inward sense of egalitarianism from a young age. It came to some extent from his awareness that there was something not right in Northern Ireland; something which he felt but couldn't fully understand or describe.

However, his love of going to the pictures was probably an even greater contributor to his nationalist and socialist inclinations. From the age of seven, Dan had discovered the magic of cinema. The Great Escape (the concept itself rather than the classic film starring Steve McQueen) was to be found in the darkened picture houses of Derry and he was an immediate convert to the wonderful opt-out clause presented by the movie heroes of that time.

Dan went as often as he could, sometimes many days in a row if he could muster the sixpence for entry. He learned words like 'muster' from the wonderful westerns he saw. Of course, they mustered posses or cattle, not sixpences!

He loved westerns, action films and epics of the Roman Empire. Those films generally had a theme of, 'A man's gotta do what a man's gotta do' running in parallel to a love interest for the leading actor. Dan wondered why they'd 'gotta do' it twice, but assumed it was for the purpose of thoroughness.

The lead character was usually a man who stood up to injustice and came out on top in the end. Gender equality was virtually non-existent in Hollywood in those days, although Doris Day challenged the patriarchal norms as Calamity Jane.

John Wayne would have taken no shite from the nuns, Christian Brothers and priests who tortured us, Dan often reflected. How he would have loved to let the Magnificent Seven loose on the whole lot of them.

The fears and disciplines of school were easily forgotten during those special hours of escape when Dan could become Davy Crockett, Robin Hood or Spartacus, all unrelenting men who stood up to be counted and who fought for the underdog. The love interest in the films bored him, so he used those moments to go for a pee or to the shop for sweets. In later years he had many love interests but considered it might have been better to have continued peeing or shopping.

But this sense of fair play was mixed with the fear, dread

and bladder issues brought on by teachers that were the underbelly to his existence in the college. And it was this unhealthy concoction of wanting to stand up but knowing you had to lie down that would eventually erupt when the boy finally became the man.

St Columb's was the place where all Derry mothers wanted to send their sons so that they could become priests, teachers, solicitors, or accountants; all acceptable and exalted professions of the time. The fact that Dan didn't make the grade for any of these lofty careers didn't concern him, as he could only imagine John Wayne, Kirk Douglas, or Errol Flynn behind guns and swords rather than altars and desks.

Dan's first day at the College was full of apprehension and expectation but wasn't memorable, apart from getting the customary ducking under the cold water tap by the second year boys, who were just passing on the induction 'hello' they themselves had received the previous year.

The College received boys from all the Derry Catholic primary schools and also catered for boarders from country areas. Following some academic tests, they were corralled into classes ranging from 1A to 1F depending on their perceived academic ability.

Dan was put into 1C, which was testimony to his ordinariness. He would have aspired to have been in 1A but expected to be in 1F, so 1C was okay by him. He was to learn that lofty aspirations coupled with low expectations corresponded with the amount of work he should have done and the amount he actually did while he was at the school.

St Columb's was undoubtedly a great place for keen academics, and the teaching staff nurtured those who were naturally talented or whose parents were upstanding middle-class professional or business people from within the Catholic community.

The teachers were a mixture of priests and laity, who brought a new string to the torture bow in the form of demeaning and degrading the students. Getting slapped or beaten was over when the pain died off, but this new punishment could last for weeks, months, or even years depending on the donor.

For Dan, some of the mental abuse seemed to be lodged forever, which is testimony to the thorough job done on him by some of the teaching staff, who could have slotted very well into the German SS thirty years earlier.

There were many occasions when Dan was to feel less than whole, but two incidents stuck out in his mind that reminded him of his days at the College. The President of St Columb's was a priest called Fr McFarrell. He was a nephew of a bishop, so was right up there in the queue for heaven. He even walked like a saint, in a slow pious movement with his arms folded and his hands disappeared up the opposite sleeve of his cassock. *God knows what he was hiding up there, but it certainly wasn't humility,* Dan reflected.

That's where his saintliness ended. Underneath the priestly garments was a pompous, pretentious, class-orientated little man who oozed the poison of superiority and snobbishness, and who seemed to have a life mission of ensuring each boy knew his pedigree, especially those from working-class backgrounds.

Dan vividly recalled his first encounter with the President. His French teacher, Mr Bardun, hadn't shown up and they had a free period. The majority of the class, Dan included, bolted straight to the football pitch, with a small number opting to go to the study. One boy asked him if he was going to the study and he replied, 'Are you off your head? I'm not going to that joint.' Even in hindsight, he thought this was a mild and reasonable response, given the option of football or books to an 11-year-old.

However, his comment was shouted just below the President's open window. Luck was not with him that day as Fr McFarrell was on spy duty and heard the comment. 'Come up to my office, boy,' he bellowed from the open window. Dan's heart sank as he climbed the stairs to 'Wee Ronnie's' office. He knocked softly on the door to be met with a stern 'come in'.

McFarrell admonished Dan for his cheek and his audacity to refer to the study as a 'joint', gave him six slaps with his sturdy leather strap, and told him to go straight to the junior study for the rest of the free period when he left his office. He then asked him his name and address. When he realised who Dan was, he asked him if he wanted to turn out like his older brothers at the college. He immediately responded, 'I hope so, father.' Boy, was that the wrong answer.

Wee Ronnie eulogized for about ten minutes on the demerits of his brothers and extended his rant to include degrading Dan's father's work as a local publican, telling him he would be watching him from then onwards. Just like the incident with Tony Stewart, Dan wanted to speak up to explain how good his brothers and his father really were and how he looked up to them, but again in those situations, at the age of eleven fear always won through over valour.

Dan walked from that room with his head bent low and his young mind pickled with all that Wee Ronnie had said. Added to that was a feeling of having failed his family by not speaking up when they were being attacked.

Interestingly, from that day Dan Feeney walked with his head low in the shape of a question mark. From then onwards he totally hated the College, and within three years he had more or less downed tools completely and turned his back on education and sport.

At that age, it's natural to think you are being singled out, but conversations in later years revealed many similar interventions with other working-class students by the President. Two former students, one of whom later became a solicitor, the other a teacher, recounted McFarrell's contempt for working-class students.

They were in their final year and studying for their A-levels. It was a sunny day and instead of going to the study they were sitting reading in the sunshine with their backs propped against the gable wall just below the 'presidential suite'. The Reverend Fr McFarrell walked by, and on noticing the two young men made just one comment, 'Creggan slags,' before walking on with his head erect.

Obviously, he didn't approve of the fact that young men from working-class backgrounds were at St Columb's, making a success of their time there and leaving with good prospects for their futures. It is also true to say that many of the boys who entered the school from more affluent areas and backgrounds were to a large extent oblivious of the class distinction that was so prevalent in those days. Such was the skill with which this particular form of apartheid was practiced.

For the rest of his life, Dan found it poignant that his early experiences of discrimination came from within the bowels of the Catholic and nationalist community, who themselves were the victims of unionist one-party domination for so many years. Reflections such as this demonstrated the complexity of the Troubles that began a few years later. At the age of fourteen, Dan recalled another pompous priest telling the class to get their parents to vote for a 'moderate unionist', an oxymoron of its time if ever there was one!

The second experience that was to brand itself into Dan's consciousness for eternity was his three years learning maths with Mr McMaher, otherwise known to the boys as 'the Hammer'. The Hammer had it all. He was a thug with a tie, excelled in verbal degradation and enjoyed watching boys suffer, and, of course, was an upstanding Catholic within the community.

He introduced Dan to valuable concepts such as the angles of isosceles and equilateral triangles, algebraic formula, the total uselessness of being a working-class

Derryman, and how to degrade a boy and ensure the effects lasted for a lifetime.

Dan didn't doubt his prowess as a mathematician but knew from personal experience how he excelled at the latter two. The three years under the Hammer's tutelage were memorable for all the wrong reasons, and even though he had a natural aptitude for figures he struggled to learn by his 'degrade as you go' system.

He recalled one day when McMaher was randomly asking questions on geometry whilst simultaneously throwing barbed comments to the students. He barked loudly at Dan, 'What's an acute angle?' As Dan tried to determine whether it was over or under 90 degrees, the Hammer closed in, menacingly spitting insults about corner boys and lowlifes.

Dan nervously gave the wrong answer, 'It's over 90 degrees sir,' he uttered. Well, it was as if he had just made McMaher's day. The easy bit was six slaps and multiple thumps on the arm just below his right shoulder. That pain subsided over the next two periods. But his next little gem was to stay with Dan for a lifetime. 'Feeney, for the rest of your life, if you ever have a choice to make between two possible outcomes, choose the one you don't think is right because you will always choose the wrong option.'

This was esteem and confidence building at its best, Hammer style. Just the way to instil into a boy the enthusiasm and endeavour required for success! How McMaher was never awarded a Nobel Prize for his sterling contribution to youth education, Dan would never know!

Dan relived (and reviled) that day hundreds of times over the years, especially any time he had a choice to make. On the plus side, he never forgot what an acute angle was, which no doubt would have vindicated the twisted logic of the Hammer. The conflict that this experience introduced into his life was akin to watching Mrs Doyle of *Father Ted* fame trying to give herself a cup of tea!

The Hammer also had another string to his bow; he produced the college plays and musicals. Dan was a member of the school choir and was picked for a minor role in the College's production of *The Mikado.*

He was chosen as Peep-Bo, one of the three little maids from school, thus ensuring that he would be under the directorship of the Hammer. In fairness, his nasty streak was somewhat dulled during the early rehearsals. There were a number of senior students involved who wouldn't have stood for his classroom antics during this production.

But one day it all went wrong for him. He was given a copy of the *Mikado* script to help learn his lines. Somehow it got either lost or stolen and Dan arrived for rehearsal empty-handed. He explained to McMaher that he had lost the book.

Within seconds the Hammer was in a total tirade and assaulted him both physically and verbally. He told him not to come to the next rehearsal, which was two days later, without the script. For two days Dan trudged the streets of Derry on both sides of the river, seeking out bookshops, newsagents and novelty shops in an increasingly Quixotic quest to find, of all things, the libretto of a Gilbert and Sullivan operetta.

Even the top shelves of some of the more seedy shops, that a young boy could only aspire to view, were searched.

The rain poured down his face and seeped through the hole in his shoe as he tried fruitlessly to get the script. He arrived at the rehearsal soaked and scriptless and McMaher tiraded once again.

One of the senior students intervened and said he would loan his script to Dan so that he could copy out the relevant bits that featured Peep-Bo. The Hammer backed off reluctantly, after further emphasizing how useless he was both in class and on the stage. And so ended another episode of his early days at college, days that were to leave scars and scores that would never heal or be settled.

Dan's time in the choir was not without dramatic incident either. The head of music was Mr Galbraith, who also taught Irish and was involved with the school's junior football teams. The students knew him as 'Wee Jimmy'.

Dan initially got along well with him and he used to sometimes take him in his car to watch the seniors play in the Ulster College Championship games. Dan was heavily involved in the class league and later became captain of the College under-14 team.

He was being groomed to captain the team in the all-Ulster Junior Championship the following year and was even training with the current team. However, early in the relationship with Wee Jimmy, Dan was to learn that he was being groomed for other extra-curricular pursuits too.

Dan was asked to stay on after choir practice one night.

Wee Jimmy produced a trunk filled with dresses and threw one at him and told him to try it on as he was auditioning for the Christmas concert. Initially, he didn't suspect anything was wrong, although as a typical 12-year-old boy he was reluctant to put a dress on for any reason.

Anyway, he began to pull the dress on over his clothes only to be instructed to strip naked and then put it on. Dan thought it was a joke at first, but as Wee Jimmy closed in he knew he'd better comply or he might get a helping hand.

Galbraith watched intently as Dan undressed. Instinctively he knew there was something not right, but wasn't sure what it was. He recalled a slow chase around the desks as he tried to get his clothes back on without Galbraith getting his hands on him. He left the classroom embarrassed, confused, and afraid – all part of Wee Jimmy's student grooming process.

Following a sharing of experiences with another student, he realised his interest in him was far from musical, educational, sporting or spiritual. Dan never went to another match with Galbraith and faded away initially from the choir, soon to be followed by a withdrawal from sport. After captaining the under 14s, he never played football again at the College.

Dan scraped through his junior exams by the bare margin required to enable him to progress to senior level. His diminishing efforts as a student brought corresponding diminishing academic success. Now 15 years old, he was gaining in a rebelliousness that often accompanies mid-teens, and in the apathy and cynicism towards learning that had been fermenting during the years when fear ruled the day.

It was 1968 and he had witnessed on TV students rising up and protesting in Paris and Newark in the past year. The civil rights movement was gaining momentum in Derry too, and Dan recalled seeing TV clips from the October 5th civil rights march that was brutally attacked by the RUC in Duke Street in Derry. Bob Dylan was right; the times they were a-changing!

College became a place to avoid and he only went there when he didn't have the money to dobb in the cafes and snooker halls of Derry. In his final year at school, he got a part-time afternoon job marking the boards in a local bookmakers. This introduced him to the world of gambling that was to plague his life for many years to come.

But in 1969, earning fourteen bob a day was not to be sneezed at. This was also the year when he discovered the escape and buzz of alcohol, and how its effect could nullify his acute shyness with girls.

Consequently, Dan flumped all his O-levels and left college with a head full of apathy and a belly full of education. Had it only been the other way around, he reckoned he would have had a better balance. But in years to come, he found filling his belly with booze was an effective, albeit temporary, antidote to all those school memories.

And so ended his formal education under the Catholic schools system. Apart from his growing disinterest in education, he also left the College totally disillusioned about the concept of God and religion and with only one abiding belief; that he was damned to burn in the eternal fires of hell, so he might as well enjoy himself on the way down.

3

Long Trousers and Short Change

Dan was born in 1953 into a big family. His father Michael was a local publican who had married Margaret, a 'blow in' from Donegal, and they'd already had four boys and two girls by the time Dan came along. Ten years after that, the last edition of the Feeneys, John, arrived, removing the mantle of being the 'wane' of the family from Dan forever.

Dan was a normal, active yet naive and innocent young boy. A testimony to his naivety and innocence can be suitably illustrated on the day John was born. Dan was almost ten and he recalled that morning vividly. As he was leaving home to head over the hill to the Christian Brothers school, his sister Alice came rushing out of the next-door neighbours' house full of joy. She called Dan and told him it was a boy.

Dan was delighted and informed Brother Desmond and the whole class that Mrs Duffy next door had just had a new wee boy. It wasn't until he came home that he found out that it was his mum who'd had the baby and that Alice had gone next door to phone the nursing home. So basically Dan's mum had gone through a full pregnancy and Dan knew nothing about it.

The Feeneys certainly knew how to keep a secret; or perhaps more to the point Dan was more preoccupied with important events such as football, marbles, fighting, and tig to notice that his mother had put on some weight and had gone a funny shape during the nine-month period.

It's strange how wee boys have such a distaste for, disinterest in, and dislike of girls when they are running free in the adventures of boyhood. Then when they hit mid-teens, their whole life seems to be dominated by getting one of those females, that they once couldn't stand, into their arms and beyond. It's funny how the freedom of boyhood never really returns after that...

Dan lived in a three-storey house that was attached to his father's pub. There were only about thirteen years between the first seven children, so most of them were at one school or another at the same time. Breakfast time at the Feeneys' house was always eventful. The boys hurtled down two flights of stairs, all vying for the top of the table and the cream of the milk on their porridge.

The two girls came down at a more sedate pace, probably wondering what they were doing amidst all this bedlam and these stampeding males. Being the youngest of the family at that time had its benefits, especially having four bigger brothers to deal with any street bullies who fancied a soft touch. The two sisters supported Dan in more feminine ways, such as taking him out the town, buying him sweets, and probably unknowingly practising their early maternal instincts on their wee brother.

One of them practised so hard that his leg got mangled on the wheel of the pram while big sis was playing mum in the street. In later years there was a suspicion she may have also dropped Dan on his head a few times, given the way he turned out, but as yet nobody has verified this line of thought. But among family members, the jury remained out!

Friday nights were special for the Feeney children. It was payday. As the youngest, Dan had the job of collecting from three aunts who all lived within a 50-yard radius of his home. First up was Agnes, just two doors away on Brook Street Lane. Dan recalled walking into her living room each week and just saying one word, 'PAY'. At that, she selected coins from her purse to be distributed among himself and three of his siblings, the others being too old for Friday night pay. The demand for was delivered in more of a boyish lilt than a highwayman's ultimatum, but it always got the desired results.

Then it was on down the lane to his aunts Bridget and Annie, who lived next door to each other in Sloans Terrace, for further contributions. As before, he asked for pay and was again rewarded with a booty of coin to share with his sister and two brothers. Dan didn't dwell too long for small talk and used to speed back up the lane to his own house to dole out the loot.

Every week it amounted to one shilling each, which was always cashed in shortly afterward for sweets and ice cream. For over a year Dan collected every Friday until one night the collection didn't go to plan. He was seven years old and had collected successfully from the first two aunties. Then he knocked at Annie's. A man answered the door, and on seeing Dan said, 'Nothing for you today, young fella.' Dan looked at this guy in front of him, shocked and embarrassed at this rejection. He immediately ran away from the door and got home quickly. In the background, he heard a call to come back but he was too hurt to respond, so he kept on running. He shared the money with his siblings in the usual way and explained that Auntie Annie hadn't paid up.

Still smarting from before, he went to his schoolbag and penned a letter with his pencil. He ran down the lane and posted it through her letterbox. Then he sped up the lane, ran across the street, and onto the safety of 'the Bankin', a steep, grassy area near his home where all the local youngsters played, and hid there until dark.

Eventually, he went home and was quizzed by his mum and siblings about the letter his aunt had received. Initially, he pleaded innocence and ignorance of the existence of this letter. But when they recited the text he knew the game was up. It read, *I won't be back for my pay ever again* (it was a sort of Arnold Schwarzenegger moment in reverse), and was signed *Mr X*. So the game was up and they all made fun of him and often called him *'Mr X'* from then onwards. Dan never collected pay on a Friday night after that event, even though his aunt explained that the guy who refused him was her son-in-law and he was just having fun and had tried to call him back. But Mr X was having none of it.

That mix of innocence and sensitivity was fairly typical of youngsters in those times. But such innocence was often exploited by the 'dodgy' people who sometimes hung around children. A few weeks after the 'pay freeze', Dan was again up the Bankin playing with his friends. An older guy called Denis was there. He was about fifteen, and in today's world might have seemed out of place. They were all converged on a large grassy mound call the Hump, just playing sham fights and rolling around and playing head over heels.

When the boys decided to go home for dinner, Dan was the last to leave along with Denis. He started a play fight with Dan and soon had him pinned to the ground, with his knees firmly holding him down and his legs straddled over him. Then he started talking about sexual things that Dan didn't understand, getting closer into his face as he spoke. Dan didn't know what was going on but instinctively knew this wasn't normal or natural. Denis persisted, speaking into his ear about how male and female body parts worked during sex. Dan recalled his stomach feeling sick and a terrible fear overcoming him.

He shouted out for help and some fishermen digging for worms nearby heard his call and looked over. Denis immediately got up and laughed it off as if they were just playing. Dan knew he'd had a close call, but didn't know from what at that time. Once he got down off the Bankin, he just put it to the back of his mind and got back to boyish thoughts and actions. But every once in a while the memory of the experience returned. He didn't tell his parents in case he would be banned from playing there. But he did tell his pals, who like him gave Denis a wide berth from then on.

Years later, looking back, he realised just how vulnerable children were in those days, and had no doubt that many secrets would remain on the Bankin forever. Other secrets exploded there in the early seventies, but not in the way that was planned!

The secret to a happy childhood, as Dan saw it, was to get out of the house as early as possible and return home as late as possible so as to miss anything remotely to do with family life. In between were unimportant things such as going to school and mass, and important things such as breakfast, lunch, dinner and supper. In hindsight, Dan's mother was probably glad that was the way of things, as she seemed to be eternally cooking, cleaning, washing and doing her stint in the bar, so the absence of a few of the youngsters was, no doubt, a welcome break.

In between all her duties as a mother she also had the pastoral shackles of Catholicism to pass on. This meant she had to ensure the family attended mass, confession, communion, retreats and benediction to enhance their chances of getting to heaven later on in life. Well, you really had to be dead to go there, but that was just another of the many mysteries surrounding religion. She was also an advocate of, 'The family that prays together, stays together,' and so everyone gathered at 8pm each night for the family rosary.

The rosary consisted of three mysteries: the sorrowful, the glorious and the joyful, and each mystery had five decades, and to Dan, it seemed like it took that long to say it. In later life he has discovered three mysteries of his own:

1) Where do odd socks come from?
2) What do the Apprentice Boys of Derry become when they have completed their apprenticeship?
3) How do you get air into a tubeless tyre?

Dan hated all these interruptions to boyhood priorities, as he had no interest in any of these religious rituals. Dodging the rosary became an art form and it was worth the odd clip on the ear to go missing around 8pm on at least some nights during the week.

The thing about the rosary was that over time it took longer to say, due to the ever-increasing litany of saints that was tagged on to it, and the other trimmings, prayers his mother had gathered up over the years. Her prayer book bulged with loose pictures of saints with prayers attached given to her by other collectors of Catholic saints.

Every time a new saint was canonised or an apprentice saint was beatified, his mum added them to her list. Most Catholics prayed to the saints, but Dan just counted them! His gift to future bored Catholic boys was not to behave too saintly so as to be added to the list when he died. He was comfortable that so far his gift was intact and he was actively working on keeping things that way.

Dan was always drawn to the world of bars and booze. After all, he was brought up in this environment. As far back as he could remember, he used to love sitting out at the windowsill inside his dad's bar playing Cowboys and Indians with bottle tops from used beer and stout bottles. He always loved the escape and the fantasy. Even at such a young age, Dan instinctively flew a flag for the Indians, who seemed to get a raw deal on the television programmes of the late 1950s.

In hindsight, he wondered how this instinct fared against the Hammer's theory. Hollywood had always depicted the Native Americans as the 'baddies' but finally began to tell the true story many years later in films like *Soldier Blue* that endorsed Dan's early instincts as being those of a decent wee boy with an inherent concern for those who suffered injustice and a propensity for being on the side of the underdog. In later years when he learned some of the history of Ireland, he appreciated even more how terribly the American settlers had treated that land's indigenous inhabitants.

All those afternoons playing with bottle tops opened Dan to other gems of life learning that he picked up from the barroom stories and discussions that were the background noise to his efforts to rewrite the history books in relation to the demise of the native Americans.

Dan's father was by trade a barman but by default a banker, confidant, diplomat, storyteller, comedian and boxer. His boxing skills were rarely used due to his diplomatic prowess, but Dan vividly remembers him disarm and eject a drunk with a knife from the premises and also 'flattening' an aggressive member of the traveller community who couldn't handle firewater. In Dan's eyes, his dad had just one role, that of hero, and he played it to perfection from his perspective as a wee boy in the midst of men.

Unfortunately he never really got to know his father from a man-to-man perspective, as cancer took him when Dan was only 18-years-old. From then onwards, he harboured regrets of missed opportunities to be the son he wanted to be but couldn't be, due in the main to his teenage self-centredness. Many years later he bought his daughter a keyring inscribed, *Ask a teenager while they still know it all.* She didn't know the significance of it, but Dan did.

As a child, Dan recalled being introduced by his dad to Billy the Kid, Davy Crockett, Wild Bill Hickock, Crazy Horse, Sitting Bull, Geronimo (before he became the popular war cry for those jumping from planes and high buildings), and many other historical and fictional characters from the Wild West.

He also brought spine-chilling tales to him about his battles with the 'Mallmootricans' and the 'Scotch Doctors', and magical moments from his stories about 'Seamus the Fairy', who always seemed to save the day with only seconds to spare. He was a sort of precursor to James Bond without the violence, weaponry, gadgetry and overdoses of testosterone.

The Mallmootricians were akin to the Morlocks in HG Wells' *Time Machine,* only they inhabited the riverbanks and hedge groves out the Line where Dan did his jogging many years later. They could only be fended off by porridge guns (which his dad always seemed to have at hand when confronted by them), which caused them to retreat squealing once the hot porridge hit their arses. Strangely, Dan never actually saw one, but assumed the toxic river Foyle had caused the Mallmootricans to emigrate even before the street drinkers and the travellers!

The Scotch Doctors used to come in motorboats from Scotland to kidnap young boys in commando-like night raids. Dan reflected in later years that maybe they were just trying to get in touch with their relatives who had been planted into Ulster centuries earlier to prop up British interests in the northern part of Ireland. If that was the case he would be happy to provide a few nominees for repatriation.

He loved listening to his father's yarns and believed every syllable. Hindsight introduced the thought that maybe his dad was just trying to keep him away from the river to avert a tragedy, given that the stories seemed to locate both these fantastical tribes close to the river.

Life living alongside a bar was great for Dan, especially on wintry, rainy days when football, tig or knick-knock were not options. He just loved the atmosphere in the bar, where men talked men's talk to other men, and women only ever entered the conversation preceded with expletives about nagging their men about the amount of time they spent in the pub. In later years Dan wondered if excluding women from pubs in the '50s and '60s might have encouraged them to become power walkers!

It seemed to Dan that lunchtime and dinner time was about calling into the local bar for a few halves and bottles, and night time was about calling in for more than a few more.

His dad was like the conductor of an orchestra as he served drinks, told stories, and partook in several conversations at the same time, usually winding the customers up unbeknownst to them, and ensuring lively encounters between the inebriated locals.

Another bonus was that alcohol seemed to loosen the pockets of the customers who often insisted on giving young Dan a few bob once they'd had a few. He used it to fund his frequent escapes to the cinema. Dan was basically shy and always refused the money once or twice, but drunken men were very determined so he always left with the loot - except once. A sailor on leave called Hugh used to frequent his dad's pub and was always worth a half dollar. Dan recalled sitting in the bar waiting for the cow to calve so that he could escape to the pictures. Sure enough, sailor Hugh produced the half-crown and as per usual Dan refused. But this time Hugh put the money back in his pocket and walked back to the bar to finish his drink. He learned a lot about tactics and expectations that day, but he didn't get to the cinema.

The language of the bar intrigued young Dan. Men cursed and swore with a fluency and acceptability that made him wonder if he should include swearing at all in his list of sins to the local priest during his weekly trip to confession. He decided to retain them, as the priest seemed more interested in issues of chastity than the odd 'fuck', which was kind of an unconscious contradiction in terms. Dan recalled one particular time when two well-oiled customers were having a far from intellectual discourse outside the pub. A lone dog was approaching on the far side of the street. 'Is that a grey-fucking-hound?' one said. 'No, it's a pekin-fuckin-ese,' the other retorted. 'Are you sure?' the original questioner asked. 'Abso-fuckin-lutely,' he was told. Thus ended that debate.

On another occasion, an old regular was marked absent from the bar due to being at his son's wedding. When asked the next day if he enjoyed the wedding he replied, 'It was the best fuckin day I ever had, Mickey. I don't mind a thing.'

Ordering drinks was also an art form. Often drinks were set up without a word being spoken, usually a nod or money hitting the counter sufficed. A half and a bottle was often shortened to the two or the both. Dan recollected hearing a drink being ordered, 'Give Noel the two and me the both, Mickey.' His dad knew exactly what to serve up, which impressed Dan immensely.

But life in a local pub wasn't always harmonious on the barroom floor. Over the years Dan saw his dad see off a few unruly 'bandits' who had overstayed their welcome. On one occasion an ornery old drunk, known as Smokey, pulled out a knife because his dad wouldn't serve him. He was wrestled to the ground and the knife was confiscated within seconds. No police needed, and the bar was back in motion within minutes. Sure what wee boy could have had a more courageous and heroic father than Dan?

Another time a traveller, known in those days as a gypsy, wasn't able to hold his liquor and threw a punch. He was duly 'clocked' and escorted out, again without recourse to police, solicitors, or courts. Those methods may have been crude, but they were effective and acceptable within the community in those days.

They were just an extension in Dan's eyes to the swift justice of cowboy heroes like the Lone Ranger et al, who always did what men had to do and stood up for the underdog. The licensing laws at that time were much more draconian than in today's more liberal world. Pubs had to close at 10pm, whereas today most people haven't even gone out by that time.

However, the drinking men of that era didn't take kindly to such an early curfew, and so while a few local pubs closed their doors at 10pm in cosmetic fashion, a few bars stayed open behind closed doors. Dan's dad's pub was one of the few. There was always the risk of a police raid and the local RUC station was based only 100 yards up the street, which increased that risk.

As a child, Dan remembered hearing anecdotes from customers about the narrow escapes during police raids. In one instance a lone drunken customer was sitting in the outside toilet. A policeman looked inside but miraculously didn't see or smell him. Clearly, the power of whiskey included rendering people invisible when necessary!

On another occasion, his dad managed to get a dozen customers down the stairs, into the yard and out the back gate as the police were entering the bar from the same side of the building just above the gate. It was akin to a Keystone Cops movie and ensured lively banter the next morning among the early-morning customers, who always sought their cure in his dad's pub rather than make a pilgrimage to Lourdes.

Interestingly, adjacent to the pub was a grotto to Our Lady where people occasionally worshipped Mary, perhaps looking for a cure of their own, but the instant results from whiskey and stout ensured that the pub was better attended than the grotto.

Dan recalled a particular incident where there wasn't time to get the customers out during a raid. Instead, his father herded them upstairs to the bedrooms where Dan and his brothers and sisters were sleeping. He remembered awakening to a room full of inebriated men hunkering in the dark. Outside he could hear his dad challenging the police who were searching the house. 'My children are sleeping in those bedrooms and if you waken any of them I'll throw you over those fucking banisters,' he diplomatically responded to their request to search the bedrooms. For some reason, the police decided to heed the diplomacy and not pursue the search any further and left.

Earlier thoughts of the Lone Ranger reminded Dan of how he once saved the day at a St Patrick's Day concert in St Columb's Hall in 1964. Some older guys from the area had managed to get a spot on the concert for a skiffle group that was hastily put together. They decided to include a few of the younger guys and he was picked. What an honour this was for him. To be accepted by the bigger guys was a huge bonus. To be selected was just mind-blowing for the hugely insecure young Dan.

And so, for about a fortnight before the big gig, the skiffle group met in a shed owned by his dad. They practised singing a medley of country and cowboy songs such as 'Last Train to San Fernando', 'It Takes a Worried Man to Sing a Worried Song' and 'Red River Valley'. No doubt the reader is impressed with this array of classics!

The fact it was his dad's shed and therefore possibly the reason he was included was a thought that occurred to Dan. It's funny how no esteem can always find a way to keep self-worth buried in its 'rightful' place. Not to worry, Dan would be performing live at the traditional St. Paddy's Day concert and that was all that mattered.

In fact, he would have to perform twice that night, as he was also involved in an Irish dancing performance on the same bill. So he would have to make a quick change from his kilt to his jeans and check shirt.

That's where the problem started that only the Lone Ranger could solve. Dan didn't possess a pair of jeans. In fact, he didn't possess long trousers. His mother was very strict about when her boys would graduate from short to long trousers and Dan fell shy by six months. Pleading and tantrums didn't work, and he was distraught that he was going to have to miss the gig due to having no jeans to wear. In those days if you had jeans it was one pair only, so none of his pals had a spare pair. Jeans were a bit like the early Ford cars – any colour as long as it was black - only with jeans in those days it was blue and Wrangler.

And then the Lone Ranger saved the day. A couple of

Christmases earlier, Santa had brought Dan a Lone Ranger cowboy outfit. It contained powder blue trousers with fringe down each outside leg. One of Dan's sisters suggested these might do for his gig. Initially, he wasn't keen, thinking it would be embarrassing to don the bottoms of his cowboy suit.

But as the days crept closer to March 17th, the idea gathered momentum in light of there being no other options. And so, on his debut night, Dan appeared on stage with the Lone Ranger trousers with the hem let down and the fringes trimmed off. If the heat in Dan's legs had matched the furnace that was his face, the trousers would have self-combusted, but thankfully the physics of embarrassment didn't travel that far down.

Dan thought the whole audience was as fixated on his custom-made trousers as he was and he spent the next few minutes singing to his shoes, but the show went on and they all sang their hearts out and left the stage to what to Dan seemed like thunderous applause. In the reality which came from latent humility, honesty and hindsight, it was really more like the polite appreciation shown to an under-card act, and significantly that was their one and only booking that year or any other year.

The main act on the bill that night was the hilarious Frank Carson, so Dan reckoned the punters got an extra laugh for their money. But no one mentioned his trousers and that was the main thing. Strangely he was glad that the Irish dancing performance was rescheduled to after the skiffle group on the bill that night. For the first and only time in his life, he was glad to get out of his trousers and into his kilt. 'Hi ho Silver my arse,' was Dan's farewell to his outfit as he binned it the next morning.

The issue of jeans arose again three years later when Dan and a pal both bought matching shirts and jeans to impress some girls, only for Dan's mum to bin the jeans which she believed were only worn by 'corner boys'. Little did she know that Dan's main ambition in life at that time was to graduate as a corner boy rather than to academically achieve and become the priest, doctor, or solicitor that his mum aspired for him to be. Somewhere deep down he thought that was the height of his worth.

Hindsight also showed that his mum's hopes for him had more to offer and greater longevity in the long run, but Dan fulfilled his ambition and wasted many hours over the next few years hanging around street corners. All he had to show for it was a few coats with the fabric worn disproportionately on the back, which didn't really position him to be head-hunted by passing company directors looking out for possible management potential.

For the next few years, Dan's priorities were all leading to infamy and failure rather than fame and success. His total apathy towards education, coupled with the craving for instant buzzes to change the humdrum of his reality, ensured that his teens, while exciting and even dangerous at times, were not included as reference sites in any guides to happy teenage living pamphlets.

As he approached his mid-teens, Dan's days of lurking around the bar listening to the wise old heads were waning fast. Instead, he pursued an agenda that included loitering in and around snooker halls, often during school hours, experimenting with alcohol, trying unsuccessfully to find a replacement for Fiona, his first love, and seeking financial success in Sammy O'Neill's bookmakers. So, his snooker prowess improved at the expense of his academic attainments.

His first drink at fourteen was a disaster. He stole four miniature bottles of vodka from his dad's cellar, and he and an equally 'cool' school pal headed to the cattle pens to party. Dan recalled the vile taste of the raw spirit. Strangely, for something that tasted so vile, he finished off his two miniatures and went home rather giggly, yet unsteady, and feeling a bit sick.

The fun really started when he went to bed. Unknown to Dan, his mother had installed a revolving ceiling that circled Dan most of the night. Memories of the spinning ceiling prompted him to swear off booze forever. For the next 20 years, he was to fruitlessly repeat that oath many times! Strangely, he never repeated it from the age of 33, when he gave up alcohol permanently and remained sober on a daily basis for decades to come.

Gambling brought even more instant results, and from a starting point of putting a few shillings on a horse, Dan was soon famous in his locality as a fearless young gambler among those who also spent their days loitering around bookies shops. The opportunity for placing large bets presented itself every week when Dan was entrusted by his dad to lodge the weekly takings from the bar into a local bank. He used to take a chance and place large bets of up to £100 on horses. At that time £5 - £10 a week would have been typical wages in local factories, so bets of £100 were noteworthy, especially from a schoolboy. These large bets all won. At the age of fifteen, he was becoming a local legend of the sewer that was gambling. Hangers-on abounded, waiting for young Dan to drop them a few pounds from his winnings. This he duly did as it seemingly increased the esteem in which he was held.

He also learned at an early age that you didn't need to lose a fortune for it to cause problems. He recalled his father giving him sixpence to get a stamp and post a letter. He put the sixpence to one he already had and placed the shilling on a horse. It lost and the letter wasn't posted.

A week or so later his father asked him if he had posted the letter. Dan lied that he had. As it turned out, the letter was an order to a supplier for stock for the pub. The stock was late as it had to be reordered and the bar went perilously low to running out of Guinness and losing customers. All this over sixpence!

On another occasion, he was sent one Saturday to the butchers for meat for the Sunday dinner. Dan ordered three-quarters of a pound less so that he could have a bet. Again the bet lost. His mother noticed that the meat was short in weight and challenged him. Again he lied and blamed the butcher. He was sent back to the shop to explain that he had been given short weight. The butcher remembered his order but Dan stuck to his story and eventually, he relented and gave him the extra meat. Deep down Dan knew that the butcher knew he was lying.

Dan played the same trick with a bag of change from the bank. His dad noticed that it was five shillings short and he had to brazen it out at the bank. He did, and they eventually replaced the bag with a new one. It was near closing time at the bank and Dan always believed that helped his cause.

Lying was essential for him to stay in business and Dan became accomplished at it. In quiet moments he used to hate himself for the deception, but the next bet soon proved the antidote to feelings of guilt. It was also a great escape from the put-downs and disapproval of the college teachers, and he became increasingly obsessed with gambling. That obsession was to take him to the gates of hell many times over the years.

By the time Dan was sixteen he was in full flight as a disillusioned student, a fearless gambler and a potential alcoholic. This was probably the only potential he ever managed to live up to.

4

Love and Heartbreak

Dan's aversion to religion and all its trappings in his teenage years was total, and he avoided prayer and church events whenever he could. But on occasion, he just had to run with it, especially attendance at mass on Sundays which was virtually policed by his mum. Questions were asked afterward about the topic of the priest's sermon or the gospel reading that made dodging mass hardly worth the hassle.

Interestingly, going to mass became much more fascinating when he turned fourteen, and it was in the Long Tower chapel that Dan spotted his first love. He used to gaze across at this girl in the opposite gallery whose name he didn't know. She wore a green corduroy coat over her mini-skirt, along with a matching 'Donovan' cap, and he was hooked at once. There was just something about her that set her apart from the rest. She would not have been out of place in scenes from the Carnaby Street fashion scene or on the dance floor on *Top of the Pops.* Those images stayed with Dan day and night for some time to come.

As soon as mass was over, he used to hurry across to the exit on her side of the chapel to get a closer look as she was leaving. Dan reckoned she looked intelligent enough to be at Thornhill, the local girls' college, and indeed he was proved right, which in turn put in question, at an early stage, the Hammer's theory about Dan's poor choices. Armed with a heart full of love and a belly full of butterflies (albeit coupled with the esteem and self-confidence of a lost Irishman abroad), he set out to win her affection.

Success wasn't immediate, probably due to the fact that he hadn't a clue where to start. But, start he did. For five months every day after school, he dashed home, got changed out of his college uniform into civilian clothes, and ran about a mile at warp speed to the Diamond to be there when the Thornhill bus arrived.

All of this for a glance at the lovely Fiona as she walked home with her friends. On reflection, Dan was probably a stalker before there were stalkers. Chat-up lines were not necessary as he wouldn't have got the 'huh' in hello out without taking flight for fear of rejection, or tripping on the nearest kerb, being the gack he was (for the uninitiated, a 'gack' is a geek with a Derry accent).

Dan soon had it timed to perfection and caught her most days. He recalled the sweaty palms, the fluttering heartbeat, the dancing stomach and the jellied legs as Fiona passed. At the same time, all his efforts were being channelled into looking 'cool'. It was just as well she didn't say hello or he'd have been ferried home in an ambulance, such was the acute conflict of mind and body.

He wondered if she felt the same, but had his doubts, as

she never seemed to notice him. But women were like that; they had an inbuilt ability to gaze north when they were really looking south. This was probably a preamble to multi-tasking. In later years, Dan wished a few of the women who came into his life had just looked north when he was in the south, as this would have saved him many a sore heart, sore head and unrequited love. And so the chase was on.

Dan's days, weeks and months were totally dominated by Fiona. Of course, she knew nothing about this, which wasn't the optimum way to progress the matter. But while Dan may have been a gack, he wasn't a quitter. In time he got to know where she lived and then he had a brainwave. He sent her a letter with a photograph inside and asked her to be his pen pal. Though she only lived ten minutes from him, he didn't think this strange, which kind of endorsed his total gackness.

Fiona never answered the letter and Dan always regretted putting the photo inside, as he thought that must have been the turn-off. In later years she told him why she didn't respond and also clarified some other burning issues of that time. Her grandmother had picked up on the fact that pen pals were usually from another country rather than another street in the same city. Added to that, Fiona's mother would have gone berserk if her daughter had shown any interest in a boy at the age of thirteen.

Dan's total focus across the chapel galleries was also exposed as fruitless. He always believed that as he stared at her, she must have been aware of his gaze. After all, he was like a dyslexic tennis fan, with his head always pointing away from the action at the chapel altar as his gaze was permanently focused on Fiona.

As it turned out, she was extremely short-sighted and had no idea Dan was fixated on her. The trips to the bus stop never produced results either, as she never gave him a second look. In fact, she never gave Dan a first look. Even if she had, he would have missed it, as he was so embarrassed and nervous that he used to look away shyly when he passed her in Bishop Street, near the Diamond. Added to that, he wouldn't have known what to do if their eyes had met, so readers will no doubt have deduced that Dan was the coolest guy in town and on the verge of becoming legendary among the girls of Derry!

However, fate was to take a turn for the better and in the most unlikely setting. Dan's mother had sent all her children to Irish dancing lessons from the age of five onwards. He hated it and hated wearing the traditional Irish dancing outfit, and while he never really mastered the art of dancing, he did learn how to fight a bit. Heading out to the local Feis dressed in a kilt always brought taunts and derision from the local boys, so Dan often arrived to the Feis or from it with the marks to prove that a boy wearing a kilt was still a man. Perhaps the Christian Brothers had done some good after all.

Dan recalled one particular incident in Rossnowlagh, in Donegal, where a gang of local lads picked on him, his brother Gerry, and two other of his fellow Derry dancers. A fight ensued on the outdoor stage, which coincidentally and fittingly resembled a boxing ring. The kilted heroes saw off all comers and went back home on the bus to Derry like returning conquerors, endorsing the fact that Irish dancers had 'balls' under their kilts.

The big event the week after Easter was the Derry Feis. The best dancers and singers from the city competed against each other and against the best from other parts of the six counties and beyond, including dancers from America and England.

Dan as usual was entered in the jig and reel and also some team dances. His solo performances were about as accomplished and graceful as a whale trying on a Wellington boot, so they never produced medals, but invariably the teams he danced with were in the shake-up and got medals. Dan was always afraid he would be the one to dance to the left when the others went right, but his girl partner usually managed to whisper the next move in time for it to compute in his brain and then reach his feet in tandem with the rest of the team.

Another traditional part of the Feis was the long waits between competitions. It was during one of these breaks that Dan finally met Fiona. As it happened, she was a singer and was in a competition that was wedged between Dan's dancing commitments. He and a few fellow dancers were sitting at the back of the great hall in Derry's Guildhall eating sweets and making noise when, as if by magic, Fiona walked on stage.

Dan immediately quietened his pals and explained that this was the girl he had told them about. He gawked at her and listened intently to her rendition of 'Baidin Fheilimih', and while he hadn't a clue what she was singing about, he was riveted by her performance. As it turned out, the song was about a little boat, so she wasn't exactly serenading him. But he was already all aboard and floating aimlessly in his romantic voyage of the mind.

She looked beautiful in her short dress and trendy hairdo. And so it was that Dan finally plucked up the courage to ask Fiona out for a date. Well, sort of. He got his friend Liam to approach her and let her know he was interested in her, in a kind of Dickensian 'Barkus is willing' fashion.

That's when his trouble really started. You see, Dan was expecting total rejection, but, in fact, he got a positive response. Fiona had sent word that she would meet him outside St Columb's Hall the next afternoon at 3pm. *Jesus, what am I gonna do now?*

The sweaty palms, racing heart and jangling nerves of his stalking days now paled into insignificance as Dan was overcome with a tsunami of fear and trepidation mixed with a cocktail of excitement and adrenaline. He wondered why, at times like this, his bowels and kidneys seemed to come under pressure. On reflection, he reckoned that God had a great sense of humour to use the same body parts for sexual arousal and waste disposal!

That night was one Dan never forgot. His mind ping-ponged between *What will I say to her tomorrow?* and *She's not going to turn up*, both thoughts bringing no peace to his tortured emotions. In the final analysis on a sleepless night, he settled for her not turning up as preferable to him having to actually talk to her.

He would have awakened early the next morning had it not been for the fact that at no stage did he sleep. He eventually crawled out of bed to begin preparations for the big date. After taking a bath on three occasions that morning, he decided to have his first ever shave. A few minutes into it, it became apparent a strong breeze would have sufficiently removed his face fluff, but Dan thought a cleanly-shaven face would convince Fiona she was going out with a real man.

Where the fuck are the Christian Brothers when you need them? What will I wear? His mother disapproved of jeans and the only other long trousers he had were his black school ones. However, he did have a pair of brown corduroy trousers that he bought with his Christmas money, so they got the vote, along with a yellow tee-shirt. Just before he left the house, he paid one last visit to the bathroom.

The nervous sweat that was now flowing freely down his chest and back nullified the three baths he had taken earlier. *She'll think I'm a minger.* At that, he emptied almost half a bottle of his brother's Brut aftershave onto his hands and applied it generously to his face and neck.

A feeling of excruciating pain ensued as the Brut connected with the shaving lacerations on his face and neck. Dan learned a lesson that day on how, and when, not to shave. This was followed by several blasts of Old Spice deodorant under each arm. He held it that close and squirted it that often, the deodorant formed a white scum under each armpit. *Not to worry, it's hardly likely that I will have my oxters inspected on a first date.*

Dan set off to meet Fiona looking like a shiny new pin and smelling like a whore at a hockey match, due to the chemical reaction of the toiletries with the relentless flow of perspiration. By the time he reached St Columb's Hall, his bowels and kidneys were also talking back to him, so as you would expect, all was not well with Dan Feeney on his first proper date.

He still hadn't worked out what to say to Fiona if she turned up. The 54-year-old Dan's advice to his teenage self would probably have been to be himself and act normal. But that would have translated to young Dan as wetting and shitting himself, having a failure of his vocal cords, and awkwardly falling down the steps of St Columb's Hall.

It occurred to him that while he knew a little Latin, French and Irish and had a modicum of geography, history and science, no one had taught him anything about the life skill of a first date. Then his worst fear and his greatest wish happened simultaneously; Fiona turned up.

The good news was that his bowels and kidneys held the line. The bad news was that he was dumbstruck. Fiona was beautiful, and here she was standing beside him and he couldn't form a sentence. Dan could feel the inferno of his embarrassment rise up from his toes to his hairline.

The next few minutes remained a blackout, erased from Dan's memory forever, but his next recollection was that Fiona and he were walking and talking their way around Derry's walls. She was even lovelier up close than she was at stalking distance. After the initial awkwardness and the pregnant pauses, they got on really well and the potential for bowel and kidney activity receded completely, as did the torrent of perspiration.

There he was on a date with the girl of his dreams and all was going well. He could have walked around those walls forever. Interestingly, some people seem to have been walking around them forever, much to the displeasure of the majority of Derry citizens!

After an hour or so, Fiona said she had to go to meet her friend. That immediately started the waste disposal units and sweat glands off again. Would he kiss her or would that be too forward on a first date? If he did kiss her, would she be a windmill or a brick wall?

He desperately hoped she would be a windmill. Dan had little experience of kissing girls, but there seemed to be two types. The brick walls were the ones who puckered their lips, closed their eyes and compressed their closed mouth against yours, with no other movement until the first one gasped for air, at which stage the clinch was broken. It was sort of a preamble to a head butt.

The second kind were the girls who took a slightly more open-mouthed approach to kissing and who moved their heads in a circular motion whilst in suction mode. Dan really liked the moistness, warmth and passion of the 'windmill' girls. And for some strange reason, kisses of that type seemed to introduce activity in other parts of his body, which was all new to Dan.

Fifteen minutes later Fiona reiterated her need to go. During that time Dan was still struggling with what to do next. He desperately wanted to kiss her but hadn't a clue how to bring this connection about. So another lap of the walls ensued. *If I don't kiss her she'll think I don't like her, and if I do she'll think I'm a dirty brute,* he thought despairingly. He didn't have the sense to know that this was traumatic, but he knew it was a predicament.

Thankfully Fiona didn't live in the dilemmas that Dan resided in. So she stopped at a quiet part of the walls near Bishop's Gate, took Dan's hand, walked to an inlet in the wall, and kissed him. It was everything Dan had hoped for and more. She was enough of a windmill girl to power up the city for a fortnight.

And so began Dan Feeney's first love affair. The next six months were everything Dan could have dreamed of and more, albeit with the restraints imposed with having to do it all undercover to keep their parents in blissful ignorance. They saw each other almost every day and their windmills were at full tilt for hours on end. In hindsight, Dan reckoned he and Fiona were unwittingly, anonymously and effectively pioneers of saving the planet from meltdown, given recent revelations about global warming.

Of course, the emotions engendered by the kissing led to other forbidden fumbling activities that just seemed normal to these seemingly in-love teenagers. Strangely, the priests and nuns from their colleges that forbade such acts were sworn to lifetime celibacy, so their baseless instructions were ignored.

But unfortunately, Dan was to become another statistic of that ominous adage, 'Anything that does that much for you will eventually do that much to you.' Funnily enough, in the process, he became more of a candidate for hypothermia than meltdown. Dan's modus operandi for arranging dates with Fiona was through her brother, Jim, who was at college with Dan. After the first six blissful months, Fiona didn't turn up one night to the back stores in Sackville Street. He assumed it was a one-off and that there would be a valid reason.

He never got to know. Not being a quitter, Dan continued to make arrangements through Jim for the next three months and every night Fiona failed to appear. Dan recalled the striking of the Guildhall clock every 15 minutes from 7.30pm to 9.30pm, at which time he decided she wasn't coming. It would have been funny if it wasn't so sad. The memories of those two-hour waits during winter nights remain. He was frozen stiff in all the wrong places!

He existed in that incompatible state of the eternal hope of Fiona turning up, coupled with the inevitable realisation and despair that she wouldn't. Perhaps three months was a long time for the penny to drop, but that's the parameters a young heart will extend to, to hold on to a dream. The dream finally metamorphosed into a nightmare when he heard one of his classmates bragging about 'getting off' with Fiona at the local hop in the Wolfe Tone Hall. Dan was stuck in that awful dilemma of wanting to deck the guy for stealing his girl, but not wanting to show everyone he was hurting. Pride won through and he chose the latter. Over the years, Dan perfected the ability to bleed internally as other relationships came and went.

That was the day Dan first became aware of the heavy burden that was emotional pain. No doubt the gurus, psychologists and counsellors of today's informed world would have fixed him in jig time with their self-help, self-absorbed, fee-driven American psychobabble. As for Dan, he just had to get used to existing with a broken heart and at the same time try to function in the teenage world he lived in. Strangely and perhaps miraculously he survived without recourse to drugs. Sex and rock 'n' roll played a part, however.

A friend had reminded him that although Fiona was off the menu, they hadn't stopped making girls. He was right. Dan didn't exactly become prolific afterward, but hanging out in Jimmy Macari's café did present opportunities, even for a gack.

Rock 'n' roll was also a great antidote, and the late '60s was a Mecca for rock and pop music and all that came with it. Many hours were whittled away by teenagers shaking their heads in that oh-so-cool way, intently listening to the rawness of the Stones or the suaveness of the Kinks, that let all and sundry know they had arrived.

That's the way it was, as jukeboxes belted out sometimes frantic, sometimes serene, sounds that could only be appreciated by those 'virtual' mods and rockers on the march to nowhere fast, with all the answers to questions that would never be asked and no answers to the ones that would.

In the midst of all this, Fiona was confined to history, except for the occasional times when Dan saw her, at which he immediately reverted back to that babbling, jelly-legged, dry-boking idiot whose heart was in Foster's Terrace, not San Francisco. But what the fuck would Tony Bennett know about such matters anyway?

There were other ways to escape from heartache and he found two of them almost simultaneously at the age of fifteen. They also proved to be the antidote to all life's problems for some time to come. Dan was content to live anywhere except in reality, and these obsessions cleared the decks of that problem.

Unfortunately, they came with a price tag that was to haunt and taunt him for many years. The instant effect and escape of alcohol and the adrenaline, danger and uncertainty of gambling soared him to incredible heights and sunk him to unfathomable depths. This ensured his maturity and ability to function and contribute to the world in any practical or sensible way was put into suspended animation for many years to come.

5

Double Troubles

1968 was a momentous and life-changing year for Dan. At 15, he was the perfect age to be sucked in by the simmering rebellion that was lurking in the underbelly of life in Derry and that was about to take centre stage and change the course of history in the North for decades to come.

Dan was always aware that Catholics and Protestants seemed to be kept away from each other in terms of schools, sport and socialising. As a young boy, he didn't know why but just accepted it without giving it much thought. He was acutely aware of the British presence in the North and, thanks in part to the Christian Brothers, had a strong sense of his own Irishness and an aspiration for the unification of his country.

Dan's nationalism was pretty basic and centred around the fact that, historically, the English seemed to feel the need to invade and take ownership of other people's countries throughout the world. Ireland just happened to be one of the victims and to Dan, it was high time they let the Irish get on with their own affairs. Following the 1916 Rising and the war for independence, they eventually let go of 26 counties but held on to the remaining six. Dan just thought they should return them to their rightful owners. Apparently, the Protestant community and their political representatives who ruled the roost in the Northern Ireland parliament at Stormont frowned on such aspirations.

That government was basically a one-party state with a few token 'Taigs' thrown in to camouflage the look of apartheid. Some rumblings had been going on in Derry about seemingly unimportant things like fairness in the allocation of houses, votes and jobs. It appeared that being a Catholic meant you were less likely to get any of these, irrespective of your need. And, given the Catholic Church's view that contraception was sinful, the Catholics of Derry badly needed the jobs and houses to keep large families fed, watered and sheltered.

Perhaps this was an oversimplification of the problem, and indeed politicians and historians of all hues have been making fortunes explaining the complexities ever since, but to Dan, it just didn't seem fair that people should be treated differently for any reason. In the midst of all the flawed teachings and the jaundiced opinions that had infiltrated him through the years, there was a fundamental principle that had always stayed with him, and it was that all men were created equal. This also applied to women (even power walkers). It may have been naive and, to some, downright ridiculous, but it was a bedrock on which his belief system sat comfortably despite the many flaws and afflictions that were at work within him as a young man in those days.

Fundamentally, he was uncomplicated in his views of the

equal rights of mankind, and that the English should give back what they had stolen. Up until 1968, he didn't have a vehicle to espouse these fine and just causes, but all that was about to change. Dan was aware of and hugely impressed by the blacks in America standing up for their civil rights under the leadership of people like Martin Luther King and Malcolm X.

It appeared that the more they stood up, the more they were knocked down by racist police and white supremacists. But what really impressed Dan was that they kept getting up again, no matter what the cost. He had heard of and was fascinated by Che Guevara too, a revolutionary in Cuba who seemed, to Dan, to be a sort of Bob Dylan with a machine gun. It didn't get much better than that. So something was simmering in his young mind.

In tandem with these romantic values about equality and the need for English restitution, Dan was in full flow pursuing the escapes and buzzes of alcohol and gambling. He was also living in hope rather than expectation of getting a new girlfriend to replace the irreplaceable Fiona. Apart from his inherent shyness and low esteem, he was also inhibited by another unwelcome appendage to his sense of uselessness. Acne didn't register as a terminal illness in any medical dictionaries, but in Dan's eyes, it was at least on a par with leprosy. The daily ritual of mirror-gazing revealed increasing numbers of these vile blemishes on his face, which to him resembled a cross between a cratered road and a pebble-dashed wall; though without the customary blue glass.

Dan, being the impatient teenager he was, wanted instant solutions, but his doctor only offered advice about eating healthier for the next 50 years and issued prescriptions for spot creams, which at best only dulled down the pebble dash. So he did his own surgery by squeezing them out individually, in so doing splattering the mirror with a mixture of acne juice and blood. This didn't work either as the squeezed spots just looked redder than before and new ones popped up to replace any that had died.

He was convinced that no girl would ever look at him again, so he just stopped trying. The benefit of this was he couldn't be rejected, so he settled for that as a good trade-off, at least for the time being. Besides, his early successes in the bookies had faded so he couldn't really afford to date anyone, as he was permanently skint except for the odd win on the horses that he used mainly to fuel his increasing appetite for alcohol.

Of course, unwittingly his dad still had a sweat each week with the bank lodgement, but any money Dan made was either reinvested on the nags with a nil return or mooched off him by the hangers-on who always seemed to turn up on Wednesdays when he was flush, but who were nowhere to be seen the rest of the week. Meanwhile, his attendance at school became even more sporadic.

In fact, he managed to get a job in the bookies marking prices on the board, which meant that he didn't attend school in the afternoons at all. He was paid fourteen shillings a day but doesn't recall ever leaving with the money. Instead, he just bet with it and was usually at least a fortnight's pay behind due to credit bets that didn't deliver. Dan hadn't been debt-free since, with countless thousands of pounds borrowed over the years to provide the ammunition demanded by a gambling obsession.

Dan couldn't understand why he rarely won. He could always pick a winner or two out of the race card. The problem was, once he made the first bet, he couldn't stop betting until everything was lost. But he just couldn't stop making that first bet. Elvis Presley unwittingly described Dan's condition in the first line of 'Suspicious Minds' when he sang, 'I'm caught in a trap, I can't walk out.' Within a couple of years, alcohol was to fall into the same category. Of course, Dan couldn't see any of it coming as he just glorified and basked in the delusion of manliness about all that was going on.

His rejection by Fiona had really knocked his life for six. Prior to winning his first love, Dan lacked confidence and was shy. Since she'd dumped him, the volume on all his negativity was turned up full blast. He was in a place where the fear of rejection was dominating his life. He always felt he was ugly, but ugly with acne was just too grotesque to contemplate. Deep down he just wanted to be normal, but the need to escape to the buzzes of booze and bets was too powerful to resist. They helped him to ignore all his perceived defects - temporarily at least.

Yet despite this, he had the odd success with girls. Well, perhaps 'success' was overplaying things a bit. Dan recalled being at a céilí in the Stardust, a dance hall in Derry. He had honed in on a beautiful girl called Gráinne whom he had briefly met once before on the street when out with a crowd. She had long blonde hair, a beautiful complexion and was, to the teenage Dan, in that lovely place where a girl is beginning to shape like a woman. Although this thought hinted at maturity, it had been fostered in the plethora of movies Dan had been exposed to over the years, so his maturity was more an illusion than a reality. Of course, Dan couldn't imagine her allowing that milky skin to come into contact with his bulging zits. And yet he so much wanted to ask to leave her home from the céilí.

The last dance of the evening was just beginning and he was still riveted to the floor. *Fuck it,* he thought. *A faint heart never won a fair lady*. He had picked that little vignette up at a local card school and had used it to good effect many times when he went all in to win at poker. It had been successful more often than not. But this was different. Losing a hand of poker was no big deal; in many ways, it was his destiny. But another rejection from a girl; well that was a bridge too far.

No matter, he walked slowly across the floor and stood next to Gráinne and her friend. *Here goes,* he thought. 'Would you like to dance?' he offered. 'I would love to,' the girl replied. They waited their turn and then joined the 'Walls of Limerick'. It went well. She smiled and laughed in his company and he even managed not to tramp on her toes. Dan was in a state of shock at how easy this girl was making friends with him. After the dance, he asked to leave her home and she said yes. So Dan and Jennifer left the céilí together.

They walked Gráinne home first, as he had bottled it and had asked her friend to dance instead. This was the beginning of Dan's new tactic to avoid rejection. From then on, he always asked the girl beside the one he actually fancied out to dance. The logic being that if she said no, it wouldn't matter, so rejection wouldn't come into it. Taking that theory to its natural conclusion probably meant Dan shouldn't have married Bridget years later, and he feels sure she would gladly have turned the clock back and passed that mantle onto whoever was beside her the night they met, given the way their marriage turned out.

Over the next six weeks, Dan discovered another little defect of his character. When he left Jennifer home from the céilí it was clear to him that she wasn't setting his pulse racing. In fact, he felt totally indifferent, not a nice place for a fully 'testosteroned' teenager. So what did he do? Well, he kissed her goodnight in brick wall fashion and then asked her for another date. He didn't know how not to ask her out. It wasn't as if he could offer to ring her on her mobile – they didn't exist in those days and neither of them had phones at home.

He really didn't want to see her again, and yet here he was asking for another date. Sod's Law had it that she liked him and accepted each time. The next six weeks were of nightmare status. He was having two or three dates a week with Jennifer because he couldn't face calling it a day. This was such an unhealthy mixture of arrogance, people-pleasing and fear and made his life miserable. His time was spent wondering how he could extract himself from this mess, but he continually dug a deeper hole after each date.

Then he came up with a plan. *I'll find a way to put her off me,* he thought. So one Friday night he called for Jennifer at her home and they headed down town on the Creggan bus. 'Where are we going tonight?' she quizzed expectantly. Dan told her he was taking her to the pictures. He was playing it cool and didn't tell her immediately what films were on. And then he unleashed his masterstroke. 'It's a double bill: *The Magnificent Seven* and *The Return of the Seven.' Two westerns – that should put her off me forever,* Dan thought presumptively. Jennifer looked across at him and gave it to him straight. 'Oh I just love westerns,' she enthused. (Years later a female friend who he recounted this experience to assured him that Jennifer didn't love westerns - she loved Dan. That information brought with it additional retrospective guilt as to how he had treated her.)

At that moment Dan would have gladly let Yul Brynner and Steve McQueen send him to Boot Hill in place of all those Mexican hombres. But there was no escape, so they sat through both films keeping their hands and mouths busy on copious amounts of chocolate, ice cream and Coke. A waste of hand and mouth activity on a date at the pictures, but when it's not there, it's not there!

After that night Dan adopted the 'Fiona' approach to extricating himself from the dilemma; he just didn't turn up for the next date. He always felt bad about that. No doubt

Jennifer got over it in a few minutes, but such was the nature of the beast that Dan still regretted such cowardly behaviour long into his 'man' years. It's strange how someone who has faced difficult and dangerous situations all through his life couldn't tell a girl he didn't want to go out with her. His only hope was that she became a power walker, which would of course render any need for belated amends void!

In the midst of all these juvenile jaunts, a budding revolutionary was trying to get out. After October 5th 1968, he got his chance. That day, around 300 civil rights activists in the process of having a peaceful march were battened off Duke Street in Derry by the RUC. Dan saw the footage of this unprovoked attack on the news that night. In fact, it was transmitted all over the world and Northern Ireland had finally registered on the global map, but for all the wrong reasons. It was to occupy that status many times over the next 30 years.

Civil rights became 'sexy' and a flame was fanned that would engulf the little northerly province for decades. In true 'Forrest Gumpian' style, Dan was there in the middle of it all. Duke Street on October 5th entered Irish folklore. In fact, if all the Derrymen who have since claimed to be on that fateful march had actually turned up, the Troubles may not have happened at all, as they could probably have taken over the country and liberated the six northern counties in a bloodless coup. But that's the way with bandwagons, everybody wants on them!

Civil rights marches and protests became commonplace,

as was the heavy-handed response of the police. Sporadic riots in Derry between young Catholics and the RUC were breaking out regularly and Dan was always at the heart of them. A local man, Sammy Devenny, was brutally battened to near death in his home by RUC officers who were in pursuit of escaping rioters. He later died in hospital. This further incited local insurrection and was followed by many more incidents where the overzealous police action exacerbated the already volatile situation in the city.

The unionist government couldn't have given the civil rights movement more support if they had devised their marketing strategy! Dan's life had become full of excitement. There was the buzz and danger of the riots, the betting sprees on horses and cards, the continued experimentation with alcohol (with dependency alarms already sounding, but of course still silent in Dan's young ears) and the daily escapes from college. Terminal shyness and acne still kept his love life on the rocks, but there was too much happening for him to notice or even care.

Dan soon found that riots had a practical side too. A friend of his, John, managed to liberate a car from outside his uncle's house one night. His uncle Charlie was a mechanic and was repairing the car. John and Dan went for what to them was a 'wee spin', which was a softer way of describing car theft and joyriding. Within ten minutes the car went out of control a couple of miles outside the city, did a double somersault and came to an abrupt halt when colliding with a salt bunker at the roadside. Miraculously, the boys were virtually uninjured.

In the Derry of today, there would have been at least six whiplash claims launched by accommodating local solicitors before the car engine had cooled down. The car was write-off material. They didn't know what to do or how to face uncle Charlie. But face him they did and he wasn't a happy man. However, wiser and older counsel found a solution to this dilemma.

The car was quietly towed into the local area and somehow found itself beside a burning bus at the bottom of Bishop Street during a riot the next night. The car owner got compensated for his vehicle being stolen and burned out and never knew the real story. Butch and Sundance were off the hook!

Scary moments like that dampened Dan's ardour for adventure and recklessness for a least an hour! He seemed to suffer from the affliction of a short and selective memory, especially when it came to learning the lessons from 'teenage kicks' that went wrong. On the other hand, John got enough of a scare to ensure he kept away from dodgy and dangerous situations from that moment onwards and he pursued a legitimate and successful career in local government as soon as he left university.

Dan loved being in the middle of everything. Apart from the craic and devilment of it all, it meant he was included and he felt 'part of', which to him was colossal in view of his acute low esteem and, of course, terminal acne. Further testimony to his seeming inability to learn from experiences in those carefree days was exemplified by some incidents that happened on the river.

Although Dan had opted out of all sport at college, he still played soccer with the local team. At a time when the Daisy Field was a field with daisies prior to its invasion by travellers, he and the rest of the 'gang' used to occasionally play football there. One day, one of the older guys, Charlie, suggested that instead of playing on the bumpy terrain that was Daisy Field, they instead look across the river to the virgin turf of the new playing fields at Prehen. He suggested they all go over in a small boat that he and a few others had 'liberated' from Inch Island a few weeks earlier.

Everybody was game for this adventure and so the 'sailors' set off across the river. About a dozen or so young men packed into the boat. Then Charlie had one of his less inspired brainwaves. 'What about leaving the oars here and using our hands to paddle across to the other side, lads?' Charlie commanded respect in the area from the younger lads, so within seconds the compliant crew were frantically paddling across the half-mile stretch, and with a favourable current, they landed safely at the Prehen pitches. For two hours they enjoyed flowing football on the bump-free turf. Dan loved the whole episode and was looking forward to the return voyage.

When the match ended it was time to head back across the pond. So, in they got and started to paddle. This time the current was not so friendly. The little boat soon gathered speed as the current carried it out and was soon in the centre of the choppy river as it sped north towards the Craigavon Bridge. Fear engulfed the rookie crew. As they approached the bridge they could see that the river was rapids-like around the bridge and they feared they would hit one of the pillars on the way under. If they had done, the boat would have surely smashed up and they could all have drowned. Dan certainly would have, as he couldn't swim.

The Christian Brothers had seen to that some years earlier when they chucked him into the swimming pool headfirst and he had to be fished out by the pool attendant. Part of their strategy to make a man out of a boy, no doubt! Miraculously the little boat got under the bridge and just shaved a pillar on the way past. This was a much closer shave than the one Dan had prior to his first date with Fiona. And this time the smell in the boat was certainly not one of Brut aftershave!

They careered on down the river, all the time paddling without paddles, panicking and, perhaps, pissing themselves. Somehow, probably by God's will, but certainly not by their seafaring skills, they managed to get the boat across to the city side of the river and they landed safely at the back of Derry's Guildhall, almost two miles from the Daisy Field. This was adventure at its height in Dan's book, especially after they were back on terra firma. It's funny how men's fear changes to bravado and ego after the crisis is over. Huckleberry Finn and Tom Sawyer weren't a patch on this lot. Having said that, deep down they all knew how fortunate they were to be alive and Charlie could paddle his own canoe next time he wanted to put his oar in, or rather leave it out! The river was a dangerous place and had to be treated with respect from then on. About a week later, Dan and another friend, Paddy, were spotted standing on an old wooden door in the middle of the river using two large poles to navigate. Lessons learned from the boat trip: zero.

Clearly, such fearlessness and courage could and should have been harnessed into greater use so that mankind could benefit from Dan's adventurous spirit. And so it was that he became increasingly wedded to the civil disturbance that was gaining momentum by the week. Well, no one approached him to circumnavigate the door around the world or climb Mount Everest, so he had to be doing with more parochial activity.

August 12th 1969 moved Dan's revolutionary status up a gear. Traditionally, the Apprentice Boys of Derry marched in the city on that day. The Apprentice Boys were a sort of hybrid of Orangeism but were not fully part of the Orange Order. To Dan, they were just Orangemen, which meant they were on the 'other side.' In later years Dan got much amusement from the fact that the Protestant/ Orange population within the city insisted that Derry be called Londonderry, including prominent members of the Apprentice Boys of *Derry.* This irony remained one of many inconsistencies that continue to baffle free thinkers everywhere. But then in a country that isn't really a country with a Deputy First Minister who isn't really a deputy, you didn't really expect clarity and common sense to prevail!

Due to tensions arising from the civil rights protests, many thought that the Apprentice Boys should have kept their march to the Waterside area of the city, away from the Catholic west bank. But these particular boys weren't very accommodating and decided to march past fringe areas that heightened tensions even further. Dan was there at the bottom of Waterloo Street when the mayhem started.

As the marchers passed through Waterloo Place they were jeered by the gathering of Catholic youths. They in turn returned the jeers and ensured their bands ratcheted up the tension by battering out a rousing rendition of 'Derry Walls' as they passed. As Dan recalled it, the Orange bands always seemed to play tunes and songs that recounted historical victories over their Catholic neighbours, especially when near nationalist areas.

Catholics, on the other hand, really only had songs of dead heroes like James Connolly, Kevin Barry and Father Murphy, as they seemed to have lost all the battles. But all that was about to change. There was a thin line of police separating the two sides. All it needed was a spark to ignite the already hostile atmosphere. The spark came, not with any militaristic genius or revolutionary strategy, but from one of the 'old heads' that used to frequent his dad's pub. His name was Artie, and he appeared on the scene with a belly full of booze and a plank of wood in his hands; probably a dangerous cocktail under the circumstances.

He staggered up to the police line and lobbed the plank over at the marchers. The rest became history and is known as the Battle of Bogside. For the next three days and two nights, the local people from the Bogside and surrounding areas defended themselves against the might of the armed state police and their notorious reserve force, the B Specials. Dan was in the thick of it throughout.

It was an electrifying time and whatever the danger of those days, there was also the overwhelming feeling of a community getting off its knees, never to return to them again. The RUC used everything they had to quell the insurgent Croppies of Derry. But this time they did not lie down. The Catholics of Derry had decided that they wouldn't be treated like second-class citizens again. All the injustice and discrimination they had endured over the years became the catalyst for this newfound collective backbone that stood up and said 'no more' to their so-called political masters. And it was the inebriated Artie who lit the touchpaper.

History books and news reports didn't record it that way, but Dan was there and that's what happened. Those few days were as exciting as they were scary. Heroes appeared from among working-class men and women to lead and direct the defence of a community. Some were named, like Eamonn McCann, Bernadette Devlin and Paddy 'Bogside' Doherty. But the real heroes in Dan's eyes were the ones with no names, those anonymous giants who fought with stones, petrol bombs and, at times, with their bare hands to protect their homes and families from a police force on the rampage that had been given a free hand by their political masters to put the rising down.

They couldn't and they didn't, and at least history recorded that bit correctly. Dan recalled petrol bombs being rained down from the top of Rossville Flats on marauding RUC men, putting any notions of taking up residence in the Bogside out of their minds. Just like October 5th, if all the men who now claim to have been on top of the flats had actually been there, the flats would have been tumbled many years before they actually were demolished, and at much less cost!

No one slept - or so it seemed. Dan was there throughout and had the scars and the trophy to prove it. He was hit on the head by a brick thrown by an RUC man. To this day he believes he was concussed as well as cut and bleeding profusely, but there was no time or inclination for a trip to the hospital in the midst of battle. If Mel Gibson could take all that Longshanks could throw at him, then a few bricks on the head in the Bogside wouldn't stop this teenage Braveheart! (Poetic licence and retrospect are wonderful things when making anachronistic comparisons!)

A quick repair from a first-aider and he was soon back at the front line. Some more astute onlookers who knew Dan before and after would suggest the concussion never ever cleared given his personal history over the next thirty-plus years. That theory, coupled with the earlier one that his sister might have dropped him on his head as a child, was certainly symptomatic and indicative that things went on in Dan's head that the rest of the world was not invited to! The other trophy that Dan acquired was an RUC riot shield liberated from a fleeing policeman after one of their many failed attempts to invade the Bogside over the three days.

After three days the defenders of the Bogside were tired and drained but still determined that their newfound backbone would hold firm. By this time riots in support of their stance had broken out in Belfast and other parts of the province. The unionist government, no doubt embarrassed by the resolute opposition to the RUC from the Derry upstarts, was planning to let the notorious B Specials loose in the Bogside. The Irish government was under pressure to show tangible support for their 'nationalist brothers' under siege in the Bogside and was making utterances about troops being sent to the border and put on standby to defend the Catholics of Derry.

The Irish government was always good at utterances, but rarely stepped up to the mark when it came to positive action. It's called politics, apparently! More importantly, Dan was eating a bag of chips and drinking a can of Coke during a lull in the fighting. Then an air of something momentous descended and rumours of troops coming in abounded. Initially, it was thought that the Irish Army was being sent in to rescue the beleaguered Bogsiders. The aforementioned 'utterances' ensured that rumour was quickly scotched.

Then it was announced that the British government had decided to send in their troops to relieve the RUC from their riot duties in an attempt to calm the escalating crisis. The Bogside went into celebration mode at the sight of the RUC and B Specials being stood down. The British Army was welcomed onto the streets of Derry by cheering Catholics. The Battle of Bogside was over and the victorious Derry Catholics were in a celebratory mood.

A Fleadh Cheoil was held in the Bogside shortly afterward, with music, dance and merriment replacing the previous danger, tension and fear. It was a great time to be a Derryman or woman and Dan soaked up every moment. He also soaked internally from copious amounts of beer over the Fleadh weekend. The world was indeed a wonderful place for Dan Feeney in August 1969, but all that euphoria was to change.

British troops on Irish soil may have solved an immediate crisis for the British government, but the clock was ticking on how long the nationalist population of the North would tolerate English squaddies on their streets. A pot was boiling which would spill over into a bloody war for three decades to come.

Worse than that, Dan failed miserably in his GSE examinations and had to either repeat them or look for a job.

6

Boy to Man?

Dan returned to college to repeat his O-levels but it was soon obvious that the academic route to fame and fortune was not going to be his pathway, so he left college as soon as he obtained a job as an office junior in an estate agent's office in the city. His salary was £8 per week. It was really only a wage in Dan's eyes, as salaries were for snobs and boring people and he didn't qualify on either account. Whatever the semantics, the £8 a week didn't go far for a young man with an appetite for booze and betting. He was paid on a Friday and usually skint by Saturday; unless he touched lucky at the horses or cards, which meant the party went on to Monday.

A typical weekend itinerary was: collect pay, bet the horses, go to the pub, get drunk, play cards to the wee small hours, sleep to lunchtime and repeat the dose for as long as the money lasted. Interspersed with this cocktail was to turn up at the riots in the Bogside and go to the odd dance in search of the elusive girlfriend.

Dan found that his fear of rejection by girls usually dissipated somewhat after ten pints of lager. So he often approached girls for a dance, but by then he was too drunk to be of interest to any Derry woman, who on instructions from their mothers went to dances in search of prospective husbands, and Dan didn't meet any of the qualifying criteria. For some reason vomiting in the dance hall, falling down stairs and staggering through a set of slow dances didn't seem to tick the right boxes for Derry girls in search of a partner! Even in hindsight Dan still recalled that lifestyle with some fondness, but he also realised that it completely imprisoned any youthful potential that may have been trying to escape.

In spite of this tumultuous, yet vacuous, existence, Dan got on well at work and was in line for promotion to his employer's nearby stockbrokers' office, which would have brought serious career opportunities. But Dan's self-destruct button was already on standby and was about to be activated.

One Friday he managed to lose all of his wages on the horses before finish time at work. Panic filled Dan's self-centred and reactive mind as the thought of no betting, no drinking and no dances created mayhem in his underdeveloped brain. However, all was not lost. He knew there was a 'good thing' running in the 3.45 at Ayr. So he 'liberated' some money from the office safe and went and placed a £40 win bet on the unbeatable Supermaster. Like many unbeatable horses over the years, Supermaster got beat, trailing in a distant second.

That day Dan discovered that the fear of being caught stealing was even more potent in stirring up bowel and kidney activity than those nervous moments preceding the first date with Fiona. To make matters worse, one of the managers in the stockbrokers' office saw him leave the bookies shop. His first instinct was to run, but some fatal sense of 'take your oil' prevailed, so he went back to the office to face the music. At the same time, he was hoping the manager would not notice the missing cash. Within minutes his fate was sealed.

The manager asked him about the missing money. Dan owned up that he had taken it and lost it on a horse. Had this been a Hollywood movie, his manager would have listened to his confession, gave him a comforting hug and told him that many young men face such difficulties in life and that he should now learn the lesson from this experience and go on to become a paragon of virtue, honesty and integrity from that moment onwards. Unfortunately, his boss wasn't a film buff, so he sacked him on the spot.

Dan left the office in abject shame and disgrace. He knew he had not only let himself down but had also brought the shame and disgrace to the door of his parents. He just couldn't face them, so, filled with remorse and guilt, he managed to gather up some money from friends and adjourned to the pub to drown his crisis in enough alcohol to allow him to temporarily forget this nightmare - or 'daymare', as it really was. Eventually, he had to leave the pub, so afterward he ensconced himself at a card school table with the few shilling he had left and played poker most of the night. By 5am he had turned the few bob into more than £80 thanks to a fantastic run of luck, coupled with the fearlessness and recklessness that enabled him to maximise his lucky streak at the expense of his more faint-hearted opponents.

Even with a pocket full of money he still lacked the courage to face his mum and dad, so with the help of an older brother he decided to go to England and seek his fortune. He had another brother in London called Hugh who was alerted that Dan was coming over. That Monday he set sail for London; a 16-year-old boy with high hopes that a geographical change would bring better fortune to his troubled life. Well, he actually had to take a taxi, two trains and a boat, but such banal details don't lend themselves to the romance and nostalgia of emigration.

Ireland is full of stories of how its young men left its green shores to seek work and wealth. Many never returned, having been sucked up in the vacuum of Irish Paddies working, drifting and drinking their way around England, always hating their fate and dreaming of home, but unable to break the cycle long enough to make it back. Sometimes they managed to visit with bulging pockets that diminished rapidly in the pubs, where they acted the big shot to receptive natives happy to have their thirst quenched by the returning heroes. But they always returned to the daily struggle of life in England, as it slowly ground many of them down to hopeless nonentities in an unfriendly land.

Dan was lucky. Within two weeks he was disillusioned. The streets of London were not paved with gold but rather by anonymous faces and not one with the time or inclination to say hello to this young Irishman abroad. Hugh looked after him well and certainly didn't try to persuade him to stay. Behind the scenes, Dan's father had done something remarkable. He had gone to the nearest telephone box and had used a telephone for the first time in his life to call Hugh. He didn't speak long. Four words were all that was necessary, 'Get that boy home.' Those four words were probably the greatest act of love a father could enact. They contained unspoken and unconditional forgiveness and a father's longing for the return of his son, undoubtedly backed up by a mother's broken heart at the prospect of another son being lost to England.

And so the prodigal son set sail for home, this time on an aeroplane! It was the spring of 1970 and a penitent Dan got off the plane to be greeted by his mother and father. Not much was said and the loss of his job with all the attendant shame wasn't mentioned. Some guys are just lucky with the parents they get. Dan was one of the lucky ones.

The spirit of reconciliation and resolve to do better only lasted a few days, as Dan once again answered the many extreme calls that were sounding in his head. His priorities again centred around the weekend riots with the British Army, who had by now become the RUC in a different uniform after murdering two young Derrymen. Of course, they claimed they were gunmen and nail bombers but the people of Derry knew different – two unarmed young men shot dead by trigger-happy squaddies, perhaps a part of some master plan to dampen the enthusiasm of resistance and rebellion.

Well, they got that plan wrong in spectacular style. The Catholics of the North were no longer dormant and would stay awake to see this struggle for freedom and equality to a conclusion.

Alongside the bubbling political crisis, Dan strongly fancied Nijinsky to win the Epsom Derby and was wondering how he could get some money to bet on this sure thing. The cause of his excursion of shame to England was now fading, just as it did so many times in the past and was to do on so many future occasions. Nijinsky duly won the Derby and Dan had his lot on it, but like so many times before and after it was just a winning blot on a loser's landscape.

As a child, Dan had heard stories of the IRA from his dad and of course from the Christian Brothers, usually in the format of songs of the brave dead heroes such as Kevin Barry, Father Murphy, Sean South of Garryowen et al. He was always impressed how these poorly armed and barely trained young men could run the Brits ragged in spite of their superior numbers, training and weaponry. Okay, the IRA volunteers were usually killed in battle or executed after they were caught, but there was no doubting their heroism. To fight with the odds overwhelmingly in your favour was one thing. To fight knowing you were sure to die or be imprisoned was another.

Only those with a just cause and a deep love and need for freedom could do battle in such circumstances. And when those young men fell, others rose up to take their place. If the English learned anything during the Troubles it was that they could kill and capture young patriots but they could never defeat an idea. Ideas of freedom and equality remained long after the colonialists have gone. Today there is peace, but Dan still awaited their departure and the return of what they stole.

IRA activity in Derry during the Battle of the Bogside was virtually nil. But in the months following and with the introduction of no-go areas by the nationalists of Derry, the republican movement was beginning to recruit and arm itself in defence of the local population and in defiance of the artificial unionist state now buoyed up by the British troops on the streets. Dan recalled seeing some young IRA volunteers coming and going from houses in his street. That all changed when Eamonn Lafferty was shot dead near the city cemetery during a gun battle with the army. From that moment Dan knew that the IRA was the only tangible means of opposing injustice and fighting for the freedom that he believed Ireland so badly needed.

The civil rights movement was fragmenting, and leaders were becoming politicians who would soon be absorbed into the quagmire of politics that was Northern Ireland. The British were masters at enticing those who opposed them into their political web and thus ensure any outcome had a British stamp and a British context. Latterly the events of May 2007, with the arranged marriage of Sinn Féin and the DUP into a power-sharing executive at Stormont, was testament to their cunning and wily ways of dealing with the Irish problem. Only the English could have veteran republicans steeped in the tradition of armed resistance and dyed-in-the-wool unionists whose only measurement stick was 'not an inch' both claiming victory in the same political settlement.

Although Dan had no time for British rule in Ireland, he had a grudging respect for the way the Brits pulled this one off. Armed struggle always ended up at the negotiating table and when it got there it was no longer a fair fight between revolutionaries and British politicians. That irony may have been wasted on the current incumbents of Stormont, but not on Dan Feeney.

1970 drifted seamlessly into 1971, with Dan's life typeset into the headlines of riots and violence in Derry. The IRA was beginning to make an impact with sporadic shootings and bombings. The unionist government was calling for internment without trial to put down the republican rising.

Dan was by then working again, this time as a storeman in a factory outside Derry that manufactured women's underwear. It was here he learned a new vocabulary working in the midst of more than 100 factory girls who ensured all his visits to the factory floor ended with him returning to the store with a face like a traffic light on stop. Even 35 years on, words like 'gusset' still brought him out in a cold sweat. Overall, the craic in the factory was great. Dan recalls his first day, meeting Mr Browne, the manager, who explained to him how important his job was. Minutes later he issued an old grey shop coat to him that said much more to Dan about how important he was to the company. He was just as important as the guy who wore it before him!

With so many girls in close proximity, Dan had high hopes that his luck with the ladies would change and to some extent it did. But he was still clueless when it came to that first step of breaking the ice and spent many hours rehearsing speeches of undying love that would never be heard. Luckily, a few of the girls didn't have his affliction of terminal shyness, so his sexual awakenings jerked along at a very uneven pace. The wages at the factory were £12 per week but with regular overtime, Dan's take-home pay often topped £20. It would have been ample for any young man had he not had such a leaning towards drink and gambling. The overtime perhaps emphasised Mr Browne's perception of Dan's importance to the company as it involved brushing, mopping and buffing the factory and canteen floors every night after work. All those years of downing tools at St Columb's College had paid off in grand style, as he became a proficient cleaner of floors. Any lurking notions of grandeur soon dissipated after a few mop strokes.

The Troubles were hotting up and Dan was usually ensconced in the middle of riots every weekend. He even introduced Peter, a Protestant friend from work, to them, and he seemed to enjoy having a go at the Brits every bit as much as the Derry Catholics seemed to. From a historical perspective what was happening was momentous, but to many, it was just teenage craic with the added ingredient of danger thrown in. Every so often that danger came home to roost in tragic style.

Dan recalled a soldier being shot dead by the IRA at a sentry post in the army barracks situated in the old Essex factory site near the Creggan Estate. That night he and a friend were out walking, a customary pastime he reverted to when the horses had once again failed to deliver and therefore the pub was financially out of bounds. So, as you can imagine, he did lots of walking in those days! Come to think of it he might have been a power walker before that activity was hijacked by those disgruntled and overweight Derrywomen.

He was walking along the Lone Moor Road approaching the top of Westland Street going towards Laburnum Terrace. It was dark. Suddenly a single shot rang out and about 30 yards in front of him a man hit the ground with a deathly thud. That man never rose again. He died on the way to the hospital. His name was Billy McGrenery. Of course, the British Army claimed he was a gunman. Billy McGrenery was no more a gunman than Dan was a bishop. He became another statistic in the rising list of innocent men murdered on the streets of his own town, perhaps the victim of another trigger-happy soldier out for revenge for the earlier event that day.

This incident, in conjunction with numerous others, had Dan thinking that maybe the time had come to fight this injustice with something more effective than stones and petrol bombs. His mind was made up soon after.

Dan and Peter had booked to go to Butlin's holiday camp in the Republic of Ireland on the second week of August 1971. They nearly didn't get there. Dan got his holiday pay at the end of July and around lunchtime the next day he swaggered up Bishop Street with over £120 in his pocket. *I'll just have a few pints and back a few horses,* he thought with the unwitting delusion of countless alcoholics and compulsive gamblers. By 3pm it was all gone. As was usually the case, it was only then he recalled the fact that he was to go on holidays with Peter the following week. For the next week, Dan dwelled in that inner abode of fear, guilt, self-hatred and self-condemnation, all mixed with a good dollop of self-pity. The days passed all too quickly prior to Peter's arrival at his house on the Friday night before they were to depart for Butlin's.

All week Dan had tried to win the money back but couldn't. Even his brother Gerry, who had pulled him out of so many holes in the past, couldn't work the oracle this time. Peter duly arrived and Dan explained his predicament. As a last resort, he decided to ask his dad for the money. Just the thought of having to do this was a hundred times worse than losing the money in the first place. He would have preferred not to go on holiday but that would have meant letting Peter down. Funny how the dictionary definition of words like 'dilemma' doesn't adequately engender the fear and panic that was engulfing Dan at that time.

To make matters worse, Peter's night went further downhill because he arrived just in time to be counted in by Dan's mother to the reciting of the rosary to Mary the mother of Jesus. This was as bad as it can get for an Irish Protestant, but Peter compliantly and considerately knelt down with Dan's family. To Dan it seemed that Catholics treated Mary as a sort of 'Wonder Woman' who had a baby without having sexual intercourse, was 'airlifted' into heaven when she died and who has since made many personal appearances to 'visionaries' in places like Lourdes, Fatima and Knock.

On the other hand, the Protestants seemed to portray Mary as some sort of disposable whore whose only importance was as a conveyance for the unborn Jesus and to look after him until he was old enough to get on with his task of saving the world. Therefore Mary apparently had no importance in the Protestant interpretation of Christianity. Both analogies disturbed Dan. His view was that the Jesus guy was pretty cool and decent and preached and practised the love of man as the solution to the riddle of life. So in Dan's eyes, his mum had to be pretty cool and decent too.

Peter tolerantly knelt with the rest of the Feeneys and mumbled with them until Dan's mum signalled through the sign of the cross that the rosary proceedings were over for another night. Just to be safe, the two pals quickly exited and went to the pub for a few pints before they went to the dance at the Embassy Ballroom in search of the elusive girl in a million. For once Dan's mind wasn't really on the drinking, although he did down several pints of lager and a few vodkas. Unlike the rosary, the dance went too quickly as Dan got closer to the impending face to face with his dad. He knew his father would still be up when they returned from the dance. After finishing in the bar he always took 'a mouthful of air' outside before relaxing on an easy chair in the living room after a long day on his feet.

They arrived back around 1.30am and Peter was

dispatched to his bedroom while Dan sat with his dad. The next few minutes were even longer than ten rosaries as Dan tried to get the thoughts in his head out as far as his vocal cords. He couldn't speak. *Fuck it,* he thought, *I can't dump this on my da. Peter will have to go alone.* Simultaneously his father said, 'So you're off to Butlin's tomorrow, then.' Now there was no way out.

It's funny how Dan faced many dangerous, difficult and even life-threatening situations in future times, yet here he was afraid to speak to his dad. The motivational difference between a just cause and shame was vast. Dan muttered in a semi-coherent voice, 'Well I don't think I'll be going on holiday.' Then followed his confession about losing all his wages and not having the money to go on holiday. His dad calmly asked him how much he needed to go. Dan replied that £30 might cover it. His father gave him £40 saying that he would probably need the extra tenner. He spoke to him briefly about how gambling and drinking didn't really agree with him and then told him to go to bed and get some sleep and enjoy his week away.

No words of condemnation or admonishment and no mention of paying the money back. Just a father being a father in that quiet, unassuming way that epitomised Dan's daddy. Almost simultaneous with the relief was an acute feeling of being humbled by this great man. Then that feeling of shame returned that he had put his father in this position once again. Upstairs in the bedroom, Peter was relieved to know that he and his 'mucker' were off to Butlin's the next morning. Dan affirmed to himself once again that this incident would mean the end of his gambling and that he would drink moderately from then onwards.

As previously, these solemn oaths were obliterated within days of arriving at Butlin's. In fact, by Wednesday, money was running dangerously low due to his excesses in Dan Lowry's pub. So he placed a small bet and all four horses won. He did the same yankee bet that night and they all won too. With over £50 in winnings, Dan and Peter were the kings of the holiday camp, although Peter didn't have Dan's appetite for alcohol and used to go to a cabaret show before joining him in the pub. Dan couldn't understand such weird behaviour but put it down to some strange Protestant eccentricity.

On August 9th 1971, while they were away, it was announced that internment without trial had been rushed through Parliament, and republicans were being rounded up, interrogated and taken to various locations and held indefinitely without any charges being made against them. It was later learned that many of these internees were brutally tortured during the interrogations. Of course, the government denial experts were wheeled out to counteract any claims of torture, but the nationalist population knew the truth long before the British government accepted the ill-treatment and torture of internees. In time Dan would see this practice up close and personal.

Internment without trial was the last straw for Dan and he vowed to come back to Derry and join the Provisional IRA. Within one day of his return, he had made contact with a known IRA man and asked to join. He recalled clearly that man calmly telling him what becoming a member of the IRA had to offer, which was basically imprisonment, internment or death. The starkness of such a marketing strategy didn't deter Dan's enthusiasm to take up arms against injustice and for freedom, and he affirmed his commitment to become a volunteer of the Provisional Irish Republican Army.

Within a few days, he and others were called to a venue in the Brandywell area of the city where they took the oath of allegiance to the IRA. Dan's next dilemma was whether or not to tell his parents. Given the likely prospect of imprisonment or death, he decided they had a right to know. His father took it well and seemed almost proud of his young son. His mother had a completely different reaction, initially hysterical, followed by stern and sustained disapproval. It's strange that this was the only time he could recall making his dad proud, hardly the normal father/son moment of pride! Yet Dan was still glad to have experienced it.

Not long after, on April 1st 1972, his daddy died of cancer. Mickey Feeney was dead far too soon, and a family grieved his loss. Dan always wished he could have added more to his father's life, but accepted that he was what he was in those days, and deep down he knew his father accepted him too. He would always have the memories of the stories, the yarns, the example and those quiet acts of unconditional love that only a parent could give. They would not be wasted.

Some weeks passed with no word from the IRA. Dan went to work and behaved normally in as far as possible given his propensity for escapes from life through those potentially fatal mechanisms of booze and bets. Then the day came when an IRA volunteer arrived at his house and he was told to attend a meeting in a house in Derry's Bogside later that night. When Dan entered the house he was directed upstairs. Altogether there were ten there. A man entered the room and gave everyone the opportunity to leave before the meeting started. A sort of 'get out now before it's too late' moment. This young man was to be their section leader and would ready them to take their place and play their part in the struggle for Irish freedom on the streets of Derry.

Nobody left. Dan often thinks about the faces of those young men. Some he knew but most he didn't. The prophecy of death, prison or internment without trial proved true for everyone there that night. Over the next three years, two were killed during a gun battle, while the rest were either sentenced to many years in gaol or interned without trial in Long Kesh concentration camp, near Lisburn.

The boy was on his way to manhood and would have to grow up very quickly to keep pace with the demands of guerrilla warfare in an Irish town.

7

Soldiers Are We

'You are now soldiers of the Provisional Irish Republican Army and my job is to train you on the use of guns and explosives,' the man said matter-of-factly. 'This is a stick of gelignite.' Dan's thoughts immediately focused on what would happen if it exploded in the room. A fire burned in the corner and the training officer threw the gelignite into the heart of it. Everyone jumped off their seats and headed for the door. The section leader spoke above the ongoing commotion. Of course, Dan's customary activity in the kidney and bowel areas was already gaining momentum. 'No need to panic, men. Gelignite will burn harmlessly. It needs a detonator to activate an explosion.' The sense of relief was palpable as the frenzy dissipated to sceptical calm.

Sean, who would be their section leader for the next few months, then produced a detonator and showed them how to insert it into the gelignite. Next, he introduced some fuse wire which, when attached, would complete the ingredients to make a simple bomb. At that time there was no real sophistication or expertise in explosives within the IRA and the bombs were crude and simple, yet potentially deadly.

Some volunteers lost their lives in premature explosions

trying to pioneer the IRA bombing campaign, which at that time was to hit the British economically by blowing up commercial targets. The Brits referred to such tragedies as 'own goals'.

Sean explained the rationale behind the IRA's bombing of commercial targets. The idea was to hit the British taxpayer where it hurt most – their pockets - to create financial chaos and bring them to their senses about returning what they stole. It all made perfect sense within the IRA, but in reality, bombing businesses in Derry or elsewhere in the province was to cause no more than a ripple in the British economy.

In addition, people in Britain couldn't care less about what happened in Ireland. History has revealed that the strategy of the early '70s had merit, but it was the location of the bombs that was going to be the influencing factor, as the bombing of Canary Wharf, the heartland of the British economy, over 20 years later proved. It's notable how English minds changed when the problem crossed the Irish Sea!

After an hour or so, Sean dismissed the new recruits with a time, date and venue for their next section meeting. They all left and went their separate ways. Dan could still feel the excitement as he walked home through the darkened streets. Inside he was now a soldier of Ireland ready to die for his country. It's ironic how freedom fighters find something exciting and romantic about dying. His up close and personal experiences of the next few years were to change those romantic notions about death forever.

To the outside world, he was just another denim-clad,

pimple-faced teenager with nothing remarkable to distinguish him from the civilian population of Derry. To Dan, the downside of being in this army was that you couldn't tell anyone. Here he was, one of a few dozen IRA men in the city on the verge of taking on the might of the British Army, and he had to keep it a secret. The pulling power that this information would have had among the 'babes' in Derry was potentially huge, but would never be measured because of the secrecy attached to guerrilla armies. These early thoughts graphically demonstrate the innocence attached to his idealism and did not bode well for the reality that bombs and bullets were about to bring. Innocence and idealism were not going to be compatible, as war was a dirty business and Dan was a soldier. It was a soldier's job to take orders. The transition from romantic republican to active soldier did not come easy for Dan Feeney.

Over the coming weeks, the training continued. Weapons were introduced. Dan's exploits in the cinema as a boy had created an understanding of guns that only Hollywood could engender. The first words of the section leader as he passed around a Luger pistol among the recruits took the gloss from guns forever. 'Never point a gun at anyone unless you intend to use it,' he warned. Dan had envisaged twirling it around his finger a few times, but those words suggested that guns were serious implements and had to be treated with a lot more respect than John Wayne ever showed.

For the next hour, they were taught the mechanics of the Luger and learned the names of all the parts as the instructor stripped it down and built it up several times. Dan vaguely recalled a poem he should have learned at college but didn't, due to his days of apathy to and escape from education. There was a recurring line which read, *But today we have naming of parts.* Here was Dan all set to free Ireland and he was being taught to rhyme off the parts of a German firearm.

Over the next few weeks, this boring routine was replicated with a .45 automatic pistol, a Lee Enfield .303 rifle, an M1 Carbine and a Thompson submachine gun. All the macho and romantic notions of a man with a gun doing what a man's gotta do evaporated amidst the boredom and technical mantra of naming parts. As much as it was probably a necessary first step to get used to handling these weapons prior to actually using them in a war situation, Dan was deeply disillusioned and despaired at the thought of Jesse James or the Lone Ranger having to learn their trade in this fashion.

In between the IRA training sessions, Dan went to work as normal and still found time for his other potentially fatal interests of drinking and gambling. He found it strange that his day job involved the handling of women's underwear, something he would have much preferred to do at night in a more recreational setting, yet at night he was a secret soldier handling weapons of destruction, but still almost oblivious to the danger and seriousness of what he was embarking on.

As the IRA gained experience, the weapons coming into the country became more varied, lethal and plentiful. Dan recalled the first time he was introduced to the Armalite assault rifle. It looked so harmless, like a black plastic toy. Yet it was a serious killing implement used by the Americans in Vietnam. The instructor emphasised its lethal nature, then showed the feature of its folding butt that was extremely useful for concealment in an urban guerrilla war setting. The bullets were armour-piercing and could kill from 1000 yards. All this information impressed Dan greatly, but still, it didn't penetrate his thinking that he might be actually using the weapon in situations where he could kill or be killed. If ever a young man was in for a shock about what war was really all about, it was Dan.

The Christian Brothers had done a thorough job in romanticising the struggle for Irish freedom and glamorising 'dying for the cause' in such a way that if you died, you almost expected you would still be around to hear the songs sung by drunken Catholics in local pubs, eulogising your bravery and ultimate sacrifice for the mother soil. Sure what young patriot could wish for a better send-off?

Dan often mused about what his funeral would be like if he were killed in action. Again his naivety obscured the seriousness of such thinking. It seemed reality was for other people, not him. But the truth was that, after all the training was over, Dan was going to experience the seriousness of waging war in Ireland, and the romantic overtones in his head would be tempered with the very real violence, victims and volcano of pain that wars outside of Hollywood brought with them.

January 30th 1972 was to accelerate the lesson that war

was a dirty business in tragic and deadly fashion. History records it as Bloody Sunday. Just as on August 12th 1969 at the Battle of the Bogside, Dan had a close-up view of the events of Derry's darkest ever day. Like many thousands of Derrymen and women, Dan joined the anti-internment march organised by the civil rights movement. There was much publicity about it, with the usual rantings from politicians on all sides as to the merits and demerits of the event. The unionists wanted the march stopped from going to the city centre and the nationalists were demanding their right to march in their own city. It's interesting that 30 years later there has been a transposition of the argument in relation to certain Orange Order marches in Derry and other parts of the North.

Dan recalled joining the march at William Street, as he had met with some fellow IRA volunteers earlier in the expectation that they might be needed for 'action' on the day. They were instructed there was not to be any interference with the march. Experience had shown that it was almost a certainty there would be a riot at some time during or after the march and Dan intended to be part of it, but his contribution would be as a civilian rather than a soldier.

The army had cordoned off the bottom of William Street and were there in strength to make sure the march didn't get to the Guildhall Square in the city centre. The unionist government had banned it. History records this as not one of their most inspired decisions, but the rationale of bigotry and dominance tends to obscure wisdom!

The march was re-routed to Free Derry Corner in the heart of the Bogside when it became clear that the security forces would not allow it to go into the city centre. This decision was taken to avoid trouble and bloodshed. With around 20,000 people taking part, the organisers wisely decided not to confront the army, who seemed particularly gung ho and up for it that day. With the marchers moving away from William Street, it opened the door for the 'recreational' rioters to have a go at the Brits.

Some 300 young rioters did battle with the army in the usual fashion, with stones, bottles and petrol bombs raining in on the soldiers who responded with tear gas and rubber bullets. Not a lot new there, except someone at some level had decided that this was the day the Brits would teach the young rioters a lesson. What happened next is subject to various experiences, beliefs, understandings and theories. Some have truth and merit, others are just lies and cover-up (in later years the Bloody Sunday tribunal report vindicated the innocent dead, and at least for once in the history of the Troubles the same truth now resides with the people of Derry and the British government).

Shortly after 4pm the British Army, led by the 1st Battalion Parachute Regiment, flooded into William Street both in armoured trucks and on foot. The rioters scattered. Dan was close to the front of the riot and cut left over Chamberlain Street hoping to escape to the nearby Rossville Street flats. As he was running up the street he heard several shots. Instinctively he knew they were not baton rounds, but deadly lead spewing out of the soldiers' SLR rifles. He had heard the crack of these high-velocity guns before.

He continued to run towards a wall beside the car park at the foot of the flats and hurtled over it to take cover. More shots rang out. Then in the lull, he heard a man shout. He tentatively put his head above the wall and saw the man going crazy and shouting at the soldiers to shoot him. There was a body lying close by. The man was remonstrating that they had murdered the young man on the ground. As he was shouting and daring the soldiers to shoot him, the army duly obliged and shot him. The man fell to the ground. He was armed only with his courage to stand up to soldiers shooting defenceless men indiscriminately.

History records those two men as Jackie Duddy, who died on the way to the hospital, and Michael Bridge, who was wounded. The world was to view the rest of this story through news clips of Bishop Daly waving a blood-stained handkerchief in a desperate attempt to get Jackie Duddy medical attention. It's a pity they didn't see footage of the shootings in that car park that preceded these scenes. Then they would have known that men were murdered by the British Army on Bloody Sunday and there would be no need for all the prevaricating, spin and fudging that the British government had been guilty of for over 30 years. Those two men's only crime was to be there on that murderous and tragic day.

Dan kept his head down after that until the shooting ceased. For a few minutes, he sat with his back to the wall in frightened disbelief at what he had just witnessed. But he saw what he saw, and outcomes of inquiries and tribunals would never measure up against the vision of men being shot in cold blood – and by soldiers paid for by the taxpayers of Britain and Northern Ireland, one of whom included Dan Feeney.

For decades unionist and British politicians, and their apologists in the media, have continued to excuse or cast doubt on the immorality, barbarism and significance of the events of Bloody Sunday. They have equivocated between these murders and the killings carried out by the IRA during the Troubles. What they seemed to miss was that the Bloody Sunday murders were carried out by the state, whose primary responsibility is to keep its citizens safe, not shoot them on the street like dogs, and therefore the actions on that day were and remain an affront to democracy.

Eventually, he got up and ran as fast as he could in crouched fashion towards Free Derry Corner, his heart pounding with the fear and expectation that he might be shot too. He wasn't, and eventually made his way home, unaware of the actual scale and impact of what had just happened. He recalled telling his father the story. In fact, his father had been listening to the breaking news and was able to give him more information about the number of casualties than Dan was aware of himself. That day the story unfolded hour by hour, with claims and counterclaims of who shot first, and the usual British media extravaganza ensued. When the dust settled, 13 men were dead and one died a few months later, with scores of others arrested, wounded or injured.

No soldiers were shot, which was not a surprise to Dan given what he'd witnessed in the Rossville flats car park and what he had been told before the march by his IRA superiors. Someone, somewhere, within the army or perhaps the government, had decided to teach the risen people of Derry a lesson. The lesson was learned all right, but not in the way the Brits had planned.

The day following the massacre was eerily sombre and surreal, with the people of Derry converging en masse on the Bogside in stunned silence, just walking around the streets where their neighbours and townsmen were murdered. A few days later the funerals took place, and it seemed like the whole city turned up to share in the grief of the families. It was a huge send-off for the innocents in that quiet and dignified way that only unbearable pain and grief can engender in human beings.

The atrocity was over and the dead were buried, but the impact had yet to start. Bloody Sunday created a recruitment surge to the IRA as hundreds of young men and women decided that the only way to stand up to injustice and murder was to take up arms against the state that presided over it. The IRA now had the supply of men and arms it needed to escalate the campaign and it did so with deadly effect. Dan only had to wait a few months for his first call to active service.

By this time he had left his job at the underwear factory and was working as a wages clerk in a local shirt factory. It was a usual Derry summer Saturday, which meant it was dull and raining, and Dan's plan for the day centred around the bookies and the bar with maybe a visit to the Stardust later in search of that woman in a million who was going to sweep him off his feet. He'd been out the night before and was suffering from the effects of alcohol that usually meant he needed some more very soon. After the pubs closed he'd gone to a card school and had managed to remain in the chair to the end and leave with over £90 to bring forward to the Saturday agenda.

He had struggled to dislodge himself from bed until just before noon to ready himself for the next phase in self-destruction. By 1pm he was washed, watered and fed, and ready to hit the pub for the mandatory 'hair of the dog' when his mother informed him there was a young man at the door wanting to talk to him. Dan went to see who it was, expecting it was one of his pals looking to join him for an afternoon in the pub and bookies. It wasn't.

At the door was a young man who Dan didn't know. He instructed him to report to a house in the Bogside at 8pm that night and to dress in a suit if possible. That was it, no other information. For all Dan knew he could be going on a blind date, but he suspected it might be something a bit more dangerous. So ended the day's plan to go to the pub. All day, his mind wandered to what lay ahead. He couldn't even concentrate on the horse racing that afternoon and lost all his money in double-quick time. Inside, his stomach was dancing with a mixture of fear, excitement and trepidation, not to mention the withdrawals from the previous night's drinking.

He knew he couldn't drink, even though the scattered thoughts of what he might have to do created even more craving than usual. But for once he controlled the urge and didn't touch a drop.

Time passed slowly at first, and then when he wanted it to slow down, it speeded up. His cheap Timex watch often behaved like that but on this occasion, it was his jittery stomach dictating the time. Eventually, 7.30pm arrived and he left the house dressed for business. He had bought a new suit for his new job to replace the grey shop coat from his previous one. As he walked towards the Bogside his mind was dominated by what might be about to happen. *Maybe it's just another meeting,* he thought. *Then why the need for a suit?* he retorted to himself. A hundred potential scenarios presented themselves, each one dissipating to his comforting logic.

When he left home he wanted to tell someone where he was going but he knew he couldn't. Secret armies were only effective when they remain secret. At 7.50pm he arrived at the house in the Bogside. There were lots of people around, most of whom he didn't know. Dan didn't like this. For some reason, many IRA men hung around this house, which to him seemed like advertising who they were to the British Army and RUC Special Branch, who were no doubt looking on from their vantage points on the city's famous walls.

One of Dan's fellow volunteers from his section approached him and ushered him into the house. Dan was too glad to get away from the 'showmen' outside to even think about what his task would be that night. He was soon to learn. In the room, there were four large suitcases, each one packed with explosives and timing devices readied for detonation. Dan was introduced to his partner for the night, a man from another city on the run in Derry. His name was Jim. He was experienced in all aspects of guerrilla war in the North and would keep Dan right during their mission. He had even escaped from prison, so Jim was a much revered republican.

Their task was to take the four bombs to a well known and widely used local hotel, set the timers to allow 50 minutes before the bombs exploded, and telephone a warning to the RUC and the local Samaritans, to ensure everyone in the vicinity was evacuated, so as to avoid civilian casualties. The IRA mistrusted the RUC, so the call to the Samaritans was their insurance against them claiming that no warning was given.

Dan was nervous but dared not show it. Paramilitaries were expected to be fearless in the execution of their duty. His bowels and kidneys disagreed absolutely. He discovered that day that courage and fear were very close bedfellows and that one emanated directly from the other. At 9pm the two bombers set off in a taxi and arrived at the hotel a few minutes later. Dan was elected to do the talking and went to the reception to check in. The booking had been made earlier and he composed himself and went through the motions of the check-in. He paid the bill in advance, then he and his accomplice headed for the lift with their cargo of destruction.

At this point, a porter intervened and offered to help.

Dan reluctantly let him carry two cases. 'What have you in these cases?' the porter remarked at the heavy baggage. 'Bombs,' Dan replied in a joking tone. The porter laughed. Dan reassured him the cases contained product samples but didn't elaborate any further. The porter accompanied them to their adjoining rooms. Dan fumbled to find a coin to tip him. He didn't have one. He had lost all his money earlier in the bookies. He pulled a £20 note from the wad he had been given to cover hotel expenses and handed it to the porter, who was amazed and delighted by such generosity and thought all his Christmases had come at once. Little did he know that this tip would be his last in that hotel - a sort of early redundancy deposit!

After the porter left, Dan and Jim went to ready the bombs in their rooms. Jim came in to check that Dan had set his timer properly to detonate in 50 minutes to ensure they exploded simultaneously. He nodded that all was well and the two men hurriedly left the hotel on foot, went to a public phone box and phoned the RUC and the Samaritans as planned, and returned on foot back to the house in the Bogside about ten minutes later. Dan's heart was still pounding as they waited for the time to pass. He wondered would the bombs go off or had they made a mistake with the timers.

These questions were answered by a sudden and huge explosion in the distance. Jim shook his hand and congratulated him on a job well done. At that Dan sauntered home with mixed feelings. He was glad the mission was accomplished but would be uneasy until he heard there were no casualties. The late news led with the bombing and added that a warning had been given and there were no casualties, but that the hotel was extensively damaged. The hotel had to be demolished some time later and became another car park commissioned by the Provos.

Dan couldn't sleep all night. He was now an active soldier in the IRA. He was dying to tell someone about the mission, but couldn't. The secret of staying alive and out of jail was to blend back into his normal lifestyle and say nothing to anyone. Two days later, he walked past the bombed hotel on his way to work. Nobody gave him a second look. There was no turning back now. His double life had begun.

The next two weeks were quiet, with Dan living as normal in his own abnormal way. Some of the IRA recruits from his section were beginning to be arrested and charged with planting bombs in the city. They were later to be given sentences ranging from seven to ten years in prison, demonstrating the short active service expectancy for many IRA volunteers. A few others were 'on the run' because they had become known to the security forces.

Dan just stayed away from all of it to maintain his anonymity. At the weekend dances, he could see the 'on the runs' were getting lots of attention from the local girls. He wanted to shout out, 'What about me? I'm a Provo too,' but that wouldn't have been a wise move. And so the dances produced the usual waste of shoe leather. He just circled the hall in search of the elusive girlfriend, knowing that even if he found her she would never know because of his deep fear of rejection that meant he would always ask the girl beside her for a dance. How could a man who could plant bombs with all the attendant danger and precision be so pathetically shy when it came to affairs of the heart?

Then, as if by some miracle, a girl in the factory called Amanda came to Dan's attention. She was a beautiful young country girl from Campsie, a village on the outskirts of the city. Amanda and Dan struck up a rapport and each made it known to the other that they were going to Borderland dance hall on a particular Friday night. To Dan, this sounded extremely promising and his rejection aversion eased considerably. With the required quantity of alcohol consumed that meant he could still speak, and perhaps even dance, without appearing too drunk, he entered the hall.

Within minutes he had spotted Amanda, who was there with some other factory girls. Even with the requisite Dutch courage, Dan was still shy to approach her directly, but eventually, he blended into the company and somehow managed to get chatting to her. Everything seemed on track, so he asked Amanda to dance. Even that was going unusually well. They say that if something seems too good to be true, then it usually is. Dan didn't know who 'they' were, but they were about to be proved right again.

Without such informative hindsight, Dan asked Amanda could he leave her home. He doesn't recall exactly what she said, as his gack streak overtook him as she spoke. All he knew was that the word 'no' was said and he had to get off the dance floor and into the obscurity of the crowded hall very fast.

For the rest of the night, he sat in the 'rejected' corner, just wishing the dance was over and he could get on the bus home. Strangely, at work the next week Amanda was just as friendly as ever. Dan just felt awkward and embarrassed but tried to act cool in her presence - not easy when inside you're a gack - but his method acting skills had improved thanks to previous experiences of rejection, so Amanda was none the wiser. He tried again at Borderland for the next two Fridays, each time with additional booze consumed to cushion the blow. Each time Amanda said no.

This hurt Dan much more than when Ulster said 'No' many years later! Whatever the reason, Amanda seemed unobtainable, except during work time flirtations that created unrequited expectations in Dan's mind, heart and nether regions. Then something really strange happened the following Friday.

Dan staggered into the dance hall dressed in his new suit and lemon polo neck sweater. Readers under the age of fifty will be excused for vomiting or making weird retching noises at this apparent sartorial 'dootness', but Dan was looking well that night and in full synchronisation with the fashion trends of that era. After the seventh pint of lager, he reckoned he was a force to be reckoned with and a handful for any woman. He eventually came across Amanda and her friends but this time he wasn't going to lead with his chin. Too many knockbacks take their toll on even the bravest of hearts, so he didn't engage in any flirtation with her.

However, she approached him. 'You're looking very well tonight, Dan,' she said. In that clumsy way that only this awkward Derryman could muster, Dan muttered something inaudible, that if translated from grunt form probably meant 'thank you'. There was an uneasy silence. Amanda broke it. 'Are you not going to ask me to dance tonight, Dan?' Confusion with or without alcohol is still confusion and Dan was extremely confused. 'What's the point, Amanda, sure you always shoot me down anyway,' he retorted. 'Well maybe I won't tonight,' she said. Dan's confusion increased. What was it about women? When you gave them attention they weren't interested, and when you left them alone they wanted attention. But the main thing was, Amanda was interested.

Maybe it was the lemon polo neck sweater that clinched it or maybe she always liked him and was just playing hard to get. Dan would never know as it appears that women were trained not to give information to men that might remove their eternal confusion. The upshot was that he left Borderland that night hand in hand with Amanda. This was the beginning of a short-lived romance that suffered from lack of oxygen, mainly due to Dan's other life as a revolutionary and his preoccupation with gambling and drinking on his days off. It was to end following an IRA bombing operation that changed Dan's life for the next few years.

During the coming weeks, Dan took part in many IRA operations, some of which involved getting large bombs into the city centre. 1972 was the year of the greatest number of bombings and shootings and he was in the thick of it.

It was getting more difficult for volunteers to operate, as the security forces were ratcheting up surveillance, and checkpoints were being established at all the entrances to the city centre. And so it became a game of cat and mouse between the IRA and the British Army and RUC. In most instances, the IRA mice escaped with the 'cheese' as they breached the security apparatus time after time. Dan recalled discovering a way to get a bomb into Strand Road in the centre of Derry without actually going through a checkpoint. However, it meant coming dangerously close to a few. This discovery came about as a result of his gambling. He observed that the Brits had left an opportunity near the bookies in Patrick Street. The target was a local electrical shop that specialised in televisions, radios and record players.

Dan recalled that there was an old discarded record player at home. He reckoned it would provide great cover as he passed close to the army checkpoints. His mother was reluctant to let him have it but he convinced her it was for a friend who liked fixing old electrical appliances. Her parting comments were to the effect that he was up to no good, but he suitably ignored her always sharp perception. Anyway, he rationalised that it wasn't working and would be better out of her way.

He took the record player to a house in the Brandywell area, near his home. There the explosives team surgically took its insides out and inserted a 30lb bomb inside the empty shell. The bomb was housed in three plastic bags which were connected by Cordtex and fuse wire to a detonator. Dan would have to light the fuse inside the shop. It was a dangerous operation in that he would have to pass by two checkpoints, at Sackville Street and Great James Street, to get to the blind spot in Patrick Street which would give him access to Strand Road.

For 'health and safety' reasons he was to have two scouts, one in front and one behind, to keep him informed of any problems or army activity along the way. They got a lift to the edge of the no-go area at William Street and set off in single file towards the target in Strand Road, with Dan carrying the record player by the handle with the grilled speaker facing downwards. All initially seemed to be going well, but as Dan approached the army Sanger at Sackville Street, the scout to his rear called that there was a problem.

He was right. One of the bags inside had burst and white powder was spilling out from the holes in the speaker. He didn't know whether to run, walk or just abandon the operation and turn back. As he looked at the trail of white powder, he had one of those Hansel and Gretel moments and wished the birds would descend to eat the powder before the army saw it and became suspicious. Unfortunately, birds weren't as fond of a diet of explosive chemicals as they were of bread, so the white line lengthened with every step Dan took.

He decided he would continue onwards rather than turn back, as he was so near the army lookout post and hoped they wouldn't notice the white trail. The sweat was flowing freely down his forehead and his shirt was showing signs of a deluge under the arms. His heart was pounding, just waiting for a British accent to shout 'halt', or even worse a shot to be fired, which this time he would never get the chance to hear. The romantics of republicanism and freedom fighting were exploding as myths often did, even before the real bomb went off -and of course, alarm signals from his bowels and kidneys were making their customary intrusions.

He passed the army post and nothing happened. He often wondered was Stevie Wonder on lookout duty that day! Around the next corner was the Great James Street checkpoint where all pedestrians and vehicles were searched. As he skirted the checkpoint and took a left into Patrick Street, fear once more consumed him. He was within feet of the soldiers but again they didn't seem to notice him or his leaking, explosive cargo. Once past, he quickened his step and within less than a minute was at the entrance of the electrical shop in Strand Road. He looked in.

It was packed with Saturday morning shoppers. He carried the record player into the heart of the store, lit the fuse and shouted to everyone that they had three minutes to get out. Panic ensued, with Dan exiting along with the shoppers and disappearing into the busy street. Within three minutes he was safely back in the Bogside, and two minutes later he heard the explosion in the distance that confirmed that the bomb had gone off and the operation was successful. The fuse actually had five minutes in length, but he indicated a lesser time to ensure everyone got out safely. Once the bomb exploded, Dan headed home quickly.

He was having lunch when the BBC One O'Clock national news reported the bomb in Derry. They even gave the detail of how it was concealed in a record player. Dan's mother put her head in her hands and then let fly. 'That was you, wasn't it?' she shouted. 'I am ashamed that a son of mine could do such a thing.' Dan tried to laugh it off and reassure her, but his mum was having none of it. She knew her son and she knew he had lied. She'd had plenty of practice, as part of Dan's career as a failed gambler involved lying on demand and she was often the recipient. He gulped his lunch and left the house to go to the dual sanctuary of the bookies and the pub. Within half an hour he was lost in the adrenaline-filled fugue that punting and alcohol brought about, pulling him back to that world of buzzes and escape where he preferred to reside - especially in times of pressure like that particular day.

Sunday nights became a regular night to go on patrol with some IRA buddies. They drove around Free Derry in a hijacked car with a boot full of rifles, always looking and hoping for an opportunity to have a go at the Brits. For four weeks in a row, they had crouched at a vantage point on the Bankin.

As a child, Dan had played football, Cowboys and Indians, war games and 'who falls the best' on that hill. Now, at the age of 19, here he was firing real bullets from an IRA rifle at the British Army who had taken over an old creamery near the Daisy Field. This to a large extent was hands-on training for the young volunteers, as secret armies didn't have rifle ranges to learn how to shoot guns in a controlled and safe environment.

Week after week, at around 7.30pm on Sunday nights, they let the Brits have it with a salvo of shots at the army post. But on the fifth week, the army was waiting for them. Dan remembered getting one shot off from his bolt action Lee Enfield rifle. Next thing he saw sods of earth bouncing around him as the army marksmen returned fire with frightening accuracy. His earlier days playing 'who falls the best' kicked in very quickly as he and his comrades tumbled down the hillside to safety. They were soon back in their car speeding off to comparative safety in the heart of the Bogside. From then onwards they were more varied and selective in the time and places they chose to ambush the Brits. Learning on the job was a must in those days if you wanted to live to tell the tale!

Shortly after planting the record player bomb, Dan got word that he had to go on the run. He was now an OTR. Apparently, one of the scouts on that operation was arrested and implicated Dan under interrogation from the RUC Special Branch. The IRA training in how to handle interrogation at that time wasn't comprehensive. In fact, it was almost non-existent. Okay, they got the message across when they told volunteers, 'If you're lifted by the Brits, keep your mouth shut and don't sign anything and you'll be okay.' Unfortunately, they didn't explain how to do that under extreme pressure from trained detectives, who often reverted to violence and torture tactics to elicit confessions from young IRA volunteers.

Now Dan had to get out of town quickly because one of his own had broken under interrogation. This brought an end to his short romance with Amanda. He met her to explain that he had to leave his job and his town and wouldn't be able to see her again. He didn't give her any specific information about what he had been doing - just another occupational hazard of belonging to a secret army. Amanda seemed stunned and confused. Dan had so much going on in his head that he probably didn't feel the impact in the way that she did.

His primary concern at the time was to stay alive and out of prison. He had considered asking her to become one of those unfortunate women who had to visit their on-the-run men in secret, but the decent streak in his nature that was wedged between the adventure and the madness took over and he knew he had to set her free. He had nothing to offer other than what was offered to him when he joined the Provos, and death, imprisonment or internment weren't exactly attractive dowry material for any young couple. In hindsight, he reckoned he did her a favour, and the long-suffering Bridget who became his wife in later years would no doubt agree. But young hearts are young hearts, and break-ups are painful irrespective of the reasons and logic of the moment. When the mind and the emotions conflict, Dan learned that the emotions usually always won. Over the years he suffered many punctures to his heart to prove that theory, but he had his escapes on hand to anaesthetise all forms of emotional pain.

In September 1972, Dan was smuggled across the border into Donegal to one of two houses at Fahan, near Buncrana, that was populated by IRA OTRs. The houses were crowded with volunteers following Operation Motorman in July when the British reclaimed all the no-go areas. Many known IRA men and women had to get out quickly and the organisation had to rethink its strategy now that the Brits were in their midst all day and every day.

Dan recalled the weeks leading up to Operation Motorman. There was a push on politically to get the army to pull down the barricades that were erected on and off since August 1969. It was obvious something big was being planned. The Provos knew this and had been preparing to give the army a 'welcome' when they invaded Free Derry. In fact, a number of bombs had been planted under the soil up the Bankin, attached to a remote control that was attended to by Dan from the skylight of his house which overlooked it.

So by night, Dan sat waiting for the army to arrive on the Bankin at which time he was to activate the bombs by pressing the remote control button. Each morning for three weeks he had to deactivate the bomb mechanism to ensure that the children who played there were not in danger. Dan used to sit up at night more in dread than in hope that the army would turn up. Deep down he didn't want to kill anyone, yet he was a soldier and this was war, so he was ready to press the button. For some reason, perhaps divine intervention, the bomb mechanism was uplifted just before Operation Motorman by wiser counsel within the IRA leadership and taken to another part of the city.

Dan was told it was for another operation. In hindsight the sceptic in him wondered was there British involvement in this decision. They had a history of infiltrating IRA ranks with paid informers over the years. Removing the remote apparatus seemed a strange decision as the Bankin was certainly an obvious, useful and strategic vantage point for the army. A few days later Operation Motorman was launched, and the Bankin was soon awash with soldiers. Their sniffer dogs found all the underground explosives and the army carried out controlled explosions in the wee hours of the morning that kept everyone awake all night. Nobody got injured and inwardly Dan was as much relieved as he was disappointed. Many young men endure such conflict no matter how committed they are to their cause. Dan was born a human being and then became a soldier, so the human side was there first. At the same time, he was aware that an opportunity to hit the enemy hard had been missed.

Living away from his home comforts in a house full of young OTR volunteers was a huge culture shock for Dan. Things you took for granted, like the use of the bathroom and your mother having your dinner ready at the same time every night, were absent. And some freedom fighters didn't associate hygiene with the war effort. Dan reckoned if one particular Provo was sent back into Derry, he would have secured a withdrawal of all British forces. Just by lifting up his arms, he reckoned that they would have laid theirs down!

Watching TV in that house was a waste of time too, with a dozen people talking or changing the channel every five minutes. It was a sort of *Big Brother* house for terrorists! Dan would have voted them all out if he had a choice. The noise of so many men talking and carrying on in that loud macho fashion used to drive him crazy. He knew a few of the men from his earlier days in training, but most of the inhabitants were initially strangers. But in life, you have to adjust to your circumstances and Dan was no exception. He comforted himself with the thought that he would be back into Derry in a few weeks. Wishful thinking!

Two months later he moved out of the house and slept in an abandoned car across the road. He called it 'Benzene' given its previous occupation ferrying large bombs that were made up of industrial chemicals, nitrobenzene, an explosive primer and the usual detonation accoutrements. It retained the smell from its previous life, a cross between marzipan and death! This abode was hardly in Dan's ' Top 20 homes to occupy' list, but he was a wanted man in the North and was ordered by the IRA not to attempt to go back over the border without permission.

Keeping the men occupied was difficult. Some, Dan included, were involved on occasion in preparing explosive mixes for large bombs that were being readied to be smuggled into Derry for the continuation of the bombing campaign. So Dan blended in well with Benzene. On one occasion he recalled mixing a room full of the chemicals with a few comrades with their hands and feet. He still wondered if the infiltration of the chemicals through his pores qualified him as a wartime unexploded bomb!

But most of the time there wasn't much to do except adjourn to the pubs in Buncrana and listen to the 'my dick is bigger than yours' type stories of OTRs' exploits on active service in the North. Dan hated all this, although the fact that it was all laced with a seemingly endless supply of beer and vodka enabled him to tolerate the muscle-flexing by some loose-tongued Provos. There seemed to be a propensity among Irish subversives to inform on themselves to impress fellow terrorists. In today's world, there might be a niche market for a self-help group to deal with such issues of low esteem among former Provos! In Dan's world of that time, loose talk of this nature could cost you your life or freedom, so he just kept his mouth shut. He even stayed silent when he heard one such volunteer take the credit for the hotel bomb he and Jim had carried out. He was dying to contradict that guy but wisely put anonymity before ego on that occasion.

He often wondered how the supply of alcohol kept coming given that the weekly wage for OTRs was £5 per week. In Dan's eyes, it was the alcoholic's version of the miracle of the loaves and fishes, and he was happy to be a recipient of this 'daily bread'. God was indeed good, as some of his pastoral bouncers within the clerical wing of the teaching fraternity used to say.

The futility of wasting his time in Donegal when he could

be doing something destructive for the cause in Derry was constantly on Dan's mind. Week after week the OC of the OTR Provos refused his request to return to the fray. Dan did make the occasional unannounced sortie to Derry. He missed his home and family and the Derry craic, not to mention the pubs, bookies and dances. It's funny how you never really appreciate what you had until you hadn't got it anymore.

Even though Dan was a comparative misfit within the family, he just missed the comforts that only home life could offer. Being an outsider didn't really bother him because his five brothers possessed degrees of difference too for one reason or another. Only his two sisters seemed to have been blessed with normality and balance in their lives. Of course, at the time Dan thought there was something seriously wrong with them. He just couldn't imagine how anyone could live happily without overindulgence in the good things in life. That at least enabled him to see his crazy, mixed-up world as normal. And his brothers' non-conformity also gave credibility to his way of thinking and living.

On one occasion he was caught by the Provos in Lifford trying to hitch a lift to Derry after a dance in a local hotel. To make matters worse, he was drunk and had been in a fight at the dance. When he arrived back in Fahan the next day he was sanctioned for all his misdemeanours. Firstly he was made to sweep the road for 100 yards on either side of the house. Considering the fact the road wasn't dirty, Dan failed to find any logic in such a punishment. He was hugely embarrassed when passing motorists sounded their horns.

Fuckin' Dad's Army, Dan thought, *giving a punishment like this to a freedom fighter.*

When the sweep was completed he was then informed that he would be on 'stag' duty for a spell. That meant, every night for the next three weeks, he had to lie on the roof with a rifle from midnight to 8am, to protect the OTRs from an attack from the loyalist UDA, who had threatened to bomb Provo houses in Donegal. Again, Dan's sense of logic didn't take well to this punishment, and worse again it meant he wouldn't get to a pub, bookies or a dance for three weeks. When he went to bed at 8am the others were getting up, so it was almost impossible to sleep with the noise, and the old car wouldn't have been an option during the daytime. He got a better sleep on the roof at night.

If the UDA had attacked the house Dan would probably have been the last to know! He recalled one Sunday night his four best mates came home in the wee hours from the dance in Borderland. It was snowing that night, but somehow he had managed to drop off into a deep sleep. They called out to him a few times but got no answer. Then Dan was woken by a barrage of snowballs. It took days before the slagging stopped. He laughed it off by saying, 'What the fuck does it matter? If the UDA wanted to kill them they would come during the daytime when there was no lookout.'

In Dan's eyes the Provo officers weren't exactly the great strategists the Brits thought they were, but the good news was the Brits didn't know what Dan knew. If they had, the war might have been over before it got started. But it did get started, and over time the Provos became a formidable foe for the British, so much so that in later years they publicly admitted that they could not defeat the IRA militarily.

Unfortunately, they didn't seem to have learned those lessons, as proved when they and their American allies tried to impose their 'peace' on the people of Iraq by saturating that country with armed troops ready and willing to bomb and shoot the citizens until they accepted an unacceptable solution imposed by right-wing moralists. Again they found that patriots rose against them and returned their violence with more of the same. Eventually, they will leave these places and history will record that they should never have been there in the first place. The increased carnage in the middle east since that invasion is testament to their unwanted interference.

Dan believed that would be the story in Ireland too, and that after more than 800 years it was time for their 'lease agreement' to expire. If it didn't happen, another generation would rise up in years to come to finish the job he and his comrades had started. Whether that is morally defensible in some eyes is debatable. But the history of Ireland was peppered with risings against British occupation, and history usually did and probably would repeat itself if the cause of conflict did not disappear.

He totally mistrusted British intentions toward Ireland. In such a political vacuum he envisaged that Patrick Pearce's famous words during his graveside oration of O'Donovan Rossa in 1915, 'Ireland unfree shall never be at peace', might once again prove prophetic.

8

The Wilderness

Late 1972 seamlessly became early 1973. By this time Dan and three other dissenters had left the OTR house and were living a mile away in a little holiday chalet owned by a republican sympathiser. They'd gotten fed up pleading with the top Provos to let them back into Derry to finish what they started. In hindsight, this was a rather tall order, but the romanticism and fanaticism of youth didn't allow for the luxury of such foresight and wisdom. Eventually, they walked away from the Provos – for a while, at least.

Dan recalled one drunken 'hero' castigating them for leaving the Ra and telling him they would miss the glory of victory when the Brits withdrew in the next few months. Dan informed him that glory was never part of his agenda when he decided to do something to fight injustice. History was to prove that particular visionary's prediction to be somewhat off the mark, given that the Brits were still there decades later! It's no mystery he wasn't selected as a budding politician when the Provos decided to abandon the bomb and bullet in the 1990s. Perhaps his flawed analysis of the early seventies had a bearing on that!

Their decision to walk away meant that they were on their

own and would no longer receive the limited support of being fed and housed, or the fiver a week OTR money. No one could ever accuse the Provos of being mercenaries! In those days they didn't own the clothes on their back, never mind the Armani suits, pubs and property portfolios that seem to be part of some contemporary republicans' acquirements!

They put their life on the line for free. That's what made them unbeatable at that time. However, when the word hit Derry that they had been disenfranchised, many friends, family and sympathisers came to their aid with parcels of food and money. In fact most of the time they were much better off than before, and with only four in the house, issues of hygiene and personal space were much less acute than further up the road. The drink flowed freely too, and Dan consoled himself that a winter in Donegal would be quite acceptable as long as the supplies of beer and whiskey kept coming.

But after Christmas, Dan was fed up being on the run with no job, no prospects and little money. He still wanted to go back to the North to continue the fight, but for the time being there was no prospect of that. His mother, who was always against the violence of the Troubles, urged him to go to Dublin for work and even arranged a job with a relative. That's the love of a mother, willing to support her son but not his politics, and the first to offer help even though it took him miles away from her. Some astute commentators call that love unconditional.

Eventually, Dan agreed to go. By this time he had met a

local girl from Buncrana, Pauline, and as usual had fallen in love within the first ten minutes. Amid notions of marrying her, he decided to take the job in Dublin to earn some money. Unfortunately, Pauline had other plans that didn't include Dan and moved on to another Provo shortly after he'd arrived in Dublin. He discovered it one weekend when he hitched home to surprise her at the dance in Borderland. He did, and he surprised her new boyfriend too!

As always, hearts didn't heal easy and Dan once again experienced the emotional pain of rejection. No other pain was quite like it. Apart from the feelings associated with the loss of someone you loved, he also managed to attach to himself feelings of guilt and blame for the actions of another.

Of course, the safety net of the bar and the bookies numbed them sufficiently to ensure life went on regardless. Dan was beginning to perfect the formula for emotional healing: ten pints of beer and a bottle of vodka seemed to provide a sufficient antidote for the lonely nights, while the daytime was taken care of by endless hours in the betting shop trying to disprove the theory that the bookies always win. He didn't, although the occasional winning streak kept him trying for many years to come.

Had he written a self-help book at the time to enlighten those afflicted with being dumped he might have saved countless thousands from the fate of treatment centres and counselling! To Dan, in those days, oblivion was always preferable to reality. His success at choosing girlfriends was just about equal to his success at backing winners, so he and oblivion got along just fine.

He rented a small bedsit near his workplace on the north side of Dublin. To call it basic was an affront to basic, but it had a single bed, a cooker, a sink and a small table with a flap to extend it in size to enable a dinner plate to be placed on it. Not that Dan did much cooking. Living alone and being responsible for himself gave him certain options. He chose to spend his money on drink and gambling. Latterly he understood it wasn't really a choice, as the obsessions he had were in total control. Nevertheless, the outcome was that the flap on the table was only ever used once.

His weekly groceries usually only consisted of bread and butter, a few other necessities and a bottle of HP sauce, which was borderline mandatory for a Derryman. On his way home from his local pub, the Brian Boru, he would sometimes get fish and chips in Forte's café in Phibsboro. Needless to say, Dan didn't suffer from weight issues in those days and wasn't being canvassed by the predecessors of Weight Watchers! He was a lean and mean drinking machine!

He was paid on a Friday and was usually skint by Saturday unless the horses produced a few winners, which they rarely did. He used to dread Monday to Friday at work. Not because of the job or the people. He was happy with both. He was a trainee manager in a small factory in Glasnevin in north Dublin and the mostly female staff there were lively and full of craic. His dread came at 10am each morning when the factory junior, Colette, used to take orders for snacks for the tea break. Dan never had the price of a doughnut and used to pretend he wasn't hungry. Then he would sit with them drinking tea and watching them eat.

Often, there were days he never ate anything if the bread ran out at home, yet he was too proud and too ashamed to ask for some help. He was sure they must have heard his stomach rumble with the pangs of hunger, and that increased the acuteness of his embarrassment. Every week he swore to himself he would buy in enough food to do for the week and keep some money for the tea breaks at work, and every week he failed to do either.

However, one Friday he finally won some money at the horses. He bought a pound of steak, a bag of spuds and a tin of baked beans and set about cooking his first dinner in Dublin. Half an hour later he sat down to the feast. Perched on the edge of the bed, he pulled out the table flap. His plate was heaped to overflowing, the beans dripping from the side. He salted his food and applied a helping of sauce, hungrily grabbed the knife and fork and placed his elbows on the table.

The next thing he knew, the flap had given way and the dinner was sitting on his lap. The fear of being burned with the piping hot food was nothing compared to the fear of losing it. With great speed and dexterity, he put the empty plate below his knees and scraped all the food back onto the plate. All that remained on his trousers was the soggy residue of the sauces from the beans and the HP bottle. He then found the table fastener he had missed the first time around and fixed the flap in place. Greedily he scoffed the lot. With no washing machine and no washing powder, he dumped the trousers in the bin as he couldn't see any alternative at the time. This incident certainly gave some credence to the popular view among women that Derrymen were lost without their mothers!

After a few months in Dublin, two of Dan's fellow disenchanted Provos, Paul and Tom, came to stay with him. Interestingly, one of the local Guards from Buncrana drove them down. He was one of a small number of the local constabulary that the lads had become friendly with. Their association was more through drink than politics. Dan often recalls leaving the Roadhouse Bar in Bridgend at 5 or 6am and being dropped off at the Provo house in the squad car by the inebriated Gardaí who were patrolling the border from the privileged vantage point of a high stool! Those friendships nurtured in beer and whiskey definitely kept a few of them out of gaols in the Republic of Ireland when their uniformed drinking buddies turned manys a blind eye as arms and explosives were being moved around Donegal.

The bedsit was a bit crowded, but with only Dan working it was all they had. In times like that, thoughts of the comforts of home returned as a means of mental torture, and Dan was indeed a tortured soul. What he wouldn't have given for a hot bath, a night in his own bed, a freshly ironed shirt and a plate of his mother's Irish stew. After a few weeks of living like overgrown sardines, Paul and Tom got jobs which meant that all three amigos were able to rent a three-bedroom apartment on the nearby Finglas Road.

It was luxurious in comparison to the bedsit, though that

didn't make it the Ritz. But with all three working, there was enough money to pay the rent, eat well and have a social life. However, they really only succeeded in the latter. So much so, that within a few weeks Dan was once again the only one working as Paul had difficulty with mornings and failed to attend his work, and Tom lost his job for punching the daylights out of a fellow worker who didn't realise he was one mean hombre - especially when he was suffering from a hangover.

So here Dan was in the wilderness that was Dublin, wishing only to be back home in Derry. The rent fell behind and eating was a luxury that serious drinkers couldn't afford. Oliver, a friend of Dan's from Marino he had met in a Dublin pub, heard of their plight. A confident, cocky, but compassionate man, yet without money or work himself, he entered a supermarket wearing a very large and very loose long black coat which contained many pockets. He left that store with an abundance of groceries concealed under the garment that now fitted perfectly and landed unexpectedly at the lads' flat.

Needless to say the hungry and redundant revolutionaries greeted his arrival with the great gratitude and huge admiration that only starvation can engender. To celebrate, they cooked and ate heartily, then they robbed the electricity meter in the apartment to take Oliver to the Brian Boru as a thank you, and to wash the food down with a few pints of Irish nectar. The liberation of the money from the meter and the food from the Dublin store remained eternally in all their minds as acts of true socialism. James Connolly would have been proud of them! No doubt the owner of the supermarket and their landlord would have taken a slightly different view, as would the Dublin Gardaí who weren't as Provo-friendly as their colleagues in Donegal, and also still considered theft a crime. But just like beauty, justification was also in the eye of the beholder, so the lads would probably forever bask in that act of reflected egalitarianism!

The justification of their socialist tendencies went to even greater extremes a few days later when they emptied the poor box at the chapel in Marino to fund another drinking spree. Their rationale at the time centred on the idea that 'God helped those who help themselves'! Externally they were full of bravado and had a 'fuck everybody' attitude, but inside Dan was full of guilt and shame at the lengths he was going to in order to satisfy the cravings within him. When the inside and the outside didn't match, it led to a pretty pathetic state of being. Dan was by now fast becoming a sad excuse for a man, and worse still he knew it. The only short-term answer he had was to further indulge his craving for alcohol to blot out anything resembling reality and responsible behaviour. This provided an almost instantaneous relief to those unwanted intrusions on his conscience.

With the rent past due and the electricity meter empty, the duration of their tenancy hung in the balance. Then providence struck. One of their fellow disenchanted Provos, John, had recently returned to the IRA fold. He and Liam, a comrade, were on a little break from the intensity of the war and they arrived in Dublin laden with cash and craic. The drink flowed freely and the lads shared stories of their experiences since they'd left Buncrana, suitably embellished and rationalised to justify the rapid moral deterioration that was taking place, judging by their recent exploits in Dublin. In the midst of the party Dan, Paul and Tom all decided they would do a runner and join John and Liam on their mini-tour of Ireland. This would take care of the looming rent and electricity issues. More importantly, John had indicated there was much talk about OTRs returning to Derry to re-engage in the conflict. That was all the three amigos needed to hear, and it cemented their decision to return (decades later John confided to Dan that he had been asked by an iconic and much-revered Provo leader to get the three men back into the fold when he was in Dublin).

Dan remembered very little of the next few days. He recalled standing on a bridge looking into a river, but to this day he remained unsure whether it was the Lee in Cork or the Corrib in Galway. In essence, he was in a drunken blackout and this gap might forever remain a mystery. Of course, for years he just laughed and joked away the significance of such a memory lapse and it became yet another part of the bravado, folklore and 'drunkalogue' that was quickly gaining momentum.

Alcoholism is that kind of illness. It had been described by those who would know as cunning, baffling and powerful, and very often the person afflicted was the last one to know. Dan certainly fitted that definition and was living in blissful ignorance in those halcyon days. The beauty of such ignorance was that he could continue on the path of self-indulgence without ever having to consider the consequences. Or at least that's what he thought.

Within a few days he was back in Buncrana, but waiting impatiently and wishing he was in Derry. Then something happened that was to change his life forever. No doubt the reader is riveted with anticipation and hope that Dan might have had a St Paul-like experience. In truth, he did fall off quite a few horses in his time (well, his jockeys did) but their destination certainly wasn't Damascus!

One Saturday night he took a risk and smuggled himself into Derry to go for a drink in his mother's pub. He just wanted to be home and this, while risky, was the nearest he could get to sampling the warmth and closeness of being there. The locals treated him like the returning prodigal son and ensured his glass never emptied all night. One of their own on the run from the Brits was always welcomed and supported. And there was a girl there who stood out from the crowd. In fact with her great figure, good looks and up-to-the-minute style, she looked distinctly out of place and would have been more at home in a trendy London nightclub than this smokey Derry back bar, populated by middle and old-aged punters whose sartorial elegance stopped at their heads on a head to toe inspection! Yet here in their midst was this beauty.

She was in the company of her aunt and uncle, who were regulars in the bar. During the course of the night the aunt,

Peggy, invited Dan into the company and introduced him to her niece, Bridget. By this stage, Dan had enough booze consumed to at least minimise, if not conceal, his gack streak. Before the night was out Peggy, knowing Dan was on the run, had invited him to stay at her home that night. Bridget was also staying there. Dan was delighted to have a safe house for the night, and Peggy's flat was as safe as it could get. She was married to an English ex-serviceman who had spent many years in the British Navy. Talk about falling on your feet: a safe house and a pretty girl all in one night.

Naturally, Dan had no preconceived notions that Bridget would fancy him. He was on the run, had no income and his acne was doing its 'Battle of the Bulge' impression on his face. Not exactly ideal mating criteria for a beautiful young woman. Then fate struck again in unusual circumstances. After leaving the bar they got in a taxi and were stopped at an army checkpoint that had sprung up less than 50 yards away. Dan and Bridget were in the back seat. Instinctively he leaned over in pretence that they were a couple so that the Brits wouldn't see him properly, and to give them the impression of normality. Bridget acted her part perfectly and kissed him. Luckily, the Brits waved the taxi on and the immediate danger was over.

It was strange that the checkpoint was there at that moment, but Dan was to have some other experiences like this over the next year, which in hindsight made him reflect that coincidence had no part to play. Derry, like everywhere else in the North, was riddled with informers. For all Dan knew, it could have been someone in the bar who tipped off the security forces. That time he was lucky, thanks to Bridget's accommodating nature. History would record she paid a high price for that kiss!

When they arrived at Peggy's flat, Dan was surprised it had only one bedroom and wondered what the sleeping arrangements would be. In the fantasy of his underdeveloped mind, he envisaged himself and Bridget would be allocated the bedroom to allow 'bonding' time! But in the reality that was Catholic Derry, he was given a blanket and shown to a corner of the living room where he would sleep on the floor. In the opposite corner, Bridget had the comfort of a large sofa.

At lights out the first ten minutes brought an uneasy silence. Dan was dying to break it but the drink was wearing off and shyness was returning at breakneck speed. He was back in that place where all roads led to rejection, so he opted to stay quiet in the corner. A short while later, Bridget spoke and a few minutes later they were both occupying the sofa having a harmless kiss and a cuddle. In today's world, they would probably have had a few lines of coke, a bottle of vodka and then gone next door for a foursome!

And so began the romance that was to eventually take Dan and Bridget to the altar. In fact, Bridget's life would be 'altered' forever! The road to 'for better or for worse' was to be fraught with much difficulty, trial and tribulation, with worse dominating better by a distance. This was especially true for Bridget, who was normal in all the places that Dan was flawed. He extended his stay in Derry for about a week so that he could see more of Bridget. The mini-skirts she wore made that objective a lot easier.

Bridget had just broken off an engagement to a local man, Terry, who was in many ways the antithesis of Dan, insofar as he wasn't an IRA man, an alcoholic or a compulsive gambler. Poor Terry, he really did miss out on so much! But as often happened in relationship breakdowns, the woman sought out someone completely different to help expunge the emotional malfunction of a broken engagement. Bridget certainly got that bit right and was to spend many years discovering her selection process for a life partner was fundamentally flawed during those times.

On the upside, life with Dan would never be dull. After he returned to Buncrana, he spent the next few weeks secretly commuting between there and Derry. This was love in technicolour, and it took no cognisance of minor details like the danger of being caught, arrested, tortured and perhaps facing many years in prison. Weekends were usually spent in her aunt's flat, with the twin sleeping arrangements in the living room being for cosmetic purposes only.

Dan even gave working in Dublin another shot for a short time in an attempt to normalise his relationship with Bridget, getting a job as a barman in a pub in the Liberties. But there was always the greater issue of liberty in Dan's mind, and he soon returned to Derry to play his role in the fight for Irish unity.

The conflict of his love for Bridget and the love for his

country was always there in his mind, but he believed they were not mutually exclusive, and so it proved to be. But there was no doubting that Bridget got much more than she bargained for when she threw her lot in with Dan.

9

Up Close and Personal

Dan's return to the Provos brought much added danger and excitement into a life already brimming with extremes. Just as John had predicted, the Provos had reversed their earlier decision out of operational necessity, and many OTRs were back in Derry to take the fight to the Brits at close quarters. Sometimes the quarters were so close that Dan could have seen their laughter lines. But the soldiers weren't laughing much, as the Brandywell Company of the Provisional IRA made life in Derry a very frightening and unwelcoming experience for the occupying troops.

This was guerrilla warfare in 1973 at its most dangerous, and Dan learned a lot about himself over the next few months. No longer a rookie, he spent most of his time planning and carrying out attacks on the Brits. After Operation Motorman, the British Army had saturated all the no go areas and made life very difficult for the Provos to operate, but in time the IRA adapted and turned what seemed like a victory for the Brits into an opportunity to send an even louder message than before to the British government. The message was that the more soldiers they sent into nationalist and republican communities, the more young Englishmen would return home in body bags.

Of course, this brought even more reprisals from the Brits. However, the British were also in secret talks with the republican leadership through intermediaries in an attempt to bring the violence to a close. This was their forte, negotiating peace while still waging war, with many of their squaddies sacrificed to die lonely and agonising deaths in a hostile land.

At least the IRA had popular support and their dead were seen as heroes; patriots paying the ultimate sacrifice for a just and honourable cause. Dan's mind often fast-forwarded to his own funeral, which at that time seemed likely to be sooner rather than later. He could see his mother crying inconsolably, his brothers and sisters walking in sombre and stunned silence. His beret perched on top of his flag-draped coffin, flanked by his fellow freedom fighters. The graveside oration emotionally delivered by some 'face' from the republican leadership, using the occasion to recruit another few Dan Feeneys. Bridget dropping a single red rose into the grave as they lowered him down (in later years he reckoned she would have dropped a ton of lead down to make sure he was there to stay). And, finally, the volley of shots fired over his coffin.

Another song would no doubt be spawned, in some smokey bar in the Bogside or Brandywell, about another gallant hero who paid the ultimate sacrifice. Sure what more fitting end could a young republican have? This question usually brought a change to his thought process, as he once again decided that living through the conflict, while less glamorous and dramatic, was still his preferred option. Thankfully the God he was no longer even sure existed was in congruence with this aspiration too. Certainly, Dan tested God's will for him to the limit, and there were many occasions when it looked as if his heavenly father was having a day off.

Living at such close quarters with the Brits breathing down your neck, though creating opportunities to take the war to the enemy, also ensured that danger and fear were part of everyday life for a Provo. Dan's movements were restricted by the fact that he was wanted and on the run and the security forces no doubt had photographs of him. But such occupational hazards had to be overcome.

Republican freedom fighters were trained, often very basically, in the use of guns and explosives, but certainly not on handling human emotions. Propaganda on all sides never countenanced that the young men and women who put themselves in danger might actually experience fear. They were seen either as ruthless terrorists or fearless freedom fighters, neither of which accurately reflected that IRA volunteers were just ordinary young men and women from within their community who believed this was their only option to change the bigotry and inequality of a failed state and ultimately bring unity to their country.

Alcohol at night-time usually temporarily numbed the emotional side of being a rebel. Not many freedom fighters talked about their feelings before, during and after battle, but Dan knew the demons which visited them during the silent dark hours: the fears, the doubts, the regrets, the guilt and the remorse. They were there in tandem with the commitment, the bravery, the pride, the passion and the raw 'fuck it' attitude that was necessary to sustain a campaign such as this. These people were human beings caught up in a struggle they didn't ask for, and not the mindless and brutal criminals the state-influenced media portrayed them as.

In the early '70s, the Showband era was still alive in Ireland, although the murder by loyalists of members of the Miami Showband in 1975 effectively put an end to it in the North. A night at Joe Dolan and the Drifters in Borderland, Mick Roche and the Arrows at the Stardust or a country and western gig with Brian Coll and his Buckaroos was the IRA volunteer's equivalent of a leave of absence. A night out in the pub followed by a few 'birls' around the dance floor proved an excellent escape from the war for many young Provos.

Many budding romances emanated from the performance of a slow set, affectionately termed in Dan's circles as 'fork busters'. However, while Dan was an ardent attendee in Borderland, the Stardust and the Metric dance halls, these nights, from his experience, were more frightening than all the gun battles and bombing blitzes put together. Because underneath the veneer of being a freedom fighter, the gack was always lurking, just waiting on any opportunity to surface. Dances provided that opportunity and Dan recalled vividly the torture of that era in his life.

Years later many eminent musicians and radio

broadcasters have maligned the showbands for their lack of originality and talent. Dan had no problem with the standard of the music or the fact that the bands just played covers. His issues were more of a psychological nature. Under the guise of entertainment, the dances were, from a man's perspective, just a showroom for women where young people met, married and mated (although at times the last two sequences were reversed, much to the displeasure of parish priests). For Dan, pre-Bridget times at the dances were just extensions of youthful frustration and unrequited passion. The priests would have no bother with him from the perspective of sins of the flesh or the mixing up of the order of mating.

Yet he religiously attended these torture sessions at every available opportunity. Borderland was a large hall in Muff, a small village just over the border in Donegal. Fridays and Sundays were Showband nights and Dan was a regular. First stop was the El Matador pub, no doubt given the name because of all the bullshit that was talked by the patrons. This was where Dan lubricated his nervous desires and prepared himself for the dance. His confidence was totally dependent on how much drink he had put away, as was his sobriety.

If he was very drunk he could usually muster the courage to ask girls out to dance, but they usually refused because of his slurred voice and staggering body. On the rare occasions he managed to get them onto the floor, they'd end up either propping him up if he fell asleep, or got their feet trodden on while he did his alcoholic version of the 'hucklebuck'. Either way, it was usually home alone at the end of the night.

If Dan wasn't too drunk, he'd spend the night circling the 'target', who knew nothing of his interest as any eye contact was immediately broken by Dan, who didn't want to be rumbled too early in the chase. As the night headed towards the last slow set, he would stand beside the 'chosen one' and practise in silence asking her out to dance in the fashion of Luca Brasi's dry run scene in *The Godfather*. Unfortunately, Luca ended up sleeping with the fishes, perhaps an unwittingly prophetic comparison at the time!

But the words always came out different when he opened his mouth. Sounds like 'ughhhh' usually resulted in the girl moving away from this incoherent babbling idiot. Sometimes he got as far as asking, 'Would you like to dance?' but in those instances, he was saying it to the girl beside the one he really wanted to dance with. That brought no solace either. If she said yes he was on the floor with someone he had no interest in, and if she said no then he reckoned he was even uglier than he first thought if a girl he wasn't attracted to refused him a dance.

Then there was the odd time when he went to the dance without any drink on board. On those nights he just lapped the girl he fancied, Formula One-style, all night hoping she would notice him and smile. Even if she did smile, Dan would have convinced himself it mightn't be him she was smiling at, and he would set off on another lap of the hall. She would also need to have been fleet-footed to put the brakes on him!

He was in more danger of getting fallen arches than

falling in love! During that circuit, he would convince himself she wasn't worth all this bother and didn't even seek eye contact for the remaining laps that night. Of course, nothing of this was ever divulged to even his closest friends. He just did his Paul Newman method act and said things like, 'The talent at Borderland was crap last night.' Interestingly, a lot of his friends used to say the same thing, so perhaps Dan wasn't the only gack in Derry.

Having Bridget as a girlfriend meant he didn't have to go through that ritual humiliation any longer, although he did still go to the dance halls any time the opportunity presented itself. Often he would just meet Bridget inside the dancehall, an occupational hazard that she had to accept as the price of dating a wanted man. Leaving her home wasn't an option either, as her parents were not supportive of her boyfriend's chosen 'career'.

Alongside all this bliss, the war went on. Following receipt of a shipment of arms from Libya, Dan recalled being secreted to Donegal with a few others to learn how to use an RPG7 rocket launcher. By the time the training was over, he could name the parts of the weapon from top to bottom, but he had no idea what it felt like to fire this deadly implement. His first and only experience came a few weeks later.

The Battalion OC assembled Dan and some others to take part in a rocket attack on a British Army Saracen troop carrier that would be returning from a checkpoint on the Letterkenny Road, on the fringe of the Brandywell. In true Provo style, they had to commandeer a getaway car at the last minute. The first one they saw was an old Hillman, which was crying out to be scrapped, but they hurriedly decided it would do okay. James Bond got an Austin Martin sports car, but here they were depending on this old boneshaker to get them to safety after a dangerous mission. The rest of the operation went in accordance with the first bit.

The three Provos concealed themselves in a laneway awaiting the arrival of the army Saracen. The plan was that one of the men would fire the rocket launcher and disable the vehicle while Dan would pepper it with bullets from his Armalite assault rifle. The third man would drive them to safety in the getaway car. After successfully pleading to use the RPG7, Dan and his comrade swapped weapons. Dan recalled seeing the troop carrier coming towards him. He placed the RPG7 on his shoulder and advanced it into firing mode and simultaneously squeezed the trigger before he had lowered the weapon sufficiently to line up his sight with the vehicle.

There was a loud bang as the rocket launched itself into orbit high over the Saracen before eventually landing harmlessly in the River Foyle. Whilst the Brits weren't in danger from Dan's prowess with a rocket launcher, local bird watchers may have recorded a few less of several species given the direction of the rocket! His lack of field training and experience, probably coupled with an overdose of adrenaline, had come back to haunt them.

Simultaneously Dan's cover man tried to open up with his Armalite rifle, only for it to misfire without a shot going off. Dan and his accomplice looked at each other in frenzied disbelief and then ran to the getaway car, jumped in and told the driver, 'Drive like fuck outta here.' The driver tried to move forward but the engine stalled. A few seconds later it started with an unhealthy chug and he nursed it up the lane and came out onto Hamilton Street, turning left in the hope of disappearing into the labyrinth of small streets in the Brandywell where safety would be almost assured.

Meanwhile, the Brits had rightly assessed that an IRA ambush had gone wrong and decided to enter the Brandywell in hot pursuit. As their car entered Hamilton Street, Dan could see the army Saracen a few yards away trying to ram them as they exited the laneway. They missed their car by inches but the chase was on and the mechanical limitations of their car were being exposed to the full as the Saracen inched closer.

The army driver positioned it sideways to enable the soldiers to point their SLRs out the slats in the hope of getting shots off at the getaway car. Thankfully they couldn't or didn't. Dan recalled their car going around the corner at the Brandywell Bar on two wheels. Their driver was absolutely amazing that day and got a performance from that Hillman the designers hadn't envisaged.

The hot pursuit continued as they exited Brandywell Road and sped across Lone Moore Road passing the famous Brandywell football ground on their left. Dan would have given anything to be in there watching Derry City FC versus any fucking body instead of being in the centre of this life-threatening drama. The next minute decided their fate.

The driver had to turn right to try to escape up Southway, which was a steep open road that ascended to the Creggan Estate and was their only possible route to safety. It was questionable whether their car would even make up this hill, but it was their only hope. The Saracen roared up behind them and all looked lost.

Dan then recalled a calm resolve descending on him. It was as if the inevitability of being shot or caught and imprisoned had kicked in. Then, suddenly, as their car chugged up the Southway hill, Dan saw distance opening up between them and the Saracen. For some reason, it had stopped a short way up the hill and the relieved Provos slowly disappeared into the comparative safety of Creggan. Many theories have been aired as to why the Brits gave up so suddenly, but Dan would always believe that they were afraid the chase was all part of a cunning plan to lure the soldiers into the openness of the hill, where an ambush would await them.

He reckoned the Brits could not have imagined that so much had gone so spectacularly wrong in the earlier ambush. If this was so, then Dan will remain forever grateful for their flawed analysis. He did appreciate that many IRA operations against the British Army were successful and therefore the soldiers' caution in this instance was understandable. In addition, they were paid soldiers, and therefore saving their own skin was a higher priority than capturing patriots having a 'bad day at the office'.

Whatever the reason, they all lived to fight another day and there certainly would be more days just as dangerous and hair-raising in the cauldron that was the Brandywell in those days. The feeling of relief was palpable and they knew they owed their lives to the driver. Interestingly, in later years he went on to make his living in the transport business!

Dan had to adjust quickly from the near-death experience of that morning to the quasi-normality of meeting Bridget that night. He recalled furtively negotiating the streets and lanes of the Bogside on his way to meet her, and the intense fear he had of being stopped by an army foot patrol. He had fake identification, but like most things with Dan it wouldn't have stood up to much scrutiny. As luck had it on this occasion he wasn't stopped, but that night his thoughts were still on the moribund experience earlier that day, rather than on romance. Deep down he knew the net was closing in and the creeping inevitability of his demise was now dominating most of his waking moments. And he had a few more close calls to survive before his fate would reveal itself.

But the war had to go on and it didn't take account of a young man's nervous system. A few days later he was back planting a bomb in the city centre. This time it was concealed in a butcher's van and his driver was not as cool as the previous one. The poor man was hijacked and ordered to drive Dan through two army checkpoints with 200 pounds of explosives concealed under some meat products and skins in the back.

As they approached the first checkpoint in Abercorn

Road, Paddy the captive driver turned about forty shades of shite. Dan tried to calm him, but it was impossible. He told him to leave all the talking to him. The soldiers duly stopped them and asked them to open the back of the van. Dan took over and after some friendly banter he got out and walked around to the back of the vehicle. His heart was pounding but he kept an exterior calm. He joked with the soldiers at the back of the van in the hope they would not ask to examine the contents, but to no avail.

Within seconds, Dan and the soldier were crouched in the back, with Dan explaining all they had was cuts of meat that they were delivering to local butchers in the city. The bomb was under some skins with large sides of beef on top. Dan recalled thinking that if this bomb went off prematurely they'd all be for the 'chop', and might be having roast beef in heaven (or hell, more likely) within the next few minutes! At that time it didn't matter to him, as he reckoned he had friends in both places.

The soldier looked around the van and was almost sitting on the meat on top of the bomb, but after a few seconds, which seemed like forever, he jumped out of the back and told Dan he could proceed. Dan thanked him and hurriedly got back into the front and told his driver to move off. Paddy by now looked in need of medical treatment as he gripped the steering wheel in white-knuckled fashion, but the operation had to be completed, so turning back was not on Dan's mind.

He explained they would have to go through another

checkpoint at the bottom of Shipquay Street. The man looked like death and began to tremble uncontrollably as they approached from Foyle Street. Dan knew this fear-ridden civilian just couldn't make it through another army search without the army catching on. Had he been able to drive, he would have let the man get out and chanced it himself. He had to think quickly to avoid aborting the mission completely.

As the van entered Guildhall Square, Dan relieved the situation somewhat by instructing Paddy to drive to another city centre target on Stand Road that meant they didn't have to negotiate another checkpoint. The man was grateful but still trembling furiously. When they arrived and parked outside the new target, Dan explained that he would go into the back to set the timer on the bomb and that after he had done so he would walk up the Strand Road and exit towards the Bogside. He instructed him to wait for one minute after Dan finished and then calmly walk 100 yards up the Strand Road to the RUC Station and tell them where the bomb was located, and that it would detonate in 45 minutes. He reiterated to him that there was nothing to worry about and nobody would be injured, given the adequate warning for the police to clear the area.

Dan certainly learned that day that you can plan the plan but you can't always plan the outcome. As soon as he got into the back of the van to set the timer, the driver opened the van door, jumped out, and ran up the Strand Road screaming hysterically that there was a bomb in the van. Dan could hear him as he quickly approached the entrance to the police station shouting 'bomb'. More pressure added to the obvious pressure that tinkering with a 200-pound bomb in the back of a van brought.

Dan had two choices: leg it to safety and leave the security forces to dispose of it, or take his chances and set the timer for the bomb. He chose the latter and within about 30 seconds the bomb was nervously set to detonate after 55 minutes. The extra 10 minutes was to make sure the area was cleared with time to spare. He exited the van and walked first slowly, then briskly, up Strand Road, turning right into Great James Street and then left towards the comparative safety of the Bogside.

As was the practice, he called the Samaritans and gave the location and detonation time of the bomb just in case the RUC didn't react in time. Thankfully the area was cleared and the bomb, whilst causing extensive damage to a number of commercial properties, didn't cause any injuries. Dan never got to know what happened when the frightened driver arrived at the police station, but he imagined it would have been a frantic scene.

For some reason, van drivers and Dan had a habit of creating difficult and unplanned situations during 1973. Following an assault on two British Army jeeps on the outskirts of the Brandywell area, the driver of a bread van came looking for the Provo leadership in the area. As it happened, Dan was involved in both the attack and the meeting with the driver. He showed Dan his van that had been peppered with bullets on the passenger side. Dan suggested that given the cargo he had on board, he should have used his 'loaf' and fired a few 'rounds' back at the Provos! Understandably the driver didn't appreciate the humour of his retort. He clearly didn't appreciate puns about guns!

In reality, those were dangerous days for everyone, even innocent passers-by such as that driver. Yet, in the midst of tragic and near-death experiences, humour and the exuberance of youth kept many young Provos in business, as to take a rigorous inventory of the nature of the war and the daily danger they were in could have broken the spirit of even the most dedicated republican. So the war continued, and Dan's life hung by a thread many more times before his time as a freedom fighter on the streets of Derry was taken away from him.

Near misses could happen at any time and not always during operations. Dan recalled taking a chance one Saturday night and calling in to see his mum in the bar. She was glad to see him but at the same time was afraid he would be in danger there.

After a few pints, he said goodbye to her and crossed the street to his neighbour Annie's house. She was a great supporter of the cause and always had an open door for OTRs. As it happened, a few of his fellow travellers were there having a few beers and a bit of craic with Annie and her family. Dan blended in seamlessly behind a fresh can of Harp lager. Around midnight, the other guys left for their respective billets. Dan stayed for a while as his bed for that night was just across the street.

Within half an hour there was a commotion at the door. The army had arrived to raid the house in search of wanted men. Dan composed himself and immediately approached the soldiers. He spoke to the officer who was leading the raid. 'Look,' he said, 'my mother and the rest of us are fed up with these pointless raids. It's just harassment of innocent citizens.' Dan insisted on accompanying the soldiers during the raid and informed them he wouldn't take kindly to them wakening his young brothers and sisters who were sleeping in the bedrooms. The officer assured him they would respect his wishes and would carry out the search as quickly and quietly as possible. And they did, with Dan by their side engaging in whispered small talk. Within 15 minutes they were content that there were no wanted men in the house. The officer apologised to Dan and said their information must have been mistaken before leaving Annie's house. At no stage had he asked him who he was or for identification. Derry people would call Dan's tight-wire act a 'brass neck' but Dan just saw it as another near miss.

A collective sigh of relief ensued. When Annie finally settled down she hugged Dan and told him that he was taking far too many chances. He reflected on the event and concluded that his survival instincts always seemed to bring a proportionate initiative. On that occasion, it kept him free. He also reflected that this was the second time a visit to his mum's pub had been followed by an army presence. He was not a believer in coincidences and decided he would give the bar a wide berth from then onwards.

The grace of God was not something Dan considered in the equation of who lived and who died in those days, but there was one situation he often reflected on which opened his mind about whether a divine being had a part to play or not.

Strangely enough, it was connected to the earlier failed attack with the rocket launcher. At that time there was only one RPG7 in the city and it was shared between the Provos in Brandywell, Bogside and Creggan. Dan and a fellow traveller went to Creggan to pick up cleaning components for the rocket launcher after the earlier incident. On their return, they took a shortcut through the city cemetery. Simultaneously an army helicopter appeared and was hovering above them.

Dan was easy to spot as he was wearing an orange jumper, bought to him by Bridget with money he'd given her after a rare win at the local greyhound track. In hindsight, this jumper was not a very effective camouflage to enable him to blend in with the majority of young Derry men who were usually denim-clad from head to toe. But Dan took pride in his sartorial elegance, even when on active service. This folly was to be royally highlighted during the next half hour.

They had hardly set foot back in the Brandywell area when the Brits swooped and saturated the area with troops. The two Provos went in different directions, each trying to evaporate into the safety of an open house before the soldiers scooped them. Dan's comrade did just that and Dan thought he had too, entering a house in Southend Park that ran adjacent to the football ground.

He knew the soldiers were in hot pursuit but hadn't accounted for the fact that they saw him enter the house. He'd bolted into the living room and vaulted onto the sofa to blend in with the rest of the family, who were watching TV. They looked shocked, but they knew the score when an on-the-run Provo arrived in such a hurry. Within seconds Dan heard a commotion in the hallway as Mrs Logue put her large frame in the way of the marauding Brits, giving him a few precious seconds to make his escape out the back door and into the mews lane that ran along the east wall of the football ground.

Dan burst out the back door and into the yard. His heart was pounding and his hands were sweating and shaking as he fumbled at the bolt to open the yard door. He looked out to the laneway but his escape was thwarted, as the lane was by now being flooded by soldiers. Quickly he returned to the yard. By this time the other soldiers had seen off the attentions of Mrs Logue and were at the rear door about to enter the yard. In an instant, he scrambled up the wall and jumped down into the yard next door.

Intellectually Dan believed the game was up, but as before the instincts of survival didn't read those types of books. The Brits were as usual offering words of advice such as, 'Stop, you fucking Irish bastard' and 'Put your hands in the air, you Provo scum,' so Dan knew the Geneva Convention was on hold. Once in the next yard, Dan tried to enter that house but the back door was locked. As he was trying to climb over that adjoining wall to try to get to the next house, the back door from the lane was kicked in and the Brits swarmed into the small yard. The game seemed finally up this time.

The Brits introduced themselves in their time-honoured fashion by dragging Dan into the laneway in a frenzy of noisy and triumphant squaddie euphoria. They had got their man. That fucking trendy orange jumper had betrayed him. From then on he vowed to pick his own clothes if he survived the next ten minutes. He was pushed down on his belly like a fallen crucifix. The soldiers above him kicked continuously at his body and stamped on his hands, no doubt part of their victory dance. The earlier bravery of his instincts for freedom had dissipated and Dan lay sprawled on the ground, once again acutely aware of what fear really was at that moment in his life. Even youthful courage and exuberance lose their potency in times like that. 'We've got the fucker, sarge,' he heard one soldier report. 'What will we do with the Provo bastard?' At that moment Dan expected to feel the muzzle of an SLR at his temple and to be spirited away to wherever dead Provos go. Strangely, there was peace in that thought and for a second he felt no fear. That second was to prove crucial.

'Bring him around to the troop carrier,' said the sergeant. 'This one's going to entertain us back at the barracks.' Dan was manhandled to his feet and his right arm was reversed and screwed up his back, secured by the cord of a soldier's baton, which the holder took great pleasure in tightening on his wrist, perhaps to see if Dan could wave at himself from behind his own back! Aesthetically it probably didn't look too good but he would have secured the part of Christy Brown had this been an audition for the role!

Dan was frogmarched down the lane to the waiting troop carrier at the foot of Southend Park. A crowd of women had come out of their houses protesting to the army to let the young man go. Mrs Logue was among them. The women of Derry were towers of strength in those days to young OTRs like Dan. Republican history should have afforded them a greater place than it has up to now. Flanked by half a dozen Brits and guided from behind by his baton-holding puppet master, Dan knew there was no hope. His mind had now turned to the torture and interrogation that lay ahead. Fear had returned and with it came that active and instinctive mind that knew only of survival. He felt the cord of the baton loosen slightly as his captor sidled him towards the open back of the armoured vehicle. In that instant, something happened that he thought was confined to the movies of his childhood.

All of a sudden Dan jerked his right arm down his back and simultaneously freed his hand from the soldier's baton cord and pushed him aside. Then came that 60-yard dash he had prepared for all those years earlier inside the very stadium that he was now being arrested outside. This time the prize was not a book without pictures, nor was there a need for accolades or acknowledgement from anyone. Matters of esteem were completely superseded by thoughts of freedom and survival.

This time he had eight or nine seconds to run for his life. The Brits were taken entirely by surprise as he ran through his 'flankers' like Moses through the Red Sea. On his right was the Wolfe Tone Hall and beyond it was a sharp right turn that would get him out of their sight and, after another sharp left turn, into the relative safety of Lecky Road. In the background, he could hear a rifle cocking and he knew that the lead going up the spout had his name on it. Dan just didn't want to be at that address when it arrived, so he kept on running.

In the midst of the frenzy, an English accent bellowed, 'Halt or we'll fire!' Dan fully expected to be seeing old Wolfe Tone himself up close and personal very soon, in the land of dead Irish patriots. Then, as he approached the right turn, a baton whistled past his head, missing him by a hair's breadth. As he took the turn, his courage was re-energised with safety now a possibility, yet the feelings of fear also intensified as his heart raced in tandem with and probably outsped his athletic limbs.

Dan arched his run into Lecky Road and sped past a few houses and Tommy McCann's fish and chip shop on his right. What he wouldn't have given to be in the stalls eating Tommy's culinary delights lavished with lashings of salt and oodles of vinegar. For once he managed to quell his hunger pangs and the arch of his run ended at Neillie Doherty's barbershop. Dan ran into the hall and opened the door at the end of the hallway. It was a downstairs bathroom and he just flopped into the empty bath. This was the end of his road.

The adrenaline of his escape had peaked and expired and he lay in the bath, out of breath and shaking with fear, and with close attention from those all too frequent visitors that disturbed his bowel and kidney activity. A modicum of pride returned and he managed to keep the bath clean. He was acutely aware of the thump of his heartbeat and wished it would stop, lest the Brits might hear it too. Outside in the street, he could hear the rampant soldiers, who by then were being harassed by a few teenagers from the area and a mini-riot was ensuing. A young man with a red jumper was arrested and later got six months in prison for riotous behaviour. Dan has always believed the jumper was what the Brits went after and this man's was the closest in colour to his.

The Brits raided all the houses that Dan had run past, even the fish and chip shop. Miraculously, they stopped the search there and didn't go next door to the barbershop where Dan lay trembling. In more than 30 years in the business, Neillie Doherty had never been responsible for a shave as close as the one Dan just had!

That wasn't the only miracle that worked in Dan's favour that day. Later that night he went to thank Mrs Logue for all she had done to help him and she told him the bit of the story that he didn't witness. As it turned out, the marksman who was on one knee and about to shoot him was pushed to the ground by a fellow soldier, who then threw the baton that just missed his head. Dan has been eternally grateful to that anonymous member of the Duke of Wellington Regiment ever since. In those days a soldier with a conscience was a rarity in Derry or any of the Catholic areas of the North. Hindsight engendered thoughts of someone up there looking after him. It took him many years to work out who that was, but eventually he came to his own belief. Whatever the reason, Dan lived that day and owed the fact that he subsequently became a father and a grandfather to this unknown soldier.

The paradox of the Unknown Soldier and the IRA man was not lost on Dan even then, although for him to extol the virtue of a British soldier in Derry during the early '70s wouldn't have done much for his street cred. So he only mentioned the experience to a trusted few. In the wrong hands, that kind of information could have led to sensationalist headlines in local or national newspapers. The Brits loved to capitalise on anything that would diminish the nationalist experience of them being an invading occupational force, happy to murder and maim to maintain the artificial state of Northern Ireland. Deep down, Dan always held the wish that he could meet that man and thank him for his act of humanity during those inhumane times in Derry. But at the time it was just another near miss, the frequency of which was getting much too close for comfort.

Some months earlier, Dan was sent on a mission to shoot two British Army military policemen (MPs). Soldiers take orders and Dan was no different, but something didn't sit right with him on this operation. MPs didn't carry firearms at that time but were still considered legitimate targets by the IRA.

Dan vividly recalled seeing the two MPs sauntering along at the bottom of Bishop Street, barely 100 yards from where he was born. He set off towards them cradling his .45 semi-automatic pistol in the inside pocket of his coat. Just as he approached them, a moment of conscience and internal conflict compelled him to abandon what he viewed would have been an unjustified assassination, even by the deteriorating standards of that bloody war.

To carry out that shooting would in Dan's eyes have put republicans in the same category as those British soldiers who executed those young men on Bloody Sunday. So Dan suddenly veered to the right onto a back lane that led to Ann Street to avoid the MPs. Those two men didn't make saving their lives easy for him when they also cut across to the back lane from an entry point 20 yards below where he entered. To make matters worse, they tried to apprehend him as he approached.

As he jogged towards them they gestured for him to stop, putting Dan into a new dilemma. Though he had made a decision not to shoot them, his instincts to remain free were of equal import. *Why could these stupid fuckers not have dandered on up Bishop Street?* he quizzed. Simultaneously his freedom impulse kicked in and he suddenly speeded up to run past them.

In hindsight, this may have been another practice spin for his subsequent and more spectacular run for his life in the Brandywell. As he tried to run past, one of the MPs reached out and tried to grab him, but Dan in full flow was not easily stopped. Again his need to be free took over and he punched the MP on the temple to ensure he got past, and in an instant, the runaway Provo was gone. Had this tactic not worked, plan B would have meant using the gun. Those two guys would never know how lucky they'd been that day.

Next up Dan had to explain to the OC of the Brandywell Company why he had failed in his appointed mission. Self-preservation outvoted the truth as Dan informed the irate OC that the MPs had caught him off guard, which was at least partly true, and the best he could do was to make his escape. His superior ordered him to go back to Bishop Street and try to catch up with and re-engage them further up the street, but by the time he got back, they were gone.

Those reporting the Troubles never really got close to understanding the type of internal human conflict that young men like Dan grappled with in circumstances like this. They portrayed them as cold-hearted terrorists or fearless patriots, depending on what tabloid they were trying to sell. Some hearing that story would call him a coward, others a hero for standing by his conscience. But Dan was neither. It was all just part of living, learning and surviving in those terrible times. What was not in doubt was that those two MPs met the right Provo on that particular occasion.

Later, Dan reflected on the incident. Had he been sent on this mission with another volunteer, he would have had to complete the job, as not risking his comrade's freedom would have taken a higher rank than shooting the MPs. Fate had intervened in everyone's favour that day.

Like most things, the incident passed and was forgotten as the Provos moved on to other engagements with the Brits on a daily basis. To the more regimented and less scrupulous combatant, he perhaps should have been court-martialed for not carrying out orders. But as only he knew the whole truth, that option didn't present itself. However, Dan remained glad and relieved that he didn't live his life with the regret and remorse on his conscience of having shot two unarmed men.

He often wondered how the Paras who butchered his unarmed fellow citizens came to terms with those actions each night as their heads hit their pillows. Maybe that was the difference between the romanticism and relative integrity associated with Dan's brand of republicanism and that of a bunch of paid assassins, dancing to the tune of career generals and vote-hungry politicians. Anyway, it appeared the Spirit of the Universe hadn't forgotten Dan's moment of conscience, and perhaps the Unknown Soldier was his reward.

10

Nowhere to Run

Trying to successfully blend the life of a freedom fighter with that of a young man dating his girlfriend wasn't easy for Dan. In between, he also had to fit in his apprenticeships as an alcoholic and a compulsive gambler, but with very little money the latter affliction was dormant most of the time. Following his latest narrow escape from the grasp of the Duke of Wellington Regiment, Dan changed the colour of his hair and grew a beard to keep the Brits guessing for a little longer. The cumulative effect of these near misses was already taking its toll. He was tormented by opposing thoughts involving staying free and being caught.

In his mind, there was a rolling inevitability that he would soon be killed, wounded or arrested, and while the ultimate blood sacrifice posthumously did lots for young Irishmen, it still wasn't Dan's ideal career path, even though he accepted and even expected that it might happen. He'd had another close call a few weeks later when leaving a local bar on the way to his safe house. The anaesthetic of alcohol was increasingly becoming his antidote, Provo style, to a day at the office. Only those who knew the effect of burnout would understand this pattern. Once again his prowess as a sprinter took him to safety as he left a pursuing army Saracen truck labouring up Bishop Street in his wake, as he disappeared into the labyrinth of side streets to safety. However, all didn't go exactly to plan when he reached his billet.

He was staying with a lady called Betty, who had offered him the sofa in her front room to sleep on. She explained it would be much safer if she locked him in the room at night so that her children wouldn't see him in the morning and talk about their overnight guest in school. No successful guerrilla war could ever be fought without those wonderful, anonymous women with patriotism in their hearts and pragmatism in their heads. They thought of everything.

This lady even provided Dan with a hot water bottle to fend off the wintry cold. A few hours into his slumber, the ten pints he'd had earlier, coupled with his run to freedom, had an alarm clock effect on his kidneys. Awaking from his sleep, he groped and stumbled in the dark room towards the door - only to be reminded that it was locked earlier in his best interests. It's funny how people keep turning the handles of locked doors even though they know they won't open!

Dan paced the floor for the next ten minutes in the vain hope of quelling this insistent urge. His kidneys were unrelenting and his knees were knocking in some frenzied attempt to ease the pressure on his bladder. Then one of his most enlightened decisions of the whole IRA campaign formed in his brain. No, he hadn't discovered a way to drive the Brits out, release all the prisoners and create a united, socialist Ireland without another shot being fired. What he did discover was that the hot water bottle was only half full and, while this wouldn't free Ireland, it might just be the vessel to free his bursting bladder.

He often recalled and recited how he watched his relief flow freely into that rubber bottle. At one stage it was questionable if the golden shower wouldn't overflow, but thankfully it stopped to a trickle at the neck of the bottle, and Dan replaced the cork a much 'relieved' man. Then followed the sleep of the just for the next few hours, before being awoken by that loud, frantic and joyous noise that only children can make of a school morning.

With the kids safely off to school, next began Dan's latest and most crucial covert operation of the campaign so far. He had to get the hot water bottle emptied without Betty noticing. That wasn't easy, as she wrestled to take it from him whilst beckoning him to a chair at the kitchen table. On the table sat a plate containing the antidote to every young man's hangover – a Derry fry. Luckily, Dan won the wrestling match and he furtively watched the golden liquid disappear down the sink. Betty watched as Dan rinsed the bottle out at least six times like some sort of Howard Hughes wannabe. No doubt she wondered what it was all about. *So now one of the best-kept secrets of the Troubles is out, Betty!*

The law of inevitability finally took its toll in January 1974. This time Dan, the runaway, had nowhere to run. And this time he was to be the author of his own misfortune. He had wrestled with the risk of going to a Wolfe Tones concert, knowing how much he enjoyed their rebel-rousing songs, many of which he was introduced to in his Christian Brothers days. However, he also suspected that the concert in the Stardust dance hall in the heart of the Bogside could be monitored by army surveillance operatives. His dilemma was whether to concede to his risk instinct or take the risk and have a much-needed couple of hours of relative bliss at the Tones concert. He decided to take the chance. Sadly, events were to show that the Hammer got it right on this particular choice. But the pressure of recent months was such that he just couldn't resist the magnetism of a night out in the bosom of republican Derry, singing songs of Irish struggle and freedom.

At the age of 14, he'd started getting into those rebellious ballads and songs of Irish freedom that the Wolfe Tones and a few other groups were performing around the country. They awoke aspirations of liberation in him that had patiently been awaiting the call. He wondered if the Christian Brothers were really the Wolfe Tones in drag, given their propensity to fill boys with blood-stirring renditions of songs to keep a nation's hopes alive at a time when nationalists in the North seemed devoid of hope, with only a token voice and absolutely no power in the unionist parliament at Stormont of those times.

Even his own city of Derry, though Catholic and nationalist by majority, was run by the Protestant unionists through their bigoted and deliberate massaging of electoral wards, jobs and voting entitlements. Dan recalled thumbing a lift in 1968 to hear the Tones at Keaveney's Hotel in Moville, and could still feel that goose-pimpled euphoria as they belted out songs of hope and independence that were about to be grasped by the nationalists in the North. Since the Battle of the Bogside in 1969 and the awakening and armed struggle that rose out of it, the band had expanded and updated its repertoire to include contemporary songs of injustice, internment and recently dead patriots.

By 1974 they were singing their way throughout Ireland and America arousing sentiments and support for the cause to even the most placid Irish nationalists.

Interestingly, they are still going strong, which is perhaps indicative that the current Brit-inspired power-sharing executive at Stormont has really just rearranged the furniture in the context of the freedom of a nation. Once again, good and courageous men have been duped by the forked tongues of British politicians, ably supported by the friendly brogues of their compliant Irish counterparts in the South, intent on keeping the North's troubles at arm's length. Dan believed the eventual reunification of Ireland would come about in spite of the efforts at Leinster House, not because of them.

On that cold January night, the Tones took the stage in the Stardust Ballroom, in the heart of the Bogside, and Dan and many of his fellow OTRs had also taken the risk to go and see them. With his recent catalogue of close calls, a night like this was bound to re-invigorate his aspirations of an Ireland devoid of British power or influence, especially at a time when fear stalked his every move. It was a welcome break from the daily threat of being shot or caught by the

Brits. For two hours Dan was free in that Ireland of poets and songsters. The Stardust shook to the rafters with rousing vibrations of, 'North men, South men, comrades all, Dublin, Derry, Cork and Donegal. We're on the one road swinging along, singing a soldier's song.' Jesus, if he could have bottled that magic blend of melody, lyricism and energy devoted to Irishness and patriotism in that hall, he would have had the whole world drink from that cup of freedom.

But concerts are concerts and reality was reality. The Tones duly finished their gig, no doubt well paid for their stirring performance. The Provos just turned up every day for free with the single agenda of uniting their country, with their lives as down payments. Dan's next challenge was how to get to his safe house in Bishop Street without being rumbled by the Brits, who he anticipated were bound to have the departing crowd under surveillance using their high-powered cameras and low-bellied touts. He and a fellow OTR, Sean, got a lift from an old neighbour directly outside the hall to try and keep their time near the venue to a minimum. Many others were gathered outside the hall enjoying their heightened spirits in the company of friends and family and Dan suspected that the Brits would concentrate on the crowd rather than on Sean and him. Another wrong deduction was 'bagged' on that occasion.

They were both from Bishop Street and were staying in separate safe houses nearby. As the car rounded the corner at Ann Street and approached the bottom of Bishop Street, it was flagged down at an army checkpoint that had been set up outside Eddie Doherty's pub directly opposite Sean's family home. Both men had been through ID checks before, but for some reason, this one felt different. It was as if the Brits knew exactly who they were looking for.

Within minutes it was obvious they did (some weeks later a local radio buff reported that he had intercepted a message on the army frequency that related to following a car from the Stardust to Bishop Street).

The abiding memory for Dan remained the anguished look on the face of Sean's mother, who was witnessing the arrest of her son and yet couldn't even remonstrate or make protest to the Brits for fear of jeopardising his false alibi. No doubt she was longing to hug him before he was taken away, but the love of a mother transcended her instincts when a son's freedom was at stake, so all she could do was to look on in silent dignity.

This time escape was impossible. Dan's prowess as a runner was totally negated as the soldiers bundled him into the awaiting Saracen and the two men were taken to Fort George army camp at Strand Road for processing and questioning. There they would be interrogated, initially about their identification documents and alibis, which, in Dan's case, held about as much water as a busted balloon. This was all new territory to him. In spite of their effectiveness as revolutionaries, they were ill-equipped and practically untrained to manage and handle interrogation by professional detectives and RUC Special Branch, who revelled in trying to break Provos. These men were almost exclusively recruited from within the Protestant community, so a few Taigs being dragged in was always a joyous occasion for them. Dan's mind was in turmoil initially, but within a few minutes, his focus turned to the fact that one of two things was now going to happen to him: release or internment. No matter what, he decided he wasn't going to admit to anything, so they would have to either release him or intern him unless they had other hard evidence to charge him. Naturally he was afraid, but in situations such as this, fear can have a positive impact, especially when coupled with an instinct for self-preservation and a loathing for your adversary. It was easy to despise his adversaries in Special Branch. In Dan's view, the word 'special' has never been so inappropriately used. It was similar to the word 'Great' in Great Britain! Dan didn't know much about oxymorons in those days, but he suspected he had unwittingly just invented two!

There was an increasing litany of stories emanating from interrogation centres regarding tactics of torture, violence and threats used by the Branch to elicit confessions to secure convictions on terrorist offences. Deep down, Dan knew he wasn't going home, but it didn't stop him from retaining a forlorn hope. It was a bit like during exam time at college when you knew that you had failed, but on the day the results came out a faint hope emerged that you had passed. Dan's initial instinct about exams was always spot on!

The RUC had the power to keep him for 72 hours and his alibi was exposed in less than 72 minutes, so from that point on it was all down once again to survival instincts and some old-fashioned 'thranness'. Dan's mum would have testified that he had the latter in abundance.

With release looking increasingly unlikely, his best hope was internment. Even though it offered no release date, Dan believed it was a better option than a 10 or 20-year stretch for a conviction for a serious terrorist offence. The Branch didn't care whose crime they pinned on a Provo as long as they got it off their books, so they were happy to offer 'a la carte' offences to anyone who broke during interrogation. An inner resolve to admit or sign nothing, no matter what happened, seemed to take over, and for the next few days, Dan focused on that alone.

Over a three-day period, he was interrogated in three different centres. After the first four hours at the Fort George army base, he was moved to Strand Road RUC Station for intense questioning by the CID. The interrogation at the army camp was relatively easy apart from one military intelligence officer, Bert, whom Dan believed to be a turncoat Catholic from Derry, who tried to rough him up a bit when he refused to give up Sean's true identity. Bert produced a photo of Sean in a group photo of a football team, pressing Dan to name the team and the other players. He conveniently said he didn't follow football so had no idea who these people were.

At one stage Bert got so angry and frustrated that he kicked Dan's chair from under him, upending him to the floor. Dan responded by lifting the chair and warning the guy that if he tried that again, the chair leg would become a permanent part of his anatomy, making bowel movements both difficult and metallic for the rest of his life! To Dan's surprise, that particularly 'heroic' offering of British rule backed off and refrained from further violence. Standing up to bullies was never easy, but it was always a better option than succumbing to cowardly thugs such as that specimen, who needed the weight of numbers to express the power and control he believed he had. Where power really lay in Dan's eyes was in not bending to injustice, but continuing to stand up no matter how many times they beat him down. Once again the connection between fear and bravery was keeping his resolve strong. That resolve was to be tested to its limits over the next three days.

At Strand Road RUC station his two CID interrogators seemed bent on stressing the fact that they were 'ordinary' detectives and not Special Branch, and that Dan would meet the notorious Branchmen at Ballykelly Army Camp if he didn't cooperate with these 'nice' guys. To him, they were just arms from the same body, and in spite of the continuing natural fear and trepidation that was driving through him, he remained steadfast in his determination not to admit to or sign anything. In the spirit of the TV police dramas of the day, the CID pair played out their good cop/bad cop routine, offering Dan a way out by admitting to lesser crimes, such as IRA membership, robbery or even a 'wee' bombing. This, they said, would save him from the spectre of the Branch at Ballykelly and offer a relatively small prison sentence of around five to seven years.

However, at just 21, donating seven years of his life to these fuckers wasn't on Dan's agenda, no matter what terrors awaited him at Ballykelly. After a further salvo of questions that brought them no information, they put him in a cell for the night. In recalling this experience Dan could still smell that odious mix of piss and disinfectant in that dungeon, and sleeping there was certainly not an option. After an hour alone, a drunk was put in with him to share the cell. But this was no ordinary pisshead. Garden variety drunks didn't sober up that quickly and ask questions such as, 'What are you in here for?' and, 'Are you a Provo?' This was something Dan had expertise in, given his current job share between Provo and drunk. It was probably one of the few positives he ever derived from such a destructive illness, apart from in later years when he was able to offer his experiences to some who sought an answer to the vile disease that alcoholism truly was.

It was no mystery to Dan that the 'drunk' was suddenly removed from the cell after less than an hour, having failed to draw any information out of him. Dixon of Dock Green in full uniform would have made a better job of subtlety than that particular drunk. With sleep not an option, he followed the artistic pursuits of many before him in that cell by scratching 'Dan was here' and 'Up the Provos' on the black tar-covered walls of his cell. In the morning he was offered breakfast, which he refused, lest it was drugged to loosen his tongue and give these clowns the confession they so desired.

The next morning one of the detectives, Sergeant Doyle, took Dan on a journey down Bishop Street as he recounted his movements. He said he had been outside his house a few days earlier. It was his way of telling Dan the cops could go where they wanted and had complete freedom of movement. For some reason, this riled Dan and he lost his cool momentarily. 'Well I hope you weren't fucking looking for me because I was up the town,' he snapped. 'Sure that's the safest place to avoid you dimwits. You think we just stay in the Brandywell and Bogside waiting for collection.'

Dan knew he'd said more than enough but for some reason, he had got into a 'dick-measuring' contest with his foe. It was true he'd often strolled around the city centre in virtual safety given that the eyes of the security forces were more concentrated on trying to thwart missions that emanated from the nationalist areas of the city. He recalled a few days earlier being in town to relax, and also to scout for potential security loopholes that could be exploited. What he didn't tell Doyle was that as he was leaving the city centre at Butcher Street near the top of Waterloo street, he met with two comrades, a man and a woman, who were lifting a pram over the dragon's teeth at Waterloo Gate. Dan helped them, and in doing so realised their journey wasn't what it seemed. The plan was for the girl to take the pram to the Diamond a short distance away. The guy with her wasn't going any further, so Dan suggested that he accompany her, which was gratefully agreed. It just didn't seem right to him that she should do this on her own.

Inside the pram was a baby doll with a blanket that covered about a hundred pounds of explosives. The timer was preset for 55 minutes. So Dan and his new 'girlfriend' walked as a couple towards the Diamond. A woman stopped, as they often did in those days, to admire the baby. She looked in, then looked curiously at the happy couple, and then went on her way talking to herself, presumably about the strange pair she had just met. They left the pram at the south-east corner of the Diamond and turned back towards the safety of the Bogside. Once there, telephone calls were made to the police and the Samaritans providing information on the location and time of the expected explosion. The area was cleared and cordoned off and within less than an hour, a large blast devastated that corner of the Diamond.

Dan would've liked to have asked Doyle if he would not have been better off catching bombers in the city centre than gallivanting down Bishop Street looking for him. But by this time he had quit the bravado contest and resumed his intransigent mode.

Several interrogations later, the two detectives threw in the towel and told him he was going to Ballykelly for further questioning by the dreaded Special Branch, and that he was a foolish young man for not taking the easier options they had offered. This was followed by a medical examination from the police doctor, who informed him he had a severe case of acne and blackheads on his face and that wherever he ended up he should seek treatment. Dan knew he had a few spots, but this diagnosis seemed a bit over the top in his estimation.

Nevertheless, he duly assured the doctor he would deal with the skincare matter at the earliest opportunity. Acne and blackheads were certainly the least of his concerns for the next three days. Surviving intense interrogation and possible torture was Dan's sole focus, and within half an hour he arrived at Ballykelly in a police Land Rover, bound by handcuffs and full of fear and apprehension, but still holding on to that invaluable thran streak that would be tested to the hilt.

Every hour there seemed like an eternity. His interrogators were definitely a step up (or perhaps down) from the relatively humane CID. Each inquisition (and there were many) increased incrementally in terms of pressure, tension, threats and violence. From a standing start, Dan's opponents ratcheted up their tactics. No doubt some police psychologist somewhere had worked out a method to take young Provos to breaking point. On many occasions it worked, as proven by the bulging prisons at Crumlin Road, Armagh and Long Kesh: full partly because so many young men and women couldn't withstand the relentless mental and physical pressure meted out by the notorious Special Branch in interrogation centres throughout the North. In Dan's eyes, this was a major failure of the Provisional leadership. Though he was trained in using explosives, rifles, submachine guns, pistols and, of course, the RPG-7 rocket launcher that nearly ensured that resisting interrogation tactics would be unnecessary, the only advice offered to counter the Special Branch was, 'keep your mouth shut.'

In hindsight, it was excellent advice, but a bit more information as to how to withstand the onslaught of the relentless Branchmen in this hostile environment would have been very welcome. Those fuckers revelled in breaking young Provos and they certainly gave Dan their best shot. Had their pay been based on the amount of fear, terror and uncertainty they could instil in a young man, they would have been millionaires many times over.

Dan found the times in between questioning almost as harrowing as the sessions with the Branchmen. Sitting alone in an empty cell left so much time to think, reflect and project. No doubt that's exactly what it was designed to do. Every noise from the corridor, every cell door opening and closing, brought fear of the next interrogation.

Strangely, as time went on, the fear of it being his turn changed to the hope that it was, so that at least he could get it over with till the next time. Sometimes the sessions seemed to last hours, while other times it seemed like mere minutes. Dan would never know how long. There were no clocks, and his watch was taken from him along with other personal items and bagged on his arrest. Even his shoelaces from his Oxford brogues were in their 'care'. It was funny how vulnerable a man could feel without his shoes tied. In later years Dan always wore slip-ons, perhaps a subconscious reaction to his days at Ballykelly.

As was the case at Strand Road, he refused the food offered. Sometime during the second day, he was brought out of his cell. He expected another hour or two of questions, insults, threats and violence, but this time it was good news. Bridget and his mother had been granted a visit after pressure from a local politician. His feelings about this went from initial elation to an unfathomable sadness that they were seeing him under such degrading and difficult circumstances, and that they had been subjected to intense and embarrassing physical searches themselves before being allowed in.

They had brought food and Dan recalled gratefully and greedily devouring a burger and chips in their presence. Seeing the pain in his mother's eyes touched him to the very core of his being. He knew she was totally opposed to his chosen path as an IRA volunteer, yet there she was once again with that most precious gift of a mother's unconditional love - not to mention the fast food! Dan's mum was to turn up many more times during his often tumultuous and problematic life, always demonstrating that instinctive love only a parent can have.

Of course, they fell out many times. That happens when a young idealist and free-flower like Dan was challenged by the experience, wisdom and pragmatism of a loving mother. Few men can ever repay their parents for their unlimited donations from the heart, and he certainly fell into that category. Unfortunately, most don't even fully understand it until much later in life. Again, Dan could have signed up for that theory too.

Seeing Bridget was a totally different experience. Just like his mum, she was not a supporter of the IRA campaign. Her only sin was to find something within this young man that connected to her heart. Her presence at Ballykelly, though visually wonderful and welcome, served only as a reminder to Dan that he would have to live without her for whatever length of time he was imprisoned. The only imponderable in his mind was the duration of his captivity, as he was sure he wouldn't be going home after the 72 hours were up. How long exactly would all depend upon whether or not he could continue to withstand the interrogations that were to follow, and manage to neither sign nor admit anything.

No sooner had the short visit with his mum and girlfriend ended than he was back in for another session with his adversaries. They seemed to alternate, with two out of three Branchmen concentrating on getting a confession out of him. What Dan wouldn't have given for an 'alternative delegate' to do some of his stints with these highly enthusiastic and over-zealous public servants. They used every trick they knew to get a reaction from him, and on one occasion they succeeded.

After failing to rattle him with cheap, nasty and perverted comments about how Bridget would spend her nights when Dan was in prison, they then remarked that his father hadn't been to see him. He knew those reprobates were fully aware that his dad died in April 1972. Nevertheless, they persisted with insults and taunts about his father abandoning him in his hour of need and followed up with some photographs of the carnage after the Claudy bomb, pressing Dan to admit to it, or for that matter to any number of crimes they had on their unsolved list.

One of the cops was fat and slovenly looking and Dan could always recall his odour and foul breath, which was like a mixture of tobacco, stale booze and sweat, during those 'in your face' interrogations. He persistently and vainly tried to get him to admit to the Claudy bombing. At that time Dan didn't even know the IRA had planted that bomb, which claimed the lives of eight innocent civilians. Furthermore, he couldn't have directed a tourist to Claudy, never mind have planted a bomb there. But the fat slob persisted.

It was then that Dan broke - but not with the confession they wanted. In a rage he shoved the fat cop back and overturned the table, squaring up to both men. 'You leave my dead father out of this,' he screamed at them. 'What kinda bastards are you anyway? Come on then, if you wanna fight, let's fuckin do it.' Strangely, neither of those state heroes obliged him. Instead, they pulled back, both physically and with the interrogation. Within seconds they ended this phase of the questioning. Dan wasn't disappointed they weren't up for a scrap. He was just as afraid as he was brave. But once again he learned a lot about the benefits of standing up to bullies. That day he had only one more session with them. It was unusually quiet and uneventful, with some pleas from his captors to cleanse his soul and admit to any one of a number of unsolved crimes they recited. Dan responded with a resounding silence. Their underhand tactics had rekindled his determination to tell them nothing.

During his second night in 'Hotel Ballykelly', there was another incident that brought home to Dan how petty, bigoted and pathetic some of the RUC Special Branch officers really were. He could hear shouts and screams from one of the cells in his row. Instinctively, he knew he would be getting a visit soon himself, but he was baffled as normally the detainees were taken to an interrogation room for questioning.

As it happened, about six off-duty Branch men were doing some extracurricular activity after a night on the booze. Eventually, they arrived with Dan. It was a terrifying experience to be lying in the corner of a dark cell and see the door burst open and the room filling up with this human vomit masquerading as policemen. Dan lay motionless and felt extremely vulnerable as they gathered round. Once the first 'hero' had kicked him in the stomach, the others joined the party. 'So you're a wee Provo bastard from the Brandywell, then,' he bellowed. Dan didn't speak or move. He was terrified, but once again after a few minutes, he was visited by that inner strength that seemed to provide an invisible defence against what these-state funded thugs were doling out.

It wasn't that the kicks to his body didn't hurt, but his awareness of how pathetic these people really were seemed to cushion each blow. *If this is all that the might of the British crown has to offer, then I fancy the Provos' chances in the long run,* Dan thought comfortingly. For the next 15 minutes or so they just asked him one question. 'Where are you from, you Provo bastard?' And for 15 minutes, Dan said, 'Derry.' Every time he said it, kicks rained in on his body from those drunken heroes. They kept on and on trying to get him to say 'Londonderry', kicking him until his intelligence and self-preservation instincts finally overtook his stubbornness, and he sat up and shouted, 'OK you fucking bastards, I'm from fucking Londonderry. Are you fucking happy now?'

At this, those drunken excuses of manhood left the cell in the darkness in which they entered, their laughing and shouting akin to some form of triumphal orgasm. While it may have been the sensible and pragmatic thing to do in those circumstances, Dan always regretted saying that word. Strangely, decades later, the question of what to call the city still divided the people here, but at least those who choose to call it 'Derry' don't get used as a football by the police these days. However, this division is indicative of how deeply rooted the problems are in the North, and Dan had little expectation the arranged marriage in Stormont between Sinn Féin and the DUP would bridge that division. No problem could ever be eradicated by treating the symptoms and ignoring the cause. In time Dan believed the current arrangements would implode, not because he was an astute political analyst, but because any settlement in Ireland needed to be worked out solely by those who inhabit the country.

The third and final day brought a flurry of activity from Dan's captors, but by then he reckoned they knew he wasn't for breaking and were to some degree going through the motions. This last round of interviews seemed to be about trying to engage him in conversation without the previous verbal and physical abuse and pressure. Dan was unrelenting and by now he was confident they wouldn't elicit a statement from him, nor would he be signing anything. Towards the end of his final interrogation, one of them asked, 'So, where do you think you're going when we've finished with you here, Feeney?' Dan replied, 'I'm going home.' He knew he wasn't, but it was his way of telling them their fear tactics had failed and they couldn't charge him with anything despite all the mental and physical pressure they had applied. It was a final act of defiance.

He instinctively knew when they ended that session he wouldn't be seeing them again. For a moment, they were the vanquished and he was the victor. It felt good deep inside to have survived their onslaught and watch the subdued Branchmen throw in the towel. (Decades later he managed to get sight of a document that related in part to his interrogation. It was heavily redacted but there was one sentence on it that he always took great pride in reading. It was, *He was not helpful.*)

Later that night as he sat in his cell, a 'friendly' cop came in and handed him a piece of paper. It was an official document called an Interim Custody Order signed on behalf of Francis Pym, Secretary of State for Northern Ireland, and it stated:

The Secretary of State in pursuance of Section 10(5) and Schedule 1 of the Northern Ireland (Emergency Provisions) Act 1973 hereby orders the detention of Daniel Feeney, 507 Bishop Street, Londonderry, being a person suspected of having been in the commission or attempted commission of an act of terrorism or in the direction, organisation or training persons for the purpose of terrorism.

This meant he was to be detained at Long Kesh without trial at the pleasure of Her Majesty's government. *She has a strange way of seeking pleasure*, was Dan's first thought. He also noted that he was being detained, not interned. Semantics were important to the Brits.

Due to the worldwide media coverage and opposition to the introduction of internment on August 9th 1971, as well as the notoriety of Long Kesh internment camp, the British rebranded the process 'detention' and the Kesh was renamed 'the Maze'. No doubt some gormless and witless underling in the civil service had come up with this insipid and inept softening of words to cloak the evil and injustice of taking away people's freedom without charge or trial in a so-called democracy.

To think that such absurd cosmetics would blind the world to this breach of human rights showed the absolute arrogance of her majesty and her government. Their duplicity in vociferously opposing similar infringements on the rights of opponents of communism in Eastern Europe was laughable. But the English language seemed to provide cover for those who want to make the unjust just, to label freedom fighters terrorists and brand the innocent guilty. Birmingham and Guildford came to mind for the latter, but long before those despicable miscarriages of justice, Irish history was peppered with Britain's bloody and tragic fingerprints.

Of course, those of a more bovine nature would always slavishly follow their political masters, or at best say nothing when injustice reigns. Democracies like this often use the votes of the people as a mandate for their double standards. Those who were incarcerated in Guantanamo Bay following 9/11 could educate the world on the double play of democracy. Then they invented rendition, where suspects were taken to other countries to be tortured, just to make the Brits and the Yanks appear 'clean'. Nobody of sound mind would attempt to justify the slaughter that was the attack on the World Trade Centre, but other people's crimes don't and can't vindicate injustice. The hypocrisy and double standards of some western democracies seemed, to Dan, to have no limits or boundaries when it came to their own national security issues.

The friendly cop came back later with a selection of books and asked Dan if he wanted to read one to shorten the wait until the next day when he would be taken to Long Kesh. Dan looked through them and asked if he had a copy of *The Great Escape*. The cop saw the humour of this request and left a book in the cell, though it wasn't the one Dan had sardonically asked for. In his own mind, not being charged was already his great escape, so Dan relaxed for the first time since he'd arrived in Ballykelly.

The next day he, Sean and a fellow traveller from Omagh, Billy, were taken to Long Kesh in a police minibus, each of them handcuffed to an RUC officer. Dan had asked to travel by helicopter, but just like his book selection, the cops didn't do requests!

It was a strange journey. They were all hungry and tired, yet their spirits were high after surviving their lengthy ordeal.

The men they were chained to would be going home for their tea that night and the three internees had no idea when they would see home again. Yet Dan wouldn't have changed places with his captors for all the world. He'd learned a lot about himself and the British during those three days. Above all else, he had discovered that the idealistic spirit that flowed from a deep quest for freedom and justice couldn't be broken by those who removed that freedom. Many have sacrificed more than Dan to remind the Brits that the Irish would have their country back. The only imponderable was when.

11

Behind the Wire

It was mid-afternoon on a dreary February Saturday when they arrived at Long Kesh. Just about the perfect day to blend in with the sea of grey that was the disused RAF airfield, now serving as a 'detention centre' following the introduction of internment in 1971. From the miles of wire and scores of Nissen tin huts to the anaemic prison screws that administered the deprivation of freedom and reflected the overwhelming greyness of their surroundings, Long Kesh was just a colourless stain on the landscape.

Dan thought only a certain breed of human being could design such a place and, in particular, make a career choice to work within a prison. They seemed to be the same the world over, almost devoid of personality, initiative and positivity as they slavishly followed the rules hour after hour and day after day, just punching in and out like drones.

Over time, Dan questioned who the real prisoners were, given that the internees basically ruled their cages from within, and who paradoxically seemed to have more freedom than the screws who 'policed' them. And the prisoners would be free eventually, unlike their gaolers who would endure a lifetime of days behind the wire until reaching pensionable age, whereby they would be dispatched and discarded to punch more grey days in the grey land of the forgotten retired prison officers, eternally trying to make sense and take value out of what appeared to Dan to be a meaningless grey existence.

He wasn't sure what he would do whenever he was released from the Kesh, but he was fairly sure he wouldn't be leading a marketing campaign for recruitment to the Northern Ireland Prison Service! Grey clothes were also out of the question!

Dan vaguely recalled being processed and then assigned to one of the compounds, known to the internees as cages. By this time he was utterly spent, physically and mentally, by his ordeal in Ballykelly. He craved a shower and a good night's sleep. All three new internees were allocated accommodation in Cage 7. As they approached the cage, Dan's first recollection was of seeing lots of men in anoraks walking anticlockwise around the interior perimeter. *What the fuck are they doing and where the fuck are they going?* were his next two thoughts. He couldn't understand the point of these prototype power walkers who seemed to be going somewhere in a hurry, but who really had nowhere to go. Internment camps were not renowned for 'way out' signs! He didn't realise that before the day was out, he would be joining them and that those 'nowhere' walks would be crucial to him enduring the next period of his life.

Once the news went out that new men were arriving, several internees gathered at the gate to greet them. The word 'greet' seemed inappropriate for such a reception, but for the first time in a few days, Dan felt in safe and friendly company. Upon entering his new lodgings, he was intensely aware of the metallic sounds of gates clanging and locks bolting shut behind him. These sounds would always be there during his stay and would remind him that, whatever his initial impressions of the screws, they still went home at the end of their shifts, while Dan was staying for an indefinite period to be determined by the Secretary of State for Northern Ireland.

Some familiar and friendly faces appeared from the gathering crowd. These were fellow travellers from Derry who had been scooped up by the Brits before Dan and who had also survived the interrogation centres to end up interned without trial at Long Kesh. For those few moments, it felt like a homecoming.

Dan's living quarters for the foreseeable future was a tin hut furnished with bunk beds and metal lockers, housing about 40 internees. The cage had two and a half huts for accommodation and one for recreation - of sorts. It was furnished with a woodwork bench and table tennis equipment and therefore would have been of much more use to St Joseph and the Chinese than to Dan, whose talents didn't involve carpentry or ping-pong.

There was also a shower facility that loosely resembled the ones in Auschwitz, albeit without the facility to filter through Zyklon B, probably a regretted omission on the part of the Northern Ireland Office! Of course the British were more subtle in how they mistreated their prisoners in comparison to the murderous terror of the Nazis. There was also a small portable building mainly used for educational and religious activities. Dan's earlier experiences with the nuns, Christian Brothers and priests were still fresh enough in his memory to ensure he steered clear of anything to do with those two subjects. In his mind, education and religion were still for those who hadn't discovered the inner sanctum of booze and betting!

After meeting all the other Derry 'wans' in Cage 7, Dan availed himself of a much-needed shower and shave. The shave brought an interesting clarity to his meeting with the police doctor at Strand Road RUC station a few days earlier. This was his first exposure to a mirror since then, and he was appalled to see his face was completely pebble-dashed with the blackheads the doctor had referred to. Dan was puzzled. He knew about his terminal acne and its apparent kinship with leprosy, and that those bulging blemishes had, over time, shifted his inherent low esteem to the basement of no esteem. But an outbreak of blackheads on this scale over a few days seemed impossible, even for his wretched face, and his first look in the mirror took his feelings of ugliness to a new low.

On closer examination, however, Dan discovered the doctor's diagnosis was fundamentally flawed. The 'blackheads' turned out to be little pieces of tar that had sparked off the cell wall when he was etching it with 'Up the Provos'. Relief washed over him in conjunction with the soapy water as he realised his sense of ugliness was not about to be exacerbated and even redefined. He could at least return to just having just the bog-standard feelings of unattractiveness that had been with him since he was a teenager. Immediately his faith in doctors diminished in equal proportion to the relief he felt.

Following the clean-up, there were two further Long Kesh initiations the three new men had to go through. The first was an intra-IRA debriefing of his interrogation at Ballykelly. The purpose of this was to ascertain what damage, if any, those coming through the interrogation centres had done to the republican movement in terms of breaking under questioning and providing names of volunteers and/or locations of weapons and explosive dumps. This was crucial to the Provos in terms of the ongoing campaign in the North. Often word got out from the Kesh before the RUC and army took action, which resulted in volunteers being tipped off and therefore able to avoid arrest and allow arms dumps to be relocated to new areas of safety. In the modern world of electronic interchange and rapid communication, Dan doubts if the RUC would have been so incompetent as to let information of that importance ferment for so long without action.

Then again, technology depended on those who used it and if their priority remained that Derrymen under interrogation should be visited by hordes of inebriated cops to pressure them into renaming their city, then there still might not be a resource available to follow up crucial intelligence of that nature. For once the bigotry and small-mindedness of the RUC might well have been an enabler for the republican struggle.

Dan's debrief, though reasonably informal, was also very thorough, with the two Provo intelligence officers grilling him for several hours on his experience at the three interrogation centres where he had been held over the previous three days. He was relieved when it was over and he was cleared and allowed to remain in Cage 7. His two travel companions also remained there too. Many who had broken under interrogation were transferred over time to another cage to ensure their safety within the camp, and also to ensure that any escape activity by the internees was not compromised. (History has shown that the Brits had infiltrated the IRA to the extent that they ran the war, and it appeared to Dan that they ran the peace too, given the current political configuration at Stormont. Was that what the sons of Róisín had fought and died for?)

The second initiation was a more unusual ceremony. The three new men were told by the cage OC that the tradition was that all new internees were advised to go to confession. There was an understandable assumption they were all Catholics. Part of the rationale was that, as good young Catholic men, they might want to unburden themselves from the effects of the war and that getting the 'pot scraped' in Long Kesh would be an uplifting, healing and worthwhile experience. Given that a priest also came on Sundays to say mass, it would enable them to receive the sacrament of communion to keep their immortal souls intact for that eventual journey to heaven. Thankfully Dan and Sean had heard about this tradition prior to arriving in the Kesh, and they knew it was just a ruse and a bit of craic to welcome newcomers. That's a trait of the Irish, especially in prisons, they make you feel at home by embarrassing the shite out of you! Initially, both said they weren't interested in the sacrament of confession given the stories they had heard on the outside, but after a little friendly persuasion, they both agreed to go along with it so that Billy, who was oblivious to everything, would fall for it and confess his litany of sins with honesty and a firm purpose of amendment.

The 'priest' was a fellow internee from Belfast called John who was dressed in the vestments of Fr Brady, who came to say mass on Sundays. John had long straggly hair that thinly and unconvincingly covered the fact that the top of his head had a deep urge to go bald. He also had a long beard which also had its own idea about where it would grow and where it wouldn't.

On reflection, he looked more like a cross between Rasputin the mad monk and Robinson Crusoe on day 99 than the more conservative image that Catholic priests embodied in those days. Anyway, Dan and Sean duly obliged and headed with Billy to the transline, a small outbuilding beside the huts, to confess their sins. A blanket with a hole in it was the divide between two chairs, one occupied by Rasputin, the other by the confessor. Dan and Sean went through the motions of a confession and received their penance from the 'priest', with Billy totally unaware it was all a wind-up, or that his winder was about to be wound tighter than a Swiss watch.

Billy slowly walked towards Rasputin, full of fear and humility. He had examined his conscience and was about to unburden all his sins to God and hopefully be forgiven and set free. Simultaneously, more and more internees quietly entered the transline to witness the event. Billy started, 'Bless me father for I have sinned. It's been six years since my last confession.'

He then recited a number of venial sins in a sort of warm-up to the big one, the mortal sin that was going to take him to hell unless he confessed it and received forgiveness. He was in deep conflict about whether or not to confess it but decided to go through with it and make a new start. Then he said those now famous words, 'Father, I'm a married man but I've been having a bit on the side with another woman.' The respectful silence in the room, coupled with its metallic acoustics, ensured that everyone in the first three rows heard every word. On reflection, it was probably the only silence Dan could recall in all his time in Long Kesh, as some genius within the cage was always proselytising about something day and night.

When Billy finished his act of contrition, Rasputin asked him to bow his head for his penance and for God's blessing. With great humility and contriteness, Billy lowered his head. At the same time, a huge boxing glove came through the hole in the blanket and hit him smack on the nose, with Rasputin shouting, 'Get out you dirty wee bastard,' as the room erupted in laughter, howls, whistles and cheers. Poor Billy was caught like a rabbit in the headlights and there was no hiding place.

In fairness to him, he accepted it very well. Within seconds the whole cage knew about it and word was rapidly filtering through the rest of the camp. Dan reckoned that if he had fallen for the trick, his only options would have been escape or death, as his pride wouldn't have allowed him to co-exist with a hundred men who all knew his darkest secrets. But Billy survived it and in many ways, he became a Long Kesh legend because of it.

Next on the agenda was Dan's first walk around the cage. Paul, one of his close friends from his on the run days in Derry, Donegal and Dublin, suggested they go out for a walk. Dan was reluctant initially as he couldn't see the point, but at least it was an opportunity to get away from the claustrophobic surrounding of the hut, and the pair could catch up on their respective lives outside and inside the wire. Dan did most of the talking, as life inside Long Kesh didn't take Paul very long to recount, with one day being much the same as the next. In addition, Paul was by nature very quiet. Dan felt strange in this place but strangely he was glad to be there.

There was a mixture of relief that he was still alive and had survived the war thus far and pride that he had withstood the barrage of interrogation from the RUC Special Branch. However, this was coupled with a dawning depression that he was no longer a free man and that his life now revolved around what was happening behind the wire of Long Kesh.

And at first glance, not a lot seemed to happen, although time was to prove that the place was a hotbed of activity, with the Provos using it as another front to fight the war. This time the war was carried on in terms of asserting their rights as political prisoners, planning escapes and generally ensuring that they proved a nuisance to their captors.

These fronts were designed to politicise the struggle within the prison and keep the Brits and screws fully occupied to ensure they were not available for their push to defeat the IRA on the streets and countrysides throughout the North. In later years the British came to accept that militarily the IRA couldn't be defeated. It was only when faced with that reality did a political settlement embracing republicans, nationalists and unionists become a serious item on the British agenda.

After a few days, Dan came to see that Long Kesh was a powder keg just waiting to be ignited, and with the touch paper being the arrogance and intransigence of the British, it meant an explosion was virtually inevitable. The Brits' colonial history ensured that whatever the Provos did would always elicit a reaction, usually disproportionate to the original action and always presenting a propaganda coup for the IRA, who were learning fast.

Of course, Dan had more pressing things to consider in his early days inside, such as the awful prison food, no alcohol, no bookies and not a woman in sight. So naturally, the history and dilemmas of governments were of little concern to him, at least for the time being.

Life as an internee soon slotted into a series of days, each one totally resembling the other. The only variation was on Sundays, when the priest came in to say mass, and on visiting days. Dan always looked forward to mass in the Kesh. Given his early experiences of the clergy and Catholicism, this appeared to be a rather abrupt change of heart.

However, on closer examination, his motivation revealed this sudden conversion was not of Damascene proportions, but rather was more practical and tactical. It all hinged on the fact that the priest always administered communion to the internees in both forms; bread and wine. So Dan got a sip of blessed booze every Sunday, which at least kept him in touch with one of his great loves. He remained steadfast that the bread stayed bread and the wine stayed wine even after the priest performed his party piece. And in the unlikely event of his analysis being wrong, he reckoned a loving God would understand his predicament and absolve his sins on the basis of his complicated Catholic childhood. A rather jaundiced view, but justification was a convenient friend during those difficult days as an internee.

The prisoners were allowed regular visits from family, friends and loved ones, and initially Dan looked forward to these days, especially to seeing Bridget, who in spite of not having republican blood in her veins was eternally loyal in making the arduous trek to Long Kesh almost every week. The visits also enabled many other things to happen unbeknownst to the prison authorities. Some were crucial to the war outside, such as the smuggling in and out of important communiqués and equipment for use in escape attempts.

Dan was hugely amused at the antics of the Cage 7 escape committee, who after lock-up used to remove hut windows to meet in the half-hut to discuss escapes. All very *Colditz* indeed, except for the fact they could have met freely before lock-up by going through the door. Having said that, escape attempts did occur regularly.

One, in particular, involved a keep fit fanatic called Eoin who, attired in jogging garb, managed to get into the back of a bin lorry and made it to the M1 heading towards Belfast. He got out of the lorry as it slowed in traffic and proceeded to jog towards the safety of West Belfast, only to be picked up about a mile from safety. Apparently, the lorry driver noticed him dismount in his wing mirror. That's how thin the line could be between freedom and incarceration in those days. Dan recalled Eoin being returned to the cage. Everyone took it personally and they were so sorry and sad to see their comrade, who had almost made it home, returned to their midst.

Other substances smuggled in were more for recreational purposes, with girlfriends and mothers concealing alcohol-filled balloons in their underwear to pass on to the internees. Under close clinical scrutiny, the passing of the illicit cargo via this method would have resembled simultaneous breast reduction and testicle enhancement, with the booze transferred from the visitor's bra to the prisoner's Y-fronts during a visit.

But it was the best way to avoid detection during the rigorous body searches designed to not only prevent smuggling in and out but also to degrade the internees and their families during visits. On both counts that tactic failed, as once again the Brits underestimated the resilience and ingenuity of a risen people. Once the 'party' balloons were successfully transported to the cage, the whiskey and vodka were transferred to medicine bottles and stored until the next shindig. Dan reckoned the medical records within Long Kesh would show inordinate cases of chest infections, as the internees regularly sought cough medicine to obtain a supply of bottles for their alcohol stash.

Alongside the spirits smuggled in, the internees also manufactured their own 'Kesh brew', with bins of fruit treated with yeast and left fermenting for weeks to produce a potent if rather congealed and concentrated concoction. Once you got used to the fact that you almost had to eat your drink, it was pleasant enough and the effect far outweighed the issues of quality and texture. Dan recalled the aftermath of one all-night session on the brew when he lost his sight for a few hours, bringing alarming authenticity to the concept of being 'blind drunk'. It happened while he was watching *Spartacus* on TV one Sunday afternoon. Having audio for only half the movie was about as useful as listening to a fire-eater or juggler on the radio! In later years Dan had watched the film many times and it always brought to mind his temporary blindness. Sadly, that freedom fighter died in both the audio and visual versions, but that aside, it remained one of his favourite movies.

Some larger 'tools' such as wire cutters and cameras were also available for escape efforts and propaganda use. Dan initially wondered how these items were availed of, but he soon learned that one of the screws had been befriended over a period of months. Once it was discovered he had a weakness for money, he was bribed to bring in some innocuous items at first, and once compromised he brought in whatever items he was told from then onwards. James Garner, who played the Scrounger in *The Great Escape,* would have been proud of them!

In the midst of the frenzy of intense political activity inside and outside of the Kesh, there was always a spirit and sense of humour within the cages. Each new internee presented an opportunity for a laugh, and many of them suffered the same fate as Billy. Dan recalled two comrades from Derry being tasked with filling the water tower with buckets of water that they drew from the taps in the washroom, totally oblivious to the fact that the tower was plumbed in. The rest of the men had a good chuckle as the unsuspecting pair slogged their buckets up and down the tower for more than two hours, the sweat dripping off them on a hot sunny day. Another martyr was given a few coins and sent to the cage gate to order 12 baps from the screw. Needless to say, the Kesh bakery didn't do baps! There were many more 'dirty Joes' played on the unsuspecting and innocent behind the wire, but perhaps the most famous was the one involving Dan and Sean.

One day after visits, Sean remarked to Toddler, a fellow traveller from New Lodge, that he had seen his girlfriend and she was 'fuckin' gorgeous'. Dan heard the comment, so later that day he sidelined Toddler and between them they hatched a plan. That night, Toddler informed Sean that his girlfriend Mary had an identical twin sister, and if Sean wanted, he would put a word in, and perhaps she might consent to him writing to her.

Sean was absolutely delighted and asked Toddler to do his best. He was a handsome fucker, loved women and was never short of female attraction. He was famous on the outside for two-hour stints in the bathroom as he groomed himself for the Friday night wooing sessions in Borderland. He was extremely easy-going and Dan was totally relying on that quality coming to the fore when the shit was to eventually hit the fan.

And so the 'dance' commenced, with an initial letter from Sean to 'Julie', Mary's twin, introducing himself and requesting that she write to him during his time in Long Kesh. Toddler promised to smuggle the letter out during his next visit, and if she wrote back he would do the same and smuggle Julie's letter in. It was perfect and Sean was hooked from the get-go. And so the letters went back and forth over the next two months, each one from Sean incrementally more romantic than its predecessor as he took the bait from Julie with alarming innocence and unawareness.

He often confided in Dan about how this girl was 'really into' him, totally oblivious that Dan was Julie and was the one answering his letters. He had even modified his handwriting to resemble the petiteness of hand you'd expect of a girl. Sean was also totally unaware that life in his hut in Cage 7 came to a standstill on letter days as each letter was passed around the hut.

Even Mickey, a ninth of August 1971 internee who was badly tortured by the Brits, and whose daily mission was to scrutinise the *Irish News* for clues to the end of internment, was giving Sean's letters priority over the newspaper. The fact that the letters were supposedly being smuggled, and therefore not subject to scrutiny by the screws, gave Sean the confidence to be open with Julie, and as each letter came back he was more buoyant about this budding love affair.

Dan bunked above him and recalled him often reading her letters and engaging him with comments such as, 'Jesus, Feeney, your woman's mad about me.' Dan didn't know whether to laugh, cry or shite himself. He reckoned when Sean found out, the latter would automatically happen first.

After about eight weeks and a build-up of correspondence, the time came when the truth had to be told. Sean had invited Julie to come and visit him, and of course Dan accepted on her behalf. Sean was hyper in a laid-back sort of way, but Dan wasn't feeling so easy-going. It was a Sunday night and he was lying in his bunk surrounded by all Julie's letters. Dan passed the word around the hut for everyone to gather at Sean's bed. By now he felt as much guilt as he did devilment, but the mission had to be completed. Even by Long Kesh standards, this was a dirty Joe to top them all. So as everyone angled around the bed, Dan went to his locker and took the pile of letters that Sean had written to Julie, threw them over on Sean's bed and said, 'Do you wanna read these too, Sean?' The hut erupted with howls of laughter and shouts of derision.

Sean was gutted, probably more by the fact that his love affair had ended than by the slagging from the internees. Dan waited, expecting a backlash, and resolved that if Sean hit him, he would take it as fair in the circumstances and wouldn't defend himself. But Sean just looked up and said, 'Ye bastard, Feeney, I hadn't a clue, fair play to you.' And it all ended in laughter, which epitomised Sean's temperament and sense of humour. It was a privilege doing time with a man like that. By morning it was all over and they all got on with another day in hell.

Despite the intermittent craic, Long Kesh was becoming more hell-like every day. Every four or five weeks, the Brits would burst into the huts in the wee hours armed to the teeth and in riot gear, battering their shields and the sides of the tin huts to put fear and terror into the sleeping internees. Then they systematically went round each bed, roaring and shouting at the men, often cracking a head, an arm or a leg with their batons as each man was forced to strip and then dress, with each item of clothing searched before he was frogmarched to the recreation hut while they searched their living quarters.

During the searches, the Brits wrecked and destroyed everything in sight. After about four hours, the men would be made to walk the gauntlet of jeering soldiers, many of whom had Alsatian dogs, gnarling, barking and straining their leashes like bloodhounds. A look in the wrong direction was reason enough for the Queen's servants to beat the crap out of an internee. There were no 'neutral' witnesses, so the Brits enjoyed a free hand and of course denied any claims of brutality and ill-treatment when the stories came out of the Kesh. This human degradation was by far the worst experience to date that Dan had suffered since being interned. But worse was to come.

By now the internees were in dispute about living conditions and their treatment and were refusing prison food and throwing the bedclothes over the wire in acts of protest. They only accepted bread, and so the Brits responded by stopping all food parcels from family. It was a grim and tense time and morale was low, with no apparent possibility of the Brits acceding to the internees' demands for better treatment and conditions, and ultimately an end to internment without trial. As the weeks went on the impasse solidified, and it was clear that something else would have to be done to break the deadlock.

It was a Sunday night in late September and they were staring into a bleak autumn and winter behind the wire. Dan was sitting talking to Seando, another fellow Derryman. They discussed the current stalemate and both agreed that something different would need to occur to increase the pressure on the Brits. They also agreed it would have to be pretty spectacular to have an impact outside Long Kesh, and in particular to engender sympathy from America and the Irish Republic. The history of the Irish struggle in prisons pointed to only one tactic that had the required potential to harness the necessary support: hunger strike.

By bedtime, both had agreed to go on hunger strike from midnight that night, and that they would present themselves to the prison medics first thing next morning to formally announce their intentions. They decided to forego the demands for better conditions in favour of one single demand: an end to internment. They would go on hunger strike - to the death if necessary - to pressurise the British to give in to their just demand. They informed the cage OC of their decision and, though very supportive, he did try to change their minds about this drastic decision. But the two young men were not for turning.

Dan vividly recalled the tormented thoughts that visited him that night. Sleep was totally off the menu. After midnight he immediately felt hungry. Then his mind projected forward to his painful and emotive death by starvation, with the Brits only giving in to the demand after the first two hunger strikers had died. He visualised the wakes and funerals with their heroic send-off from the republicans of the North.

Then he imagined his mother, siblings and Bridget crying inconsolably at the loss of their son, brother and boyfriend. For a moment all the insecurity and low esteem he had suffered throughout his life just ebbed away, as he finally felt he was worth something and that his life mattered.

The irony of obtaining self-worth from glimpses inside

his own coffin was not lost on Dan in later years. These thoughts were closely followed by an intense fear of slowly dying by starvation that caused him to sweat profusely as he lay awake in the horrific reality that was day one of a hunger strike. Events were to take place over the next two days that would completely change this situation, but that night Dan was resolved to die on hunger strike if the British did not end internment and release all internees.

By morning all these demons had left him, and all that remained was a steely resolve to see it through to the end, whatever the consequences. Seando and Dan again affirmed their decision to the OC of Cage 7 and set off to see the prison medic. The Long Kesh doctor was unprepared for anything more taxing than dispensing cough mixture and paracetamol, so the announcement of the commencement of a hunger strike engendered shock, surprise and a look that said, 'Why couldn't you have done this on someone else's shift?'

He asked what he was expected to do. Seando and Dan explained they just wanted him to formally record that this was day one of their hunger strike and that their single demand was for an end to internment without trial. Then they suggested he should report everything to the prison governor. At that, both returned to their cage and tried to act as normal as possible so as not to affect morale any further with their fellow internees, who by now knew of their grave decision.

Dan recalled how that day seemed never-ending and

how he longed for food. Over the years he learned that it's usually when you can't have something that you seem to crave it most. As far back as his crush on Fiona, he could see this theme play out in his life. In later years a broken marriage and few failed love affairs emphasised his penchant for slow learning in respect of his numerous wants over the years. He also learned that, often, when you get what you think you want, you stop wanting it. If only he had known that in the Kesh, he wouldn't have felt so fuckin hungry! But help was on the way.

Unknown to Dan, the unrest and protest over conditions in the Kesh were being scrutinised at a high level by the Provo leadership, and they had decided on a different course of action that was going to impact greatly on the hunger strike that the two 'boyos' had just started.

As he walked around the cage yard on Tuesday evening, Dan noticed messages being passed by semaphore between the leadership of the internees and the sentenced republicans, who held overall authority within the Kesh. By nightfall, a decision had been made to get them to call off their hunger strike to enable a more spectacular, coordinated and effective action to be taken, one that would bring the plight of political prisoners back to the international stage.

Seando and Dan were duly ordered to cease the hunger strike and told that something big was about to happen in the coming weeks, and when it did they would understand why their protest had to end. Dan had mixed feelings about the decision, but an order was an order so he complied.

On the one hand, he could eat again, but on the other, their sacrifice for the cause was being stood down. Additionally, he knew that both he and Seando would get a hell of a slagging about quitting the hunger strike so soon. They couldn't explain the reason in case something leaked to the prison screws that could jeopardise the imminent republican plan for alternative action in the Kesh.

The next morning they officially ended the strike without giving any reason to the prison authorities or to their fellow inmates. And they took their slagging as best they could. It felt cruel in many ways, but this was a time to accept the consequences and say nothing and they just had to nurse their bruised egos in silence. In Dan's mind, he could hear how the news was conveyed in Derry. 'Dan Feeney and Seando Meenan are on hunger strike,' then, 'Dan and Seando are off hunger strike,' and finally, 'I knew that greedy fucker Feeney would never stick it!'

Less than three weeks later, on the night of October 15th after an incident in Cage 13, the order to burn the Kesh to the ground was given by the prison OC and quickly communicated to all cages. The order was also given that no one should attempt to escape, as the prison would be ringed with trigger-happy British soldiers just itching to exact revenge on the rebellious inmates. This was a mission to burn down the prison, not an escape plan. Dan and Seando shared a smile, both knowing the reasons behind their abandoned hunger strike was no longer an issue or a secret.

Within minutes, most of Long Kesh was in flames. To

the authorities, this represented anarchy and destruction. To the republicans, it represented taking the war right into the bowels of British rule. It was a signal that this revolution could not be broken.

That night belonged to them. After some brief skirmishes with the screws, the authorities withdrew their staff to the perimeter, leaving the marauding republicans to it. Everyone knew that their 'freedom' would be short-lived, but for one night Long Kesh belonged to republicans and they diligently showed how much they appreciated their lodgings. As the screws and Brits hurriedly withdrew, they even left their dogs of war in their kennels. Soon those kennels were ablaze too, and the Alsatians that had been used to terrorise the internees barked no more.

Following the fire, the Brits tried to use the killing of the dogs to demonise those who burnt the Kesh, but there was no sympathy coming out of republican and nationalist areas at the demise of those savage animals, whose sole purpose for being there was to frighten and intimidate the inmates. Even dog lovers in the Kesh, of which there were many, understood, accepted and agreed with this action.

Internees and sentenced men converged at the football pitch, with many old comrades meeting for the first time in years. Dan recalled meeting Eddie, a fellow Derryman, who was doing time for trying to aid the escape of another comrade, 'Big Mickey', a prominent republican from Derry. Eddie and Mickey had tried to switch roles as visitor and prisoner during a visit, but Mickey was quickly spotted as he tried to leave with other visitors. So they both ended up in gaol.

How they chose those two to swap places would eternally mystify Dan, as their resemblance was as close as that of Clint Eastwood and Lulu! But no doubt Big Mickey's leadership and experience were being missed in Derry, so they had to try something to spring him. Eddie always had an innocence about him, which kind of contradicted the fact that he was a convicted felon, but those who knew him understood him. He was a larger-than-life character, with a huge frame and a voice to match. He prided himself on his jiving prowess in the local dance halls and for a big guy, he was a brilliant dancer.

A few months prior to the burning of the Kesh, intelligence came to light which indicated that loyalists intended to poison Big Mickey. The screws said this was impossible and they were sure that nobody could tamper with the food. However, to avert further protest and disruption they agreed to sample the food in front of a prisoner. Eddie was nominated for this job. After less than two weeks the screws went to talk to the Cage OC and informed him it was time to stop the tasting trials. The OC thought it a bit too soon but the screws pleaded that it had to stop. After being quizzed further, they divulged that Eddie was getting them to sample the dessert first, then the dinner and then the starter. Eddie saw this as just another way of bringing the fight to the enemy. The rest of the prisoners just thought it hilarious. Thus ended the tasting episode, no doubt to the relief of the screws' digestive system!

Dan recalled hearing Eddie that night amidst all the fire and frenzy, bellowing, 'Burn the football pitch!' This would have been difficult, given they were all-weather pitches with metal goalposts and with nothing flammable in sight. The humour and naivety of that moment have always remained with Dan, and was often recounted over the years when old comrades met in pubs and shared memories of that night in Long Kesh.

Dan recalled the looting of the prison shop at the sentenced end of the prison. He exited with a box of chocolate biscuits and shared them around. Ironically the biscuits were called 'Breakaway'. But for every fond memory of October 15th 1974, there were multiple horrific recollections of the next day to complete the picture.

If the night of the fire belonged to the republican prisoners, then the day after belonged to the Brits. Dan knew that daybreak was going to bring a concerted effort from the British Army to restore order to Long Kesh, but the damage was already done. The news of the burning was spreading all over the world, so the embarrassment for the British was total. The genie was out of the bottle.

And, like all true Brits, they tended to react badly against those who embarrassed them. Dan could just imagine the Whitehall brigade demanding that, 'The rebellious Irish peasants in Her Majesty's Prison Maze be brought to book for their impudent behaviour.' The outworking was somewhat more violent than the rhetoric, though.

The republicans could hear the soldiers as they reinforced the perimeter fences of the prison. It was clear that there would be a full-scale invasion of the prison to restore order. They knew that they wouldn't be able to stop them, but they weren't prepared to go down without a fight. Dan and a few others were given the task of selecting some older and less healthy internees and placing them in the prison hospital for their safety. Later in the day, it was reported that the Brits did not treat those guys well, beating, ill-treating and degrading most of them.

As dawn broke, the Brits attacked in their hundreds, firing tear gas and rubber bullets at will as they entered in armoured vehicles and on foot. The republicans fought fiercely and valiantly, but in reality, they had no chance against the sheer numbers, weaponry and machinery of the army. The battle went on for hours, with the main fight happening at the football pitch. For a while, the rebels held their own, but the turning point came when the army helicopters were sent in and hovered above them, dropping hundreds of tear gas canisters on top of the rioters. Everyone was choking and in pain as the marauding army, protected by their gas masks, just battened everyone in sight. In later years it had been claimed that CR gas was used on the rioting guinea pigs. Dan didn't read the labels on the canisters, but in five years of street riots, he'd never experienced anything like the potency and effect of the gas that day.

Eventually, the Brits split the prisoners, with just over half being caught at the pitch and the remainder escaping to the next compound that fringed the loyalist cages. Dan was with the ones who escaped. They could hear the screams of their comrades being beaten at the pitch and tried to come to their aid, but the Brits were too strong and pushed them back further every time they charged.

Then came one of those moments that could only happen in Ireland. As the republicans neared the 'orange' cages, the loyalists appeared armed with shields made from locker doors and batons made from bed legs. It initially looked like the Fenians would have to fight on two fronts. After all, the loyalist prisoners were in there because they had killed and maimed republicans, Catholics and nationalists. That was their raison d'etre.

But after a brief negotiation with their leader, a man known as Gusty, all of a sudden the loyalists handed over their shields and weapons to the republicans to help them in their bid to try to free their comrades at the football pitches. Gusty said he couldn't join them, but had respect for their valour.

For a brief moment, there was unity in that part of Ireland when the humanity and camaraderie of being political prisoners transcended the hatred and sectarianism that had blighted the North since its inception in 1921. Dan recalled his pride that Irishmen were helping Irishmen in a battle against the British. Not many shared this anecdote in the decades that followed, but it was an experience that Dan often reflected upon.

It remained a poignant memory, with those who witnessed

it experiencing a fleeting sense of kinship that only the underdog can truly experience. In comparison to the fiasco of the marriage of convenience at Stormont decades later, the unity of that day was born out of a brotherhood that only ever appears when there's truth and real identification, and when the political choreographers are having a day off. Interestingly, one of today's 'dance leaders' refused the order to burn at one end of the camp on that night, and he didn't get involved in the ensuing riot either. He was eventually overruled by the internees in his compound, who partially burned their cages but were too late to join their comrades at the football pitches, having been cut off by the Brits.

On the downside of such a seminal moment, Dan was handed a shield and therefore had to go to the front in their charge against the Brits to try to gain ground. Within minutes he was virtually toe-to-toe with the soldiers, and seconds later he was hit with a gas canister fired at point blank range that started at foot level and spun up his leg and body underneath the shield, spewing its toxic gas and rendering him unconscious. He was dragged away by two comrades, one of whom was John, the driver who had previously saved his life in the Brandywell. He seemed to be making a habit of steering Dan to safety.

During a lull in the fighting, the Brits and the republicans negotiated a cessation of hostilities, with the army undertaking that nobody, including those already caught at the pitch, would be ill-treated if the riot ended. The exhausted prisoners agreed, and the burning of Long Kesh and the prison riot was over.

Of course, as usual with the British, their word turned out to be just that; mere words. Dan remained amazed as to how Britain retained such credibility with the world's major democracies, given its propensity to go back on its word. But then maybe the secret of politics was that they all used their word frivolously! Without glamorising or even being supportive of the fundamentalist Islamic suicide bombers, they do at least tend to keep their word!

The next phase of this surreal episode was all about reprisal. Once the Brits got the men rounded up and split into manageable numbers within the burnt-out cages, they ensured the prisoners wouldn't forget the day after the night before. Dan recalled squatting with his arms above his head in Cage 22 for hours.

He and the others could only watch as comrades were singled out and beaten. Others had to run a gauntlet of baying Brits with swinging batons just to go to the toilet. Finally, everyone was taken back to their cages and spread-eagled against the perimeter wire for several hours.

How long it was Dan would never know, but he remembered hallucinating in the darkness. His visions veered between seeing family on the other side of the wire to rats climbing up it eating bread. Lack of sleep, trauma and hunger probably contributed to the experience but for Dan it was all part of the price to pay for burning Long Kesh, and for him, that was a price worth paying.

Anyone who moved a muscle got beaten. Eventually, the

Brits secretly withdrew, leaving the exhausted and famished internees still straining at the wire. Nobody dared look around, so it must have been at least half an hour before they even knew they were gone. Someone, aware of the silence, sneaked a look behind and alerted everyone that the soldiers had gone. The relief was palpable, although the prospects for a good night's sleep weren't too good.

All that was left of Cage 7 was the remnant of the hut used for woodwork and sport. Much of the roof was intact due to the fact that there hadn't been much to burn, so at least they had some cover from the October cold and rain. Everyone just filed in, and within minutes the exhausted men were sleeping on the stone floor using their coats to try to keep warm.

Dan recalled the initial comfort of just getting lying down. The lack of beds and bedding was of no consequence that night. After about an hour they were harshly awakened. The Brits stormed in wearing full riot gear, roaring angrily and beating the corrugated tin with their batons to maximise the impact of their mission to terrorise the internees. Dan and his comrades were ordered outside and lined up for a headcount, the first of four that night. In between counts, the Brits threw stones at the hut to ensure sleep deprivation and continue the torture tactics. Dan recalled that the Brits didn't have any dogs with them that night!

The brutality and the degradation that the army inflicted remained with him, as did the dignity and fortitude of his comrades who took all that was coming. Deep down they knew that internment in the North was well and truly fucked, and for them, the prize was worth the price.

A few months later the British government announced it was phasing out internment without trial.

12

Out of the Ashes

After a few weeks existing among the ashes of Cage 7, the prisoners were moved to the end of the camp that hadn't been completely burned to enable the destroyed cages to be rebuilt. Dan was housed in Cage 2, which was bursting at the seams with the influx of internees. There was a strange atmosphere there with the aftermath of the fire still very much in the minds of everyone.

In addition, some internees felt confused and even angry that some of their comrades hadn't successfully burned their huts when the order came, and this led to some mistrust and disharmony below the surface. At times it resulted in minor tensions between comrades, but Dan steered clear of it all. He knew that in spite of the internal issues, the enemy remained the British and all their paraphernalia of power in the North. Until that was collapsed, injustice and discrimination would continue.

Besides, it would have been the decision of a very small number of IRA officers, perhaps only one, at that end of the camp not to burn immediately when the order was given, so the rest of the men couldn't be held responsible for the dubious choice of one or two. It was a case of 'there's no fire without smoke,' and Dan saw it as some sort of a power struggle within the Kesh.

Even Provos had egos, and at times they popped above the parapet. Whatever the cause of the delay, it meant that not all internees met up with their sentenced comrades on the night of the fire. Dan didn't like any of it, as he believed that unity inside a prison was imperative to ensure everyone came through the experience together and that morale and unity of purpose weren't hampered by political ambition within the republican movement.

The Brits had set up tribunals for internees wanting to avail themselves of the opportunity to be released. Of course, like most British initiatives in the North, they were purely cosmetic and designed to give an appearance of justice to the outside world and sanitise the process, rather than actually delivering fairness or freedom. This process meant that periodically, internees could attend a tribunal where they would hear damning statements about IRA activity from RUC Special Branch men who cowered behind screens to protect their identity and their sources. They would then make allegations about IRA operations they believed each internee had taken part in.

For their part, the internees had to prove their innocence and convince the judges that they should be released. In criminal law all over the democratised world, the prosecution must prove guilt; but not so at the tribunals in this bastion of British democracy, where internees had to prove their innocence. It was just another way to justify internment without trial and was designed to ensure releases were few and far between, which they were. The inhabitants of Guantanamo Bay would no doubt identify with this method of stealing the freedom of individuals in 'the land of the free', without having evidence presented to convict them, in order to placate public feelings at difficult times. Politicians have always excelled at such actions. Dan reckoned they'd all had lobotomies of conscience prior to entering politics.

The internees were allowed legal representation at the tribunals, as the Brits attempted to legalise and give credibility to the whole sham that was taking place. But republicans knew that you couldn't legitimise the illegitimate, and you couldn't make the incredulous credible. In the early days, the order from within the camp leadership was that the tribunals were to be boycotted, and in the main everyone toed the line, although a few did attend. These were either internees with no affiliation to the Provos, or some who were struggling to do their time who wanted out at any cost.

Prison in Dan's view was actually an excellent sifting mechanism in terms of who could be trusted on the outside after their release. Men who struggled inside were not to be condemned, but in Dan's opinion, those who broke ranks with something as serious as the boycott shouldn't have been allowed back on active service on the outside, both for their own good and that of their comrades. The assurance was that anyone who went to the tribunals was suspended from the movement and would not be reinstated when they were released.

Dan strongly agreed with this measure. He considered it crucial to morale inside the Kesh, and to the security and safety of future IRA operations on the outside. Dismissal was not an option inside prison, but the suspensions in these cases would result in dismissal on the outside. That's what Dan was told anyway. Interestingly, Dan's future as a Provo was decided on this issue at a later date, not because he broke ranks, but because two Derrymen who did were reinstated back into Provo active service, even though they had attended the tribunals at the time of the boycott.

The Provo leadership rescinded the boycott at a later date, due to the high number of casualties outside, to try to bolster the numbers needed to maintain the impetus for waging the war. Daily the ranks of republican prisoners were swelling, and experienced operators were badly needed to continue the struggle. Dan was never comfortable with this departure in policy, but as a volunteer, he respected it and complied.

Dan attended his own tribunal not long after the boycott was lifted. His was noteworthy mainly for the information he received in his allegations paper. It highlighted and specified a number of IRA operations in Derry that the Special Branch had attributed to him. Given the level of accuracy, it was clear the IRA was leaking like a chip basket. Next followed visits from a solicitor who discussed methods that might help him obtain his release. This involved the solicitor talking to Dan's mother and urging her to come and speak for her son at the tribunal. Dan expressed his opposition to this, as he didn't want his mother exposed to this sham trial that he believed could have only one possible outcome. But naturally, his mum grasped at the opportunity to help get her son released.

On the day of the tribunal, Dan's mother arrived with another witness who would speak on his behalf and provide an alibi for one of the allegations. The solicitor expressed some optimism, but Dan had none. He urged his mum not to participate, but in her desperation to assist the release of her son, she insisted on going in. Dan watched as his mum begged those beacons of British justice to release her son, expressing that she had a job lined up for him in the family bar. She'd come armed with several references from priests, teachers and business people vouching for Dan's good character. Under cross-examination, she was bombarded with information to counteract her assertion that Dan would keep the law if released. Dan got angrier as the legal vultures picked holes everywhere they could. In the end, his mum just said, 'Dan's a good boy.' He could just imagine that the Branch men cowering behind the screen were lapping up the sight of this Catholic mother pleading vainly for the life of her terrorist son.

Dan felt emotion that he couldn't control, but knew he had to let the process continue. He forever regretted letting his mother go through that humiliation, but forever loved her for the efforts she made. The innocence of a loving mother set against a loaded judicial system was never going to end in anything but tears. He was so glad when it was over for her.

Next up it was his turn, and he stonewalled allegation

after allegation made by the hidden policemen. At times they produced some so-called evidence they said would compromise them or their sources if provided in public, so Dan and his solicitor were removed from the room and their bile was heard in camera. He knew there would be only one possible outcome and he was right. Later that afternoon the sham was over and Dan was given a sheet of paper which stated:

In the matter of Daniel Feeney, Appellant
I am instructed to inform you that the Detention Appeal Tribunal, having heard the appeal of Daniel Feeney, has dismissed the appeal.

Years later he became a fan of the film *The Shawshank Redemption*, and Red's visits to the parole board always evoked memories of that tribunal in the Kesh. He just wished he'd had the vocabulary in those days to echo Red's, 'So you go on and stamp your form, sonny, and stop wasting my time, because to tell you the truth I don't give a shit' speech. Dan was still too concerned about his mother to be disappointed by the outcome. He was taken back to his cage and continued life behind the wire. He always regretted obeying that order to attend the tribunal, especially after seeing the state of his mother in the midst of all that legal farce and shenanigans.

However, there was one occasion when he did refuse an order, and it was a decision he never regretted. One of the Kesh's senior Provisionals (the one, incidentally, who had initially refused the order to burn on the night of the fire) was now the OC in Cage 22 where they had been relocated following the camp rebuild. He instructed that all Provo internees would have to march every day around the cage as a means of ensuring discipline. Dan couldn't understand how an intelligent man, such as this one undoubtedly was, could come up with such a ludicrous decision. He and a few comrades remonstrated that marching around the cage in military fashion would be incongruous with any attempts to obtain release at the tribunals, as all the Special Branch had to do was to show photos of the marching internees as evidence that they were still Provos, and therefore they would be re-detained by the tribunal judges. So Dan and his comrades refused to march and were suspended by the OC.

This man in later years was pivotal in orchestrating the peace process and the eventual ending of the war for Irish freedom. Unanswered questions remained in Dan's mind as to whose agenda this man had been pursuing, and the fact that the one true solution to the Irish problem had been stalled by the eventual British in-house solution in Stormont just fuelled his fears about British influence within republicanism. But those were just Dan's thoughts. Like most opinions, they may have been right or may have been wrong, so he mainly kept them to himself. He accepted that the efforts to end the conflict were necessary and that the republican participants were honourable but probably out of their depth against seasoned politicians.

Outside, support was high after the fire and the prison

riot. Word was getting out about the injuries and ill-treatment, so the focus on internment was strong both at home and abroad. Inside it was a matter of surviving in the cramped conditions. Morale was low, but as always it only took a few to lift the spirits. A concert was organised, as were quizzes, and they had a very positive effect on everyone. Paddy Barclay stole the show with his bronchial rendition of 'Music Man'. Paddy hadn't a note in his head and his voice made Ronnie Drew sound like a soprano, but he almost single-handedly lifted the mood in the cage night after night with his asthmatic 'lullabies'. Paddy was just one of those characters with an infectious likeableness who was born to excel in times like this. The quizzes were always good craic too. Dan recalled offering a few trick questions to the quizmaster, and the answers to, 'Who wrote Brahms' lullaby?' and, 'What did you call the ship in *Mutiny on the Bounty?*' got the variety of wrong guesses that they'd hoped for before somebody realised the obvious.

The Brits mainly kept a watching brief, with a few searches at night to discourage tunnelling or other escape plans, and of course to continue their terror tactics on the Croppies. As usual, neither worked. In fact, all the while a tunnel was progressing in Cage 5, which if successful would enable a massive escape. Morale was increasing within the camp as the horrors of October faded, and external pressures continued to centre on internment. Rumours of talks between the Provos and the Brits were rife, with the end of internment being linked to deals on a ceasefire.

On November 6th, Dan recalled significant Brit activity around the camp and in particular near Cage 5. Within minutes a mini-riot had started within the bottom end cages, and once again the internees were on the rampage. It soon became apparent that the disturbance was linked to the escape bid in Cage 5 and was designed to distract attention from the escapees to maximise their chance of success. Huge optimism abounded. Thoughts of scores of internees breaching the security of one of the most secure prisons in the world just played like music to Dan. It would be especially spectacular so soon after the fire.

This time the Brits quelled the riot within a couple of hours, and like before they took their revenge on the inmates with the usual violence and degradation. Then word circulated that the tunnel escape wasn't as successful as first thought. The tunnel had come up short, and the Brits discovered the escaping internees and caught most of them within an hour. As usual, the escapees were beaten and degraded. The three that actually made it out were rounded up the next day on the outskirts of Belfast. The next piece of news stunned everyone. A soldier had shot dead one of their comrades, Hugh Coney, as he ran from the tunnel towards cover. He was of course unarmed. Word circulated that the Brits foully abused his body as he lay shot. A dark depression descended and Dan recalled the stillness of that night as the men came to terms with this murder. Of course, it wasn't reported in that way in most of the media, but everyone knew murder is what it was.

On the outside, Dan had been in many scrapes and could and should have been killed in action on a number of occasions. That was acceptable to republicans. But being murdered by your captors in prison didn't stack up in Dan's war ethics. All they had to do was stop him and bring him back to his cage, charge him and convict him of an attempted escape. Clearly, the Unknown Soldier who had spared Dan's life was the exception and not the rule, and Hugh Coney became just another despicable notch on their bloody guns, as were so many before him. War was a dirty business and Dan's romantic notions of fair combat were once again smashed.

After that incident, the gloom remained for weeks, but life inside had to go on. Prison was like that; if you stayed down for too long you might never get up again. On the outside, the talk was of a Christmas ceasefire with potential for an indefinite end of hostilities. Clearly, internment was a bargaining chip. The Brits needed the war to end, and the Provos needed men out of Long Kesh to bolster up their capability to wage war if the talks failed. By January 1975 the British government announced the phasing out of internment, which was soon followed by substantial releases, and then modest trickles of internees were freed on a weekly or sometimes daily basis. By the end of the year, all internees were free.

Dan's turn came in mid-February 1975. He recalled lying on top of his bunk in Cage 22, reading the novel *Papillion.* Someone shouted that the screw at the gate wanted him and it looked like it might be his release. Dan ignored the shout, thinking it was likely a hoax, as false alarms like this had become common since the releases started. For over an hour he continued to read and ignore the numerous calls to go to the gate. It was only when Seando swore on the grave of his dead brother, Colm, that Dan accepted it might be his time.

Dan had known Colm well and had been with him two nights before he was shot dead by the Brits during a gun battle in the Bogside. He knew Seando was sincere, so he got up and went to the cage gate. Wee Davy, the so-called 'friendly' screw, informed him in his distinctive county Derry accent that it was the real thing this time. He was taken into the screws' hut at the cage perimeter, where the prison governor handed him his release document, signed by the new British Secretary of State, Merlyn Rees. Dan accepted the paper, told the governor he couldn't thank him for this as internment was wrong and unjust and he should never have had his freedom taken away without being charged and convicted. Dan reckoned the prison authorities never really understood the men they kept inside. They were used to ordinary criminals bending to their every command, but political prisoners were a totally different breed. In the years to come, they were to learn much more about this difference when political prisoners chose to die on hunger strike for their beliefs.

He then went back to his hut, packed up his clothes and bits and pieces, and was then escorted to the prison car park, where he was left to find his own way home. Even then the

Brits couldn't end the evil of internment with generosity and magnanimity. Dan stood in the empty car park penniless, with no idea of how he would get home. Soon some cars arrived, and lucky for him they were visitors for republican prisoners. Within minutes Dan was taken under their wing, and after the visits were over was taken to a west Belfast pub where he supped his first pint in 13 months as a free man. He felt safe in the bosom of republican fellowship and alcohol. From there he was taken back in the mid-afternoon to the Kesh car park, where he met Rita, a friend from Derry who was visiting her husband Billy at the prison.

Rita drove him home to Derry and the journey down was almost surreal, with his freedom established but not yet fully accepted, and the longing to go home tainted with the knowledge that he had left many friends behind in Long Kesh. He recalled thinking that it would have been better if Rita had been driving Billy home, and he would have understood if Rita was thinking that too. However, as the car approached Derry, his thoughts of seeing his family, friends and girlfriend created that beautiful butterfly feeling that only happens a few times in a man's life. The feeling intensified as the car crossed the Craigavon Bridge, drove up Abercorn Road and turned left onto Bishop Street, just a few hundred yards from Dan's home.

Rita started blaring the car horn as they approached Feeney's Bar. A small crowd had gathered to welcome him home. Dan felt embarrassed, yet proud and honoured that his homecoming was marked with such warmth. He recalled the smile on his mother's face and in her eyes as she welcomed her son home. For her, this was the end of a nightmare, but Dan would give her many more sleepless nights in the years to come. But for that moment at least, she was in her own heaven as the prodigal returned home. Bridget was there too and they hugged and kissed openly. Then it was all hands to the bar as Dan, his brother Gerry, Bridget and a few old friends went to toast his freedom for the rest of the night. Most of that night remained a blur to Dan, probably due to too much adrenaline and even more alcohol. He recounted stories of life in the Kesh to captive listeners. No embellishment was needed to impress that audience, and Dan felt some worth about himself for one of the few times in his life. People respected and cared about him and turned up to see him. *Wouldn't it be great if it could have been like this all the time, Van?* But homecomings end and people disappear back into their own lives, and even the family bar closes eventually. In a few days, Dan's popularity would be over and his life would take a new shape - one very different to what he'd anticipated - over the coming months. The spectre of the Long Kesh tribunals would determine that.

The next morning Dan woke in the comfort of his own bed with clean sheets and a room all to himself. He so appreciated these comforts on that first morning. He would also have appreciated them the previous night, were it not for the fact he didn't remember getting home. That probably had something to do with all the excitement and the alcohol, but whether excitement caused blackouts was probably up for discussion, whereas the other ingredient had a track record in respect of memory loss! During his time in the Kesh his mother had moved to a new and bigger house, and Dan recalled being hugely impressed with a bathroom with carpet on the floor. Dan had a long soak in the bath that was virtually overflowing with bubbles. It was his first bath in 13 months and he loved everything about it, particularly the privacy and silence.

His brother Gerry was asleep upstairs and probably may not have had a bath in 13 months either, but for very different reasons. In those days bathrooms to Gerry were like crosses to vampires, though in later years he changed and embraced the concept of washing. Dan still wasn't sure if it was a voluntary lifestyle choice, or whether he was forced to either wash or decompose! For all of that, Gerry was a brilliant brother to have. He had a great capacity for alcohol, a caustic wit and he usually took the blame from Dan's mother for leading his younger brother astray in pubs and bookies.

Dan recalled his sharp wit and often recounted his favourite story that illustrated Gerry's ability to deliver a line. In later years he delivered many more as an excellent local actor in Derry's vibrant drama scene. It led to television roles and Dan believed if Steven Spielberg ever needed to cast a 'crabbit wee fucker' for his next epic blockbuster, then Gerry was his man! In their mid-teens, when the wheels of moderation were punctured forever, Mrs Feeney always slated Gerry for introducing Dan to the demon drink. For some reason, she seemed to have forgotten that Dan was reared in a bar and therefore needed no introduction.

One particular Saturday morning when Dan was sixteen, she stormed into their bedroom and launched into a tirade at Gerry, ranting, 'I'm just about fed up with all this drinking and gambling,' to which Gerry put his head outside the blanket and retorted, 'Do you not think it's about time you gave it up then?' Strangely, she didn't appreciate his rapier wit as much as Dan, who was doubled in two laughing in the adjacent bed. She went totally berserk and laid into Gerry with her trusty right hand, as he cowered under the bedclothes until she tired. She probably had a laugh in the quiet herself later, but Gerry or Dan wouldn't have been invited to witness that scene.

In fairness, her worry about her sons' drinking was well-founded, and all six sons had their own challenges with alcohol over the years. Gerry was a legend of unpredictability once he went on the razzle. On one occasion he came home from the Silver Dog bar with a dog in tow, much to the displeasure of Mrs Feeney. The fact that it was an Irish Wolfhound, coupled with the fact that it was Christmas Eve, kind of justified her alarm at this new addition to the family. Gerry ensconced it at the bottom of the stairs near to where the coal was kept, and for a short period, he was no longer the dirtiest member of the Feeney clan. However, that dubious accolade was restored to him when the dog died of distemper a few weeks later.

Gerry's total disinterest in cleanliness or his appearance could be best illustrated during their dad's wake in April

1972. His father had died of cancer after it recurred in his life for a second time following a five-year reprieve. The Feeneys were all in mourning, and the sadness at losing a parent can never be adequately described. But Irish wakes are Irish wakes, and things happen that non-Irish would never understand.

As was the custom, most of the Feeney men went to the pub the night before their dad was buried. Dan didn't accompany them, surprisingly; he felt duty-bound to see out the wake and funeral soberly. He believed he had let his dad down so much when he was alive, so he felt it might help square things up if he acted responsibly and was dependable, at least for the period up to the funeral. A strange logic no doubt, but somehow it squared in Dan's head, a place where unusual thoughts were always welcome. The brothers returned from the pub well mixed, and the craic at the wake that night was great, with stories of his dad being recounted by all. Dan loved to hear about those exploits of his dad's drinking days and tunnelling in London and Scotland, and there was no doubt that Mickey Feeney had lived a bit in his time.

Eventually, around 3am, Gerry fell asleep and Dan and his brother James decided to play a trick on him. They took a cork from a whiskey bottle, rubbed it up the chimney to gather soot, then painted it onto the sleeping Gerry's face. Dan reckoned he wouldn't even notice it the next morning. He never moved a muscle during his makeover, as he slept the sleep of the just. In hindsight, Dan reckoned there was more chance of his dead father stirring than Gerry, who no doubt had consumed his obligatory 24 bottles of stout earlier that night.

The next morning everyone went downstairs for breakfast before the funeral. Gerry was last to arrive and he went straight to the bathroom. Dan felt sure the game would be up once Gerry washed his face or looked in the mirror. But consistency won the day and he came out of the bathroom and joined the Feeney's at breakfast with his Al Jolson face still intact. A dirty bastard is always a dirty bastard, and bathrooms were just for toilet activities! Understandably Mrs Feeney didn't see the humour of it, but it was a very funny moment in the midst of a very sad time.

Gerry's life from mid-teens to late thirties was just a catalogue of bizarre experiences, mostly fuelled by alcohol. His exploits with his great pal Martin during their years at university in Belfast in the late '60s and early '70s were legendary, and none of that acclaim related to academic achievement. Some of their student antics included Gerry dressing as an Arab to deflect the bank official when cashing a cheque, hosting a wine and cheese party with 3lb of cheddar and 13 bottles of cheap Red Ruby wine and making 'Lassie stew' for his roommates because he'd drunk the dinner money earlier and the well-known dog food was the only meat within his budget. So Dan was looking forward to spending time with his brother in the knowledge that it would never be dull.

Day two of Dan's freedom set the tone for the next few

weeks, with most of the day spent with Gerry and a few friends visiting pubs in Derry. The drinking was punctuated by trips to the bookies courtesy of the generosity and prudence of his mother, who had saved the weekly £5 provided by the Prisoners Dependants Fund to help ease the financial burden for the families of political prisoners. Though he enjoyed the fruits of her generous nature at the time, he latterly admonished himself for his wasteful and selfish behaviour during those days, and indeed for many years after. Having said that, she wisely only gave him the money in instalments, knowing full well that a few hundred pounds would last just as long as thirty in Dan's carefree hands.

Dan's nights mainly involved dates with Bridget, where he usually topped up on the drinks of earlier that were dying in his system and needing rekindled. In hindsight, the writing was on the wall, even then, for the life that lay in store for them. The impending train crash was on track for Dan and Bridget from the get-go, but young love only saw what it saw and only heard what it heard.

On day three Dan was informed that his friend and comrade Paul had been released from the Kesh. That resulted in another drinking session, and there were many more as internee releases continued to trickle out. Paul was two years younger and Dan always felt a duty to look out for him. With the demons that were already knocking at Dan's door, having him look out for you was probably not guaranteeing anything other than turmoil and chaos, but he always meant well. They had been together in Derry, Donegal, Dublin and the Kesh, so the bond was total and it always remained so.

The other big issue for Dan was how and when to resume his life with the Provos. He was still a fervent republican with a personal mission to contribute to the freedom of Ireland. He knew he was a marked man in terms of being well known to the security forces, so his role would have to be defined in a way that optimised his operational effectiveness, while at the same time minimised risk to the organisation's safety and security. He knew his relationship with Bridget could also suffer if he decided to remain with the IRA, but he hoped that her strength of feeling and respect for him would sustain them. However, the events that took place in Long Kesh around the tribunals were about to come to the fore in terms of Dan's future within the IRA.

Within four days of his release, Dan informed the local IRA leadership that he was ready to report back for duty. The first feedback he got was that they wanted him to be used in a political and educational role rather than a military one. Even as early as 1975 the Provos were executing the dual strategy of warfare and politics in the knowledge that all wars ended up at the negotiating table, where pens became mightier than swords and words overtook military actions. Dan's immediate response was that he still saw himself as a soldier of Ireland, and wanted to continue in that vein. Apart from the freedom of the nation, there remained hundreds of political prisoners incarcerated in prisons in Ireland and England, many of them his friends, who needed the fight to continue to gain their eventual release.

In addition, Dan felt that politics was for older and wiser men than him, men who no longer had the will or bottle to wage war against the British. He still had both and was relieved when he was informed that his wish to remain on active service was granted. Of course, he had political awareness and had educated himself further through reading many books while interned, but he believed that greater military persuasion was needed before the politicians took over. Just before he was about to embark on phase two of his activism in the struggle, he heard on the grapevine that two of his comrades from Long Kesh, who had broken ranks and attended the tribunals during the time they were boycotted by the IRA, had been welcomed back into the Provo fold in Derry. Dan was infuriated by this decision but suspected it was just a rumour. In his view, those men were compromised and hugely vulnerable, and could be easy prey for the Brits. Dan liked both men personally, but a guerrilla war didn't leave much room for such sentiment, so he knew that he had only one course of action available to him that would square with his conscience.

He asked for a meeting with the Brigade OC of the Derry Provisional IRA, and met him in an upstairs room of a house in Lone Moor Road the following Sunday afternoon. He believed that when he recounted the experience of the Long Kesh tribunals and the promises made at that time, then the OC would see the error and dismiss the two men if indeed this rumour was true. The man was hugely respected by the republican community in Derry, and Dan had no doubt at that time of his bona fides as a dedicated republican, and therefore fully expected a positive outcome to the meeting. Ideally, he would be told that his information was wrong and he could get back into action.

Dan explained the situation and asked if his information that the two men were again active was true. He was informed that it was and that the IRA needed all the men it could get, and therefore the decision would not be overturned. Dan asked if that decision was final. The OC nodded and Dan replied, 'Well if they are in, then I am out.' He was shocked on a number of levels by the response he'd got. In his mind, this man was compromising the internal security of the IRA, not only by letting the two men back in but also by diluting the quality of volunteers by allowing vulnerable people into their ranks. Dan didn't doubt the proficiency of the two men as operators, and in fact, one of them was an extremely brave man. But if men can't do their time, they are vulnerable and should not be put in that position, for their own good and that of others. He felt the British would make hay with this sunshine, and to this day he believed they exploited weaknesses such as this.

From that moment onwards, Dan was much less convinced of the OC's credibility, and he became an onlooker at many other compromises and inconsistencies from that individual over the years that strengthened this view. Time would tell in the end, but the direction of the war and the way that the British infiltrated and to a large extent dictated how it was waged and how the peace was structured, just fuelled his suspicions. On the other hand, the OC might have been just playing the numbers game, and those two guys in and Dan out gave the IRA a plus one!

And so Dan Feeney walked away from the IRA and concentrated on being Bridget's plus one. In his heart, he always remained a Provo and a staunch and traditional Irish Republican, but from that moment he was and remained no longer active. It constantly pulled at his heartstrings, but the principle on which he walked away, in his view, was honest and true, and therefore could not be rescinded. Over the years Dan came to see that the one thing he couldn't compromise on was a principle. It cost him dearly on many occasions, but a man had to live with himself, and even with all his flaws and demons, principles remained a bedrock in his life. He became an onlooker as the war became more ugly year on year, with the Brits ensuring that the republican aim of a united Ireland got lost in the mire of sectarianism, which Dan believed they sponsored so cleverly to ensure the end game was one they controlled, irrespective of what the warring factions believed.

In later years, to see republicans strutting around Stormont as if they'd arrived somewhere pained him deeply. And it wasn't because these men had compromised; that was always going to feature in any peace talks. But he believed they still didn't see how the British duped them once again to ensure that any possibility of a united Ireland was as far away then as it was at the onset of the Troubles. When the soldiers stop fighting the politicians shape the peace, and boy have they shaped it with the deformed democracy of the Stormont executive. In Dan's eyes, true democracy would only be delivered at the birth of a new Ireland, agreed upon without British interference.

Those who dissented from traditional republicanism to seek political power in a British institution now saw those republicans who disagreed as dissidents. Traditional unionists fought with other traditional unionists to capture traditional unionist support. All the while the British could sit back watching them try to piece the jigsaw together, safe in the knowledge that they couldn't because they were holding back the corner and centre pieces. The outcome also suited the Irish government, who would collectively shit themselves if they thought national unity would ever come back to haunt them during their watch. Of course, they publicly espoused a united Ireland, but as long as they weren't doing the heavy digging to achieve it, then life was sweet.

Dan reckoned it would go round and round and on and on until someone on the hill copped onto the web of spin and deceit that the North's political institutions were founded upon. To top it all, they had the arrogance to point to this bastardisation of peace as a beacon and a template upon which other ancient feuds could be settled. Dan would not be holding his breath for peace in the Middle East! It was interesting that nationalists seemed to side with Palestine and unionists with Israel, so Dan wondered how they would square that when exporting the Northern Ireland peace model.

Dan's self-exclusion from the Provos created a vacuum in his life. A normal man would have used it as an opportunity to settle down. Indeed, he also believed that would be his path with Bridget, but the lurking, insatiable and patient vultures of alcoholism and compulsive gambling were to have their say too in how the vacuum would be filled. Bridget was stuck in the middle of these rapacious predators who were determined to extract their price, and she was destined to be an innocent casualty in Dan's battle with the rolling inevitabilty of obsessions of the mind.

Dan had to look for work, and his first post-internee job was as a labourer on the site of the Templemore Sports Complex. This was a new Council-built leisure facility that was underway. He was put to work on the playing fields area that on workdays resembled an ex-prisoners' outdoor reunion gathering.

The pay was shite but the craic was great and Dan always remained mystified as to how 'the Complex', as it was referred by all in Derry, ever got built and in particular how the public ever got to play football on those fields that were certainly not created by men of the soil!

Arriving to work late and worse for wear from the night before was almost compulsory, as was disappearing at lunchtime. Somebody always managed to clock you in or out, so nobody ever seemed to work but everybody always got paid.

The biggest hassles were dodging the site engineer and keeping the workers and British Army apart. The latter proved the most difficult as the Brits loved to taunt the 'Paddies', and Dan and Co were always glad to oblige in the sharing of insults and the odd scrap.

In fact, the tensions between the two factions got so serious that the site engineer created two security jobs for the sole purpose of keeping the peace. Dan and a fellow ex-internee, Billy, volunteered for the jobs and were duly appointed. This job made dodging the site engineer much easier given their mobile role. Billy and Dan often took the mobile element of the job to extremes as they headed off over the border to play pool in Buncrana.

While it didn't actually fulfil their job description they were always vigilant for any stray British soldiers who had a penchant for playing pool in a foreign country!

After about six weeks in the job, Billy went back to his trade as a barman and he also used an old contact to get Dan a job. And what a job it was. He became a bookies clerk, which was a mixture between his best dream and his worst nightmare. He had a flair for figures and could count most bets in jig time which meant he was excellent from a functional perspective.

However, his tendency to gamble his wages every week ensured that this career wouldn't last. Dan often recalled balancing his till to the penny at the end of the day, only to counter his accuracy with the confession that he owed the till several hundred pounds after a few bets he made had lost.

So Dan spent most of his time there skint and in debt to the manager (who always covered for him until he could repay the debt) and apart from the exceptional win, his 18 months in the job was not fruitful.

He had to supplement it with a part-time bar job that ensured his other demon was well exercised too. Dan thought it couldn't get any better, being so close to his twin loves. He loved the bar job as it allowed him to bask in the pub atmosphere both drunk and sober. He worked there on Tuesdays, Thursdays and Saturdays and drank there, and in other watering holes, on the other days. Somehow in between, he managed to keep Bridget interested.

Opportunities sometimes presented themselves to Dan that only he would have seen that way. One Thursday night, the manager Toni and her friend Maureen wanted to leave early to go over the border to the Ture Inn to enjoy the Coasters, the best local band around in those days, and have a few late drinks. Dan was glad to help and said he would clear up and lock up. It was a quiet night so he knew it would be a breeze. After he had cleared the bar of customers and tidied up, he noticed that the spirit optics appeared to get larger and larger. They grew so big that he couldn't see anything else. In fact, they seemed to be winking at him. He had, on occasion, fantasised about what it would be like to drink out of every optic, and now his chance had arrived. So for the next 45 minutes, he poured a drink from each one, sampling a concoction of vodka, whiskey, rum, brandy, port, sherry and various liqueurs. All in all, between the bar and the lounge, he drank from thirty-odd optics. It was a photo finish whether he would get drunk or sick first, but drunk seemed to prevail and the drinks stayed down. As he locked up the bar, his head was spinning with the effect of this fast and gluttonous rampage through the optics.

He set off to walk home and was aware of his unsteadiness. He knew he was extremely drunk and this was reinforced when he stopped in the Lone Moor Road beside the city cemetery. He didn't live out that way. In fact, he was walking in completely the wrong direction. He sat down at the cemetery wall and fell asleep for a while. When he awoke it was still dark. At that, he groggily struggled to his feet and staggered home. That journey of about a mile and a half seemed never-ending. When he arrived home the clock showed a time of 4:10am. He had left the bar before 1am and the rest remained a virtual blackout. When he hit his bed it was just that, a drunken and exhausted collapse onto the bed, still fully clothed. Sometime later he woke up when the potent mix of booze he'd swallowed was in the queue to come out. That awful retching and vomiting brought moans of 'never again', but in those days that just meant until the next time. He had indulged and survived a fantasy. Had there been satnavs in those times, he reckoned he would have made it home quicker!

A Thursday night was also to present his next opportunity. Dan arrived for work just before 6pm and Paddy the bar owner called him aside. He knew he wasn't late, so wondered what Paddy wanted. At this, his boss said, 'Dan, we've just completed the sale of the bar today. Just you work away as normal under the new owners. It's a pity you weren't in here earlier as we were having a wee celebration. However, I just want to let you know that the bar stock hasn't been checked and was just included in the handover as seen.' It took Dan a minute to decipher what Paddy was telling him, but interpret it he did.

Dan spoke to the other barman, Jim, about what Paddy had said, so they decided that they would 'liberate' some stock before the night was over. The problem was how, as well as how much they could take away. Neither of them had cars, so Dan was pondering his options when two acquaintances landed into the bar about an hour before closing time. He asked one of them, Brendan, if he had his car outside and was relieved when he heard that it was. So Dan consulted with Brendan and his friend Gerard about his plan to remove some spirits. Over the next hour, Dan passed more than seventy bottles of assorted spirits to Brendan, packed into brown paper carryout bags. Brendan took each one and deposited it in his car boot. They had planned that all four would go to Gerard's house and divvy up the treasure. Jim wasn't all that happy to get involved in this scheme and said all he wanted was a couple of bottles. Brendan and Gerard were delighted at the prospect of getting a few bottles too for providing the transport.

After closing the bar, all four set off in Brendan's car and arrived at Gerard's house. While carrying the bags up the steps, Jim dropped a bag and six bottles smashed, sanitising

Gerard's step forever. Dan just shrugged and said, 'Not to worry boys, plenty more where this came from.' They counted their loot in the living room. In spite of the breakage, there were 69 bottles of assorted spirits. The others said they were happy with a few bottles and seemed delighted splitting 24 bottles of 'nectar'. Dan had to work out what he was going to do next.

Within an hour he had sold 30 bottles to a local publican and kept 15 for himself. Dan arrived home very contented with his night's work and even had a few brandies to celebrate before going to sleep. The next morning he woke up for work but detoured first to the sports complex and arrived there with three bottles for the lunch break. A few of his old workmates secreted themselves in a small forest near the site and drank down their sandwiches with the whiskey, brandy and vodka. Dan didn't join them, instead heading off to his work in the bookies. Before the day was out he found out that the secret drinkers in the woods weren't as anonymous as planned and had set the forest on fire when drunk. Of course, everyone on the site denied any knowledge of the incident. It was suggested to the site engineer that it might have been the army trying to create an incident. As a fervent Scottish nationalist, he was content with that theory and the matter was closed instantly.

Dan wasn't a natural house drinker, so the remainder of his stash stayed intact in his bedroom for over a month. Then Seando, who was still interned, got temporary parole to attend a family funeral. On his last night before his return to the Kesh, Dan arranged to meet him in his mother's bar. As the night went on, about seven comrades enjoyed a drink together, with Troubles incidents high on the menu. The craic was great. In fact, it was so good that Dan thought they should adjourn to his house to imbibe his spirits collection. During Dan's internment, his mum had moved house to the leafy suburbs of De Burgh Terrace, and this big house was perfect for a wee party. All Dan had to do was get consent from his mum. He approached the bar and explained that he wanted to take the guys home for a drink to give Seando a send-off. She wasn't keen on the idea, but after some persuading acceded to his wishes, warning him not to bring too many or stay too late. Dan assured her that they would be gone by the time she locked up the bar and got home around 2am.

The bush telegraph was soon in action and by the time Dan's mother got home, she was met with overspill into her garden and a man urinating on her roses. Inside the house every room was packed with inebriated bodies drinking, talking and singing. On trying to enter her bathroom, the door opened and a guy and a girl hurried out. Mrs Feeney tried to move with the times, but this was way over the top and unacceptable. At that, she quickly emptied the house. All in all, there were about eighty at the party, many of whom Dan only knew casually or didn't know at all. He knew he was in trouble with his mum and had let her down, and took her admonishment when it came. By morning she found some humour in the melee that had descended the night before, but the incidents with her roses and the bathroom were not easily forgotten. Dan just kept his head low for a week and behaved semi-normal around the house.

His life just became a series of drinking and gambling events interspersed with work and dating the ever-patient Bridget. Somehow, he managed to juggle things to keep the 'madness' to the nights he wasn't seeing her, but controlling obsessional behaviour was virtually impossible, so the odd row crept into the relationship. However, she always seemed to see the better side of Dan and quickly forgave his transgressions.

Dan's mum had a closer view of it all and often pleaded with him to give up drinking and gambling, but ironically, just like her pleas at the Long Kesh tribunal, they were ignored; this time by Dan himself.

13

The Missing Years

Dan continually struggled with his withdrawal from the conflict. In many ways, his inner conflict ensured that, while no longer a soldier of the Irish Republican Army, he would for years deeply regret not finishing what he started.

Once he had made his choice to walk away, he consciously decided to keep clear of it all by word and action, and so, just faded into the background of quasi-normality in his totally abnormal life. He became an onlooker as the war deteriorated into what he believed became a sectarian morass managed and controlled by British spooks and agents - many of whom had Irish accents!

But his personal regrets were significantly tempered when he looked at how the war had eventually ended and what republicans settled for in the end. Chances were that, had he stayed a Provo, he would have ended up a Sinn Féin politician spinning victory out of a questionable draw and cosying up to political opponents in a sham partnership that cemented the retention of partition for generations to come. Intellectually he understood why republicans settled for the Good Friday Agreement. The violence had to stop at some stage and this offered a way out. Emotionally and intellectually he would always believe that republicans were outwitted by the British, who were the masters of spin, deceit and sleight of hand.

In conjunction with his view of life in a world dominated by his twin obsessions, his love interest, Bridget, had a different vista of it all. Life with Dan was either a feast or a famine, with the latter winning out in a ratio of about 1 to 10. She was everything he wasn't: sensible, mature and ready to settle down. She had just come out of a relationship with a rather staid and normal individual and Dan was the total opposite. This was probably what the attraction was. Though Dan was reasonably okay on the eye in an ordinary sort of way, any attraction aesthetically would never have compensated for his progressively mutating and defective personality resulting from booze and bets.

To say he was a confused young man wouldn't be totally accurate. He reckoned he knew what he wanted. The only problem was that it changed dramatically from day to day and indeed often from hour to hour.

Dan recalled having a wonderful Saturday night out with Bridget and had arranged to see her the following night. He had won a packet on the horses and was planning to take her out for a meal, after which they would head over the border to the Ture Inn outside Muff to hear the Coasters, his favourite local band.

On the Sunday afternoon he went for a walk out the Line, where he met some of his friends from Mailey's bar who were drinking a few cans of beer at the river's edge. Dan shared a couple with them and then his metamorphosis began.

Within half an hour he had decided to go to the Ture Inn with two of his friends, Robert and Paul. Of course, the date with Bridget had to be sorted, so Dan asked Robert to take a note over to her house so that he could get out of the date.

Composing the note wasn't easy, but after giving it careful thought and weighing up all the options Dan handed Robert the final version. His pal asked whether there would be an answer and Dan said there might be. Bridget read the note at the door and told Robert, 'You tell that bastard never to come near me or speak to me again.' Robert was shocked and confused and asked Bridget what was wrong. She showed him the note that read, *Bridget, we're finished, Dan.*

Robert left the doorstep sharpish. His only remonstration with Dan was to shake his head and say, 'You're a wile man,' something they said many times to each other over the next few years as they both grappled with the effects of alcohol on their young and wild lives.

To Dan, being called a wile man sounded like an accolade as it conjured up feelings of acceptance and acknowledgement, something he longed for all his life but, in his mind, could never seem to achieve. It seemed that notoriety did the trick, so Dan replicated that moment many times over the years.

Each time he did, it took him further from who he really was and who he really could have been, but Dan knew nothing of this as he milked the feelings of being 'a part of' through his pathetic efforts to impress and fit in.

After a few pints at the Ture Inn, the note to Bridget became a distant memory as the lads did what lads do. So too was Bridget, as Dan anaesthetised himself in a sea of beer and vodka. The next day the significance of the note hit home with alarming awareness and Bridget became his only waking thought. Apart from the guilt of being so immature and inconsiderate, Dan had to work out how to get her back. Eventually, after a week of grovelling and contriteness, the two were back in harness.

And so it went on with many more signs that Dan wasn't a good bet for Bridget, but for some reason she ignored the form and just followed her heart, personifying the old adage that love is blind. When it came to Dan, Bridget had the near-sightedness of Stevie Wonder and the peripheral vision of Ray Charles.

On one occasion, Dan arrived at her home to take her on a date totally blitzed from an early drinking session, only to be ushered upstairs to bed where he woke at 6am and tip-toed out before he would have to face Bridget or her parents. He often wondered why she stuck his behaviour. The relationship seemed to be one of eternally falling out and making up which preambled a marriage that was to follow a similar pattern for the next 20 years.

In spite of all the early warnings, Dan and Bridget got married in September 1976. She could probably write a book on their 20 years of marriage and maybe she would someday, but Dan mainly recalled his inadequacy as a husband, the effect of his drinking, his gambling and the pain, rows and separations caused by his inability to normalise for more than short periods. Bridget, a natural homemaker, tried to keep the marriage going as best she could. Of course, there were good times and deep down he loved and respected her, but his actions on the surface spoke a very different language.

In the midst of it all, Dan became a father to a beautiful daughter, Marie, in 1986. By this time he was having some success in his battle with the booze and he recalled vividly how Marie at the age of 10 months was instrumental in him finally throwing in the towel on alcohol.

Dan had been through six weeks of treatment in 1985 in Northlands, an addiction treatment centre in the city, and had been sober for almost a year.

He had predictably lost his job in the bookies due to too many losing bets that couldn't be covered up. However, he managed to get a junior clerical post within the public sector and soon after gained promotion to a junior management position.

Although the bottle was corked, the obsession to drink was constant as Dan sought to escape from some of the realities of life, past and present. He had learned a lot about alcoholism in Northlands and about the inadequacies he had that seemed to make oblivion a better option than reality, but in spite of the knowledge of his condition, the urges to drink always proved more powerful than his desire to stop.

He was living a life of tactical sobriety to keep his marriage afloat. To satisfy the cravings he centred more on gambling to change the way he felt and became a secret drinker by going on benders when Bridget went to visit her sister who lived out of town.

His days as a secret drinker after the Northlands experience were the worst of all, not because of the volumes of alcohol, but because of the deceit. During that time, Bridget, his mum and others within the family often praised his successful fight against the booze. This devastated Dan as he felt a total fraud and a phoney.

So on 19 December 1986, Dan had his last encounter with alcohol. He was at a Christmas party in the work canteen and the drink was flowing. Initially he abstained, but his desire for booze was too strong, and within a short time he was gulping down a glass of wine as the dinner started. Another two glasses rapidly followed it, and then something inexplicable happened. As he downed the third glass Dan got a glimpse of the future, with Marie seeing her drunken father staggering home night after night and the ensuing rows and arguments with Bridget. He didn't want Marie to witness what her mother had. He didn't want her growing up amidst the ugliness and despair of alcoholism that would brand her for a lifetime.

And so, inexplicably, Dan found himself saying a silent prayer asking God for the strength and help to stop drinking. As prayers go, it was nothing special or orthodox. All he said was, 'Jesus help me.' He knew exactly what it meant and believed if there was really a God, then he would know too. This was a completely new departure for Dan, who had given up on God all those years ago at college. Yet here he was acknowledging that self-will wasn't enough and that he needed help to beat the obsession for alcohol that had neither mercy nor brakes that he could apply.

What happened next bordered on miraculous. He put the glass down, never to lift another one. Within days he sought help and through it managed to maintain a sobriety that seemed impossible given his previous failed and fruitless efforts to stop. Had he offered up all his obsessions including gambling in that simple prayer, chances are his marriage would have survived too. But Dan wasn't one for getting too good too quick and he still needed his extremities to change the way he felt.

Living on the edge of something always seemed more attractive than normality, mainly because Dan wasn't emotionally equipped to walk anywhere other than on the edge. Those gaping holes of low-esteem, fear and self-loathing that he fermented in his youth needed instant gratification, and gambling provided that in spades. Eventually, his high wire living would exhaust Bridget's stamina and resolve; she loved him deeply, but even she had her getting-off point.

Dan firmly believed that the fact that Marie was the catalyst to him corking the bottle and interestingly resorting to prayer was deeply rooted in Bridget's story of the lead-up to her pregnancy that happened before Dan had his epiphany.

At that time they had been married for seven years with

no sign of a child, and Bridget was on the verge of throwing in the matrimonial towel as Dan's drinking and gambling were getting progressively worse.

She had tried everything to cope and became especially attracted to prayer and religion. By this time she and her friend Bernadette were attending charismatic prayer meetings. Dan derided this and referred to them as sky pilots and water walkers.

He recalled one particular night being woken out of his sleep by Bridget who said, 'Do you know what you just shouted out?' A grumpy Dan, who was trying to sleep off a fresh cargo of beer said, 'What?' and Bridget said, 'You just shouted in your sleep, "Mathew, Mark and John".' Even in a state of semi-consciousness, Dan could always conjure up a modicum of sarcasm and he retorted, 'Well what the fuck happened to Luke?' before returning to his drunken slumber.

What he didn't know was that the next day Bridget went to see Bernadette and recounted the unusual events of the night before. Bernadette immediately suggested that they look in the bible at Luke's gospel.

And there, in the very first chapter, was the story about a couple, Zachary and Elizabeth, who had been childless for many years and an angel told Elizabeth that she would have a son and he wouldn't take alcohol. Bernadette immediately interpreted Bridget's dream as a sign that Dan was going to stop drinking and Bridget was going to get pregnant. But they decided not to tell Dan who would have surely mocked at such a prophecy.

The outworking was that some months later Dan went into treatment for alcoholism. A few months after he came out, Bridget got pregnant and Marie was born on 31 January 1986. Bridget did tell Dan the story sometime later when his drinking had stopped. He was speechless, which said a lot for Dan!

Whether it was a coincidence or the work of something more powerful than that, no one would ever know, but what it did at the time was give Bridget the hope and strength she needed to hang in there with her drunken husband and the rest just unfolded.

One thing was for sure, Marie's later entry into the world had a massive effect on Dan. Whatever his failings as a husband, he had much success as a father both before and after the eventual break-up with Bridget. He loved Marie unconditionally and that love was returned tenfold over the years. Even in his darkest hours, and there were many, Marie's existence was a beacon and guiding light, taking Dan from the brink of self-destruction on a number of occasions, all of which was unknown to her.

But he also learned that even the intensity and purity of this love couldn't quell his obsession to gamble that haunted and tortured him for many years to come.

Against this background, his missing years as an active republican also caused him personal anguish, hurt and pain, especially in the midst of major and tragic events such as the Long Kesh dirty protest and hunger strikes that culminated in the 1981 hunger strike when ten republicans were allowed to die by Maggie Thatcher before the strike was eventually ended by the men's relatives.

Sometimes it's harder to do nothing than to take action, especially when your pedigree is that of an Irish republican. In later years there were claims by authentic republicans who were in Long Kesh at that time, that six of the deaths could have been avoided if those managing the hunger strike in Belfast from the outside had acted on an acceptable offer from Thatcher's disciples. This served to reinforce his views on the path taken by the leadership of the republican movement at that time. Of course, that same leadership quickly rebutted the claims and created enough doubt to ensure that the real truth may never surface.

From Dan's perspective, he made his own judgement on who had a history of lying to its members and supporters, and the republican leadership had certainly done that, at least to some extent.

However, his total distrust of the black arts of the British far outweighed the blemishes he attributed to the republican movement. Issues such as this burnt deep into Dan's soul.

Even though he was no longer active, his heart remained with the struggle for Irish freedom, and to see the custodians of the 1916 proclamation eventually negotiate away any possibility of the end of partition for generations to come hurt deeply.

He watched as the war became tangled and embroiled in a mire of sectarianism and espionage. Republicanism sought a peace settlement and was pressured from its leadership by those who chose a strategy that they believed would bring about a just and lasting peace. Once in that process, those still wedded to the armed struggle were worn down or ostracised. Dan watched on as the IRA was pushed aside for political careers to blossom. This saddened him but he understood that it was inevitable that not everyone would agree with or slavishly follow the direction the peace process had taken.

Sinn Féin now proudly sat in Stormont, the same Stormont that was brought down all those years ago by the IRA campaign. They castigated dissenters who had identified the peace process as treachery and sell-out to the Republican cause. The argument that republican dead were betrayed was held by many. Politics was not a natural resting place for romantic republicans with eyes on centuries of British treachery. But all peace settlements required compromises, especially when nobody won the war.

In Stormont, they seemed to accept scraps from their unionist masters, who vetoed anything that might further the unity of Ireland and even stymied inoffensive cultural and language advancements because of their in-bred 'not an inch' mentality.

The transition from revolutionaries to politicians was certainly not an easy one. Dan believed that once former comrades took on the mantle of politicians, then they would be absorbed into and become part of a system designed to assure unionism that partition remained certain and at the same time offer the aspiration of the unity of Ireland to nationalists and republicans.

But those incongruent positions were sold not only to the politicians but also to the people of Ireland, north and south in referenda. So, in spite of his misgivings, Dan accepted the vote of the Irish people in 1998. It was the first time since 1918 that all the people of Ireland had spoken and therefore in his eyes they had to be listened to, irrespective of his reservations.

In the midst of all that, Dan's attempts at a normal family life continued to be thwarted by his frequent escapes to gambling. Even though the drinking was over, his demons still raged as he sought new highs to quell the internal torment he felt, eventually committing the cardinal sin of infidelity.

This was the straw that broke Bridget's resolve and although they stayed together for a number of years, the writing was on the wall. Their split in 1997 was acrimonious, as these things often are.

Dan accepted that his life had changed forever and did his best to be the father that Marie needed him to be. He probably fell well short, but at least he remained present and active as a loving father, something he often took comfort from.

He also threw himself into his work and prospered accordingly. But for every plus, there was always the destruction caused by his gambling to ensure the bottom line was always in the red.

This scourge to his very soul managed to take Dan to bottoms that even his marriage bust-up couldn't. Only a fellow gambler would understand the feelings of despair, fear and shame that follow a failed gambling spree.

The compulsion to gamble became his reason to live and often his excuse to die. It stripped Dan of so much more than money. It took him back to those early days at school and college, where his self-esteem was eroded by those Neanderthals in the teaching profession who fostered and reinforced his feelings of uselessness. The extreme lows that followed losing everything were excruciatingly painful. Living alone and in isolation with that pain increased it twofold. Self–hatred was certainly an inside job.

Yet no sooner was the last rock bottom over than Dan was fuelling the next one. There was something in that thrill of putting everything on the line on a horse and watching it run that just did it for him.

Of course, he also bet many winners and had many profitable days. But a compulsive gambler never stops on a winning note. He is duty-bound to lose everything and re-enter that dark place of loneliness, despair, torment and chaos that only those with obsession and addiction can ever truly know.

For many years Dan juggled a life of fatherhood and employment with the abyss of gambling, always undoing any good feelings from the first two with the latter, ensuring that internal turbulence ruled the day. The contradictions of his life were aptly exposed by the concept of an agnostic praying to a God he didn't believe in for that elusive winner that would take him out of his latest crisis, only to bring him to the next one if the God he didn't believe in actually turned up.

Socially, Dan hardly existed. His interest in the joys around him was completely submerged under the sea of self-destruction. Music lifted his spirits at times but it always played second fiddle to his destructive afflictions.

After the break-up of his marriage, he did have a number of doomed relationships. The demands and expectations of sharing life between a woman and gambling always resulted in a resounding win for his addictive nature. No woman could co-exist with the atmosphere of tension and mood swings that resulted from living on the cliff edge of chance.

Those who knew and loved Dan often pleaded for him to stop, always to be disappointed and astounded at the choices he made. But little did they know that Dan didn't have a choice. He was to learn that the nature of the compulsion to gamble meant that logic and good sense were expelled when the gambler's short memory kicked in. All the disasters of past experiences were conveniently forgotten and sucked in by the rapacious predator needing its next fix. Gambling was an inadequate response to life, yet for Dan, it was the only escape he knew.

The adrenaline rush that preceded the bet, the expectation of watching that horse romp home and the relief of being right for once in your life, superseded those memories of past disasters. Then, the total fixation as the horses fought out a finish, the tension in the neck and body, willing your horse to exert to its limit and get its head over the line first. All followed by either agony or ecstasy depending on the result. In Dan's experience the agony won out at least 90 percent of the time, but to a gambler, a loser was only one race away from the next winner and a winner was exactly the same. And so the cycle went on, with Dan in constant states of rawness, hope, expectation, self-loathing and despair.

Everything outside of this was just a distraction from the buzz and escape, a buzz that engulfed the gambler day and night. At least when he was in that state, his past of failure as a husband and a provider as well as his tortured republican soul was expelled for a while.

If only Dan could have stayed in that state, he wouldn't have had to feel the emotions and experiences of reality, but life wasn't like that. Just as he had to sober up for a while during his drinking days, so too the gambler had to have off days too. Running out of money was an occupational hazard that all gamblers of Dan's ilk faced. He was acutely accustomed to those days when all the money was gone with not even the price of a loaf of bread, and being too ashamed or too proud to ask for help. Those were the times that visited all addicted punters and yet not even the pain of those days could resist the next urge once the gambler obtained more ammunition for the next bet.

Dan's intellect could never excuse it, but that need to fill those emotional holes could never resist it.

Financially Dan's life was a catalogue of loans followed by loans to pay loans, followed by even more loans from loan sharks, all of which ended up in the bookie's satchel. He prided himself on being able to take his oil and not show

how much losing hurt. A fellow punter once referred to him as an internal bleeder, a perfect description of his deep and silent emotional pain. That awful pain that can make suicide seem like an attractive option. For years his suicidal thoughts were only tempered by how selfish it would be to leave Marie behind to pick up the pieces.

Years later when Marie had her own child, Martin, Dan's self-destructive thoughts created double the guilt. Becoming a grandfather in 2005 was a massive experience for Dan. From the moment his teenage daughter told him of her pregnancy, Dan knew that his life, as well as hers, would change forever.

He clearly recalled her telling him that she was going to have a baby. His first words were, 'Are you going through with this?'

When she said she was, he hugely admired her youthful bravery and told her that from then on she would have three daddies, one behind her, one in front of her and one beside her. He privately worried about the pain of childbirth on Marie, his wee girl. For a time he was able to stop gambling as an offering for her safe delivery.

Those were tough days for a man who had never mastered his emotions without some form of escape. Dan recalls penning a poem about a father's experience of his daughter's teenage pregnancy. He called it 'Always Be My Baby':

Why do they call it 'good news' when it makes her feel this way?
It makes her sick, it holds her back – the price she has to pay

Acceptance is the answer, just support her every step
Keep smiling through the pain – don't let them know you wept
The law says she's a woman now, they even let her vote
But you'll always be my baby – there just aint no antidote
One day a teenage student, the next you'll be a mum
I look on with mixed emotions, sad and glad wrapped up as one

But we'll get through this darlin; sure that's what I'm here for
To hold you close and ease your pain and then love you all the more
This time will pass; new life will come and look you in the eye
And happiness will be with us; so baby, don't you cry.

This journey is a short one, but each day seems so long
Funny how goods days just fly in, but bad days linger on
But understand you're not alone, I'm here to hold your hand
And you'll know the days I carry you, by the footprints in the sand
I'll never forget the day I heard of your new condition
So young and so afraid, yet so brave to face this mission
And then we cried and hugged again and did what we do best
We'll see this through; we always do, lean on me and take a rest

But, we'll get through this darlin; sure that's what I'm here for
To hold you close and ease your pain and then love you all the more
This time will pass; new life will come and look you in the eye
And happiness will be with us; so baby, don't you cry

Perception is the problem now, then reality will be the answer
It holds you back and cripples you but inside you're a dancer

To give this life a chance to breathe won't be the end – just the beginning
Your world will change forever more, it's then you'll know you're winning
So let's look forward and not look back, the future shines through the clouds
Then count your blessings, not bad days, head erect and sing aloud
Something beautiful will come from this and change your life forever more
So let's not weep, let's just stand tall, as we walk through this open door.

Yes, we'll get through this darlin; sure that's what I'm here for
To hold you close and ease your pain and then love you all the more
This time will pass; new life will come and look you in the eye
And happiness will be with us; so baby, don't you cry.

Dan looked back on those words with fatherly pride coupled with a bit of macho awkwardness at this gushy prose, but the dad in him was always glad he wrote it.

During those days, he wrote many poems and lyrics that helped him to get rid of some emotional cramps that continually grated in his stomach. No man could live through the array of emotional chaos that Dan manufactured through his lifestyle without needing an outlet for it all.

Without the escape of gambling, his writings and rantings brought some sanity to his insane past during those months without a bet. If only he could have written forever. But he couldn't.

After Martin's birth, a new normality descended and the baby completely took over. Marie and her partner Adam became doting parents, and as Dan was already approaching dotage, given the wear and tear of his life, being a doting granddad was effortless and seamless!

Dan's next gambling spree brought even more guilt and shame than those before, as once again he discovered that he couldn't stay stopped even for those he loved, which now included his beautiful grandson.

His relationship with Martin was special. Being a grandfather was like being a father after the training course, and the fact that it was a part-time contract made it so easy and fulfilling. Yet there he was, back on that merry-go-round that had no stop button and wasn't that merry anyway. Dan's thoughts of suicide increased and at times he even developed those thoughts to the point of wondering how a man could drown himself without using his arms to save himself. Even the selfishness of leaving Marie and Martin behind could now be rationalised by his belief that they would be better off without him. A few more failed attempts at stopping gambling exacerbated the financial, emotional, mental and spiritual disintegration that engulfed his being.

It seemed that being in action was keeping him alive, yet how could the thing that was killing him keep him alive? It was a paradox not lost on Dan.

The despair and disgrace of his disintegration just took him to even greater depths. He reckoned two bottles of vodka by the side of the River Foyle would enable him to finally expire. He didn't need the booze for courage, it would be used to numb his love of Marie and Martin for that vital second that would get him in the river. Gravity would take care of the rest once he opened his mouth.

There was something very requiting about not having to feel more pain and not having to cause more pain.

To a disturbed mind, insanity seemed sane and selfishness seemed generous. But maybe the next bet would change all this. That elusive big win would enable him to make practical amends to everyone he had hurt, especially Marie. Yet Marie had no idea what was going on in the depth of Dan's mind. She just experienced a loving father and the degree of his internal torment remained hidden from her.

Dan envisaged handing her a bag full of money and saying, 'There's a few bob for you,' in his own inimitable and understated way. He often mused on such moments to the extent that he thought they were happening.

Then, reality would kick in and he would realise that he was once again skint. Dan was like a boxer who had taken too many punches to the head and had forgotten how to duck. It was strange how his demise wasn't coming from a bullet to the head, a premature bomb going off or alcohol-induced destruction. It was strange that four-legged dumb animals could take Dan to such depths.

Soon he was back into the bookies to expunge those crazy thoughts and get the big rise that had eluded him all those years. Rationalising the irrational and justifying the unjustifiable was totally necessary in that fantasy world of the addict. Then out of the blue, it happened.

Dan had 'invested' his last £100 on five horses that he had studied meticulously the night before. Had he studied half as well at college he would have had a doctorate in any chosen subject by now.

More in faint hope than in positive expectation, he folded the docket and put it in his trouser pocket, almost resigned that he would soon be short of bread again, both physically and metaphorically. The emergence of satellite TV meant he could watch the races at home and there he could show the emotion that a 'cool' gambler couldn't in public.

There wasn't much adrenaline flowing when his first selection, Godspeed, scooted in at the Curragh at odds of 6/4. His next horse, Unforgiving, got him going a bit by collaring Show Me The Money on the line at 3/1.

After this, he dared to dream a little but shrugged it off by remembering all those times that he had been visited by false prophets with four legs. All the same, he made a mental note that he had a £1000 treble running on the last three.

An hour passed and the third horse Guilty Secret won by a cosy length at 9/2. Dan's heart began to race. *Three down and two to go,* he thought. *If the next one wins I can lay off and be guaranteed a good few grand,* he projected.

The 15 minutes to the next race just dragged and seemed like an hour. Eventually, the 4.15 at Ascot went off with Dan's horse Many Regrets settling at the back. It had drifted in the betting to odds of 6/1 from an opening show of 5/2, so he was very despondent.

Usually, drifters in the market reflected a lack of confidence by the trainer and owner, so Dan wasn't at all hopeful. But in spite of the drift, it came with a late run to beat the heavily-backed favourite by half a length.

Dan did a quick mental calculation and realised he had £38,500 rolling onto the final leg of his accumulator. He mightn't have been able to impress the Hammer all those years ago at college with his knowledge of angles, but his mental arithmetic was always rapid and accurate when it came to calculating a bet.

His last choice had been a difficult one. He was stuck between two horses. That, to the non-gambler, probably sounded quite dangerous, but all punters know that dilemma when you fancy two horses but have to pick just one.

Dan had been there many times and he always remembered the aforementioned Hammer's advice. 'Feeney, for the rest of your life if you ever have a choice to make between two possible outcomes, choose the one you don't think it is because you will always be wrong.' He thought it would be just like that twisted aul' fucker to once again be his nemesis.

He then remembered his earlier thought that he could lay this one off and still win a packet for the day. That's what any normal gambler would do. Even most compulsive ones would too.

But this had become more than a bet to Dan. This was his opportunity to lay to rest the Hammer's influence that had tortured him throughout his life. It was also an opportunity to deliver on those fantasies and tangibly change Marie's life. He called his best gambling mate, Joe who advised Dan to lay off, as did everyone else in the betting office when he went in to watch the final race in the arena where gamblers love to be.

The betting came in for the 6:20 race at Sandown Park. Dan's selection, Endofanera, opened at 7/2 and drifted to 5/1 before shortening again to 4/1.

All those old adages of his teenage years that he picked up in card schools and bookies shops filtered into his brain. 'Never send a boy on a man's errand', 'Whole duck or no dinner', *'A faint heart never won a fair lady'*.

In an instant, Dan made his final decision. 'I'm letting it ride, Joe,' he whispered. It was the only decision that he was ever going to make in spite of all the debate in his head. He could feel his friend's panic, tension and heartbeat as well as his own. Endofanera was a seasoned sprinter who liked to jet off in front and stay there. On reflection, Dan thought that Sandown's stiff uphill finish might just catch the old nag out, but the race was now off and he was stuck with it.

He thought the Hammer would be delighted if he knew all this was going on. Sure enough, the old horse came out of the stall a length in front, and after two furlongs was three lengths clear of the field.

Dan's heart was thumping and his days with Fiona returned with a vengeance as his bowels and kidneys started to motor in tandem with the horse and his heart. He was just as uncertain if he could hold on as he was of whether Endofanera could.

As they entered the final furlong the horse was beginning to tire and he could see its stride shortening. His worst fear looked like happening as the horse he discarded in favour of Endofanera, Right Decision, was cutting down the lead rapidly along with two other horses. The whips were out and the jockeys were frantically trying to get that last ounce out of their mounts. Right Decision came alongside and marginally passed Endofanera with 30 yards to go but somehow Johnny Fallon galvanised the old horse and the two flashed past the post together.

By this stage, Dan was holding on to his life by his fingernails and simultaneously holding on to his continence with his hands!

Soon the experts were giving their opinions. 'I think you just got done by a nose,' one commented. Another genius offered, 'You're up, Dan.' Others suggested a dead heat. All of this meant that nobody really knew what had won, but as bookies shops are full of experts after the fact, Dan had to listen to their drivel.

He looked across to Joe. 'What do you think, mucker?' 'Jesus, Dan, it's too close to call, but I wish to fuck you had laid off as I think my aul' ticker is about to pack in,' his ashen-faced pal replied.

Then the result flashed on the screen. Winner number two, Endofanera. The place erupted and Dan was surrounded by a host of new best friends who all knew the horse was up anyway. He stood motionless, but other motions were about to descend. 'Can I use your toilet?' he asked the clerk. Luckily he made it on time or a memorable moment would have been soiled forever! As he squatted, he buried the legacy of the Hammer forever, as he flushed away motions and emotions to emerge a free man, at least for that moment.

Dan opened the docket, aware that he was just about to take £192,500 out of the bookie's coffers. At last, he had that big win and now he could do all the things he'd dreamed of.

The manager of the betting shop called him aside and said he would have a cheque for him in the morning. Dan informed him that in his forty-odd years of gambling no bookie had ever accepted one of his cheques, so he wanted paid in cash.

This caused consternation in the local office, but after several phone calls, he was finally told that if he would come to the head office in Belfast the next day, he would be paid in cash. They also asked if he would like to be photographed for the newspaper as the biggest winner that year. Dan declined. He wasn't in the mood to provide free advertising to this multinational operator. What he was getting was a mere fraction of what he had 'donated' to them over the years. Furthermore, he didn't want his piece of luck to be the catalyst for some other young Dan to innocently wade into the hell on earth that his first bet created for him.

He had learned that if you don't take the first bet, then the second one wouldn't be a problem. Although he was a beaten docket on that score, he certainly didn't want to aid and 'abet' anyone else to enter the arena of chance.

The next day he and Joe set off for Belfast. Finding the Badblokes head office wasn't a problem. Gamblers have an antenna that seeks out betting shops in an instant.

They presented themselves at the counter and asked for

the manager, Jimmy Timoney, and were ushered upstairs to the office. Jimmy greeted them in that brash, yet friendly, manner of a west Belfast man. He congratulated Dan on his win and said that his assistant was at the bank getting the cash. He was interested in his reasons for not taking a cheque and perhaps was a little taken back when Dan voiced them.

All around them were screens with both live and ante-post betting flashing like a beacon at Dan. It was the equivalent of a beautiful woman winking at him.

Jimmy said to Dan to feel free to have a bet while he was waiting.

Dan looked at one screen and saw that Last Hurrah was starting at 4/6. He immediately knew that £180,000 would win him £120,000. He knew the form of this horse inside out. He believed it would hack up. 'Jimmy,' he said, 'if I decided to put a hundred and eighty grand on Last Hurrah would you take the bet?' Jimmy turned a sickly white as he made an urgent call to the London office. Meanwhile, Joe turned about forty shades of shite!

Within seconds, Jimmy said, 'That's a bet if you want it, Dan.' He spent a minute in deep concentration and then made his decision.

14

Last Hurrah

It was a cold and sharp September Sunday morning and Mary Powers, Tina Donaghoe and Debbie O' Kane were at it again.

Three of Dan's worst nightmares were in step as they marched along the Foyle embankment. They were talking quite low as they passed Dan's apartment building, so someone was obviously getting a touch from the power walkers.

The river was high and still as they proceeded onwards past Mandarin Palace, *nearly* On the Waterfront. Further on, near the Guildhall, the Oneean Too was permanently moored. It hadn't moved for over two years after running into financial difficulties and was looking rusty and desolate. No doubt Dan would have deduced that it ran into too much shite, given his obsessive observations of the river.

Further on out, they passed the street drinkers, who were now back on the city side of the bridge, so obviously their move to the Republic of Ireland had been halted. Perhaps in the shadow of the banking and property developer collapses Brian Cowan had decided he couldn't afford them, so the move to Donegal had been cancelled.

As they headed out past the Foyle Valley Railway

Museum and approached the Daisy Field - which was still a daisy-free zone - they could see a lone male walker approaching slowly with his head held low. One of them commented that his wife must have dumped him the night before because he looked so sad. As proud 'Amazons' they still associated male sadness with female rejection. Little did they know that this man had more bothering him than a lover's quarrel. In fact, he had been divorced for years, the result of overindulgence in drink, gambling and infidelity.

As they passed the man, one of them noticed something emerge from the water. 'What the fuck's that out there in the water?' said one. 'I've no glasses on,' replied her companion, 'but it looks like an aul' carpet or something to me. You'd think people would stop dumping in the river, especially with the Council facility being re-opened in the Brandywell.'

At that, the man they had passed heard them and immediately turned around and started running towards the carpet. Joe had been walking in this area for days and now wondered if he had found what he didn't want to see.

He shouted to the women to give him a hand as he waded into the water to retrieve the river's offering. Within seconds Joe knew it was Dan. He would recognise that corduroy coat anywhere. 'Jesus Christ, I knew it,' he wailed. 'That's my best friend, Dan. I've been looking for him for days and thought I might find him wandering out here where he always comes to find peace. By fuck, he's found it now.'

The women were crying and squealing relentlessly as Dan's body was pulled to the riverbank. 'Ah Jesus, we know him,' Debbie said to the other two. 'That's that nice quiet fella who we used to see jogging on Sunday mornings. You know him, Mary, 'cause you said there was something nice about him. Remember we used to slag you and say, "There's your fella, Road Runner, coming." Tina found out his name from the man in the office at the apartments. He told us he was called Dan Feeney.'

Slowly and nervously the three women went closer. They asked Joe what they should do now. 'I really don't know,' Joe said. 'I guess we need to phone the police and the doctor. Dan has a daughter and a grandson and this will break their hearts. I just knew something was wrong when I got his text on Friday. It just said to tell Marie he'd left a wee message for her in his training bag.'

'Me and him had been in Belfast the day before to collect a bet, but it got a bit complicated. It's really strange you three being here today. I know Dan had a weird opinion of power walkers and yet just listening to you it looks like he might have got that one wrong after all,' Joe reasoned.

'You know, when he left me on Thursday he gave me £25,000 in cash and said he hoped that it might take the sting outta my life for a week or two. That was Dan, ever the understater. He had a gambling problem, ye see - just like myself to be honest. He won over a hundred and ninety grand the other day on a hundred-pound bet, but when he went to Belfast he put £180,000 on a 4/6 shot that he thought couldn't be beat. Fuck was he right, or what? It romped home by eight lengths and we left Belfast with over £300,000 in cash. He said he wouldn't be around for a few days because he wanted to quietly sort out a few friends and family. I thought nothing of it as I know the kind of him. He never valued money and if he wasn't betting it, he was giving it away.'

The women looked on in sadness and amazement at how this man who had just won a fortune had seemingly taken his own life. It didn't make sense to them but it was beginning to, to Joe. He knew Dan couldn't stop gambling and he knew Dan's life story from childhood. They had been to the same primary school and always seemed to cross paths in pubs and bookie shops before becoming even closer in the last ten years.

Joe wondered if Dan had decided to get out in front for once in his life. On the other hand, Joe considered that maybe he had made another bet that lost after they had parted company. That was more like the Dan he knew.

At that, the police arrived and took over the scene. They took statements from Joe and the power walkers.

The tears consumed Joe as he walked away from his aul' mucker, too distraught to even know the direction he was travelling. The three women went over to him and immediately called a taxi. They took him to Mary's home where he talked about Dan for hours as they sat open-mouthed at this man's life story.

A few days later Dan was buried in the city cemetery.

He was given a republican funeral, which was attended by many old comrades. For that time, at least, it didn't matter what side they were on. They were just there to pay homage to an old friend who did a wee bit to free Ireland and suffered in silence for years at the settlement he believed meant his country would remain partitioned.

But now it didn't matter, his suffering from all of his demons was over. Marie stood at the graveside with her husband and wee Martin. They were inconsolable.

Even Bridget seemed distraught. Since the arrival of their grandson they had become friends again and had spent many hours talking through past hurts, and even reminiscing about the good times too. A lot of healing had taken place.

Dan's brothers and sisters didn't see it coming either. They had done all they could over the years to help and understand, but Dan's addictions were more powerful than the love of family. His demons fuelled isolation of mind and body, but now he was at peace. They looked on in tears and sadness as his coffin was lowered and Dan was laid to rest.

The next day Joe called Marie and gave her the message that Dan had left. She went to the apartment immediately, hoping for something that could explain the suicide of her daddy. She was hurting and angry, yet somehow deep down she knew this was possibly the only way he was going to get peace. His soul was tortured by so many experiences and the gambling just seemed to get worse and worse over the years.

As she walked into his apartment she could sense her daddy's smell, a mixture of aftershave and manhood. The tears were tripping her as she opened the cloakroom door where he kept his training bag. On top of it were two envelopes, one addressed to Marie and one addressed to his dead father. Marie opened her envelope and read through the tears.

My Darlin Marie,

By the time you read this, you will have put me to my final resting place. No doubt you are hurting deeply and totally puzzled and angry at the way I left things. If I were here I would understand that. The fact that I'm not here means I considered all those things but still decided to go away.

You see darlin, I finally worked it out that if I stayed alive we would both be troubled for the rest of my life. On top of that my legacy to you and our wee man, Martin, would have been one of a tortured human being who failed at the things he wanted to succeed at and succeeded at the things he should have failed at.

So please don't be angry, my death is only a beginning and I'm finally in a better place. If there's a God he'll take me in 'cause he knows I'll need some looking after. And if there isn't, sure at least I'm no longer tormented. I couldn't live on hurting everyone I love so dearly, especially you. If that sounds selfish I guess I'll have to take it on the chin. But my intention was to take this cross away from us all.

Please forgive me and live out the rest of your life free from my demons. My love for you is forever no matter where I am.

Hope to see you and Martin in 100 years or so. Tell your ma she was lucky to get out early!

Eternally yours,

Daddy.

PS *I left you a few bits and pieces in this training bag to save you looking for mementoes later.*

PPS *will you leave this wee note up at my daddy and mammy's grave. It's for him but I'm sure she'll have a wee juke too.*

Marie opened the bag and found a host of photographs of better times, a few of her school reports and all her daddy's writings, including the poems and lyrics he wrote over the years. Underneath was £240,000 in cash with a note attached. *Have a wee drink on me and see your mammy okay too, and for God's sake buy that wane some new socks!*

Simultaneously, cheques totalling £47,500 were delivered in the post to several family members and friends of Dan with similar advice, minus the bit about the new socks.

Marie took the envelope addressed to Dan's daddy up to the cemetery the next day. She opened it and left the note at the graveside inside a clear plastic cover with a few stones on top to keep it from blowing away. It read:

That boy finally got home, Da.

Printed in Great Britain
by Amazon